The Man from Autumn

A Psychological Novel

Mario E. Martinez

Llumina Press

Requests for permission to make copies of any part of this work should be
mailed to Permissions Department, Llumina Press, PO Box 772246, Coral
Springs, FL 33077-2246

ISBN: PB 1-59526-097-8
        HC 1-59526-098-6

Printed in the United States of America by Llumina Press

Library of Congress Control Number: 2005923816

The Man from Autumn is a work of fiction. Characters and institutions in this novel are the product of the author's imagination. Real persons or entities are presented fictitiously, without any intention to depict their actual conduct. The scientific information introduced in this work is real, and when factual statements about individuals and institutions are presented, the sources are included.

*To my son Patrick, and my daughter Lauren,
who are my heroes and my inspiration.*

Acknowledgments

The completion of this book solidified my gratitude toward those who so diligently supported my dream. I cannot imagine my professional development without the support and wisdom of my dear friend and mentor Dr. George F. Solomon. Sadly, Dr. Solomon is no longer with us, but his pioneering work in the field of psychoneuroimmunology lives in the minds of scientists, who continue to advance human knowledge of how our subjective reality affects our objective biology.

I also want to thank my associates D.J. Drake, Larry McGlothlin and Amber Ribble, for their unwavering support. And, I must not forget Lynne from Lancaster, who knew I had this book in me, before I did.

I am not what happened to me, I am what I choose to become.

– Carl Jung

Be not afraid.

– H.H. Pope John Paul II

*Defensive action to prevent violent action
is non-violent action.*

– H.H. The Dalai Lama

*God is a comedian performing for an audience
who is afraid to laugh.*

– Nietzsche

Preface

The *Man from Autumn* is a navigational chart for the private journey of *Self,* concealed in a psychological novel. My intention is to take you, the reader, on a path that explores a non-linear world of meaningful coincidences and other mystical experiences, where joy is the rule and anguish an exception. The imagery this work can elicit transforms a mundane existence of the known into portals of discovery that affirm love, health and longevity as our inherent rights, rescued from a dimension of fear.

When a parallel reality is introduced, it must offer a language to establish horizons for the *bioinformational field* it creates. This alternate reality known as *the drift* has portals of entry and rules of engagement to be accessed only through a compressed perception of time and space. Within the chaotic archives of *the drift,* there is implicate wisdom that can be retrieved to understand the power of *inclusive compassion,* the *biocultural* aspects of *psycho-spiritual* conflicts and the *covenant of safety,* for a concept of relationships I call *Guardians of the Heart.*

Although there is more than enough misery, violence and hopelessness in our modern world to last us an eternity, as stewards of our free will we are masters of choice rather than victims of chance. The archetypal characters you will encounter in this novel within a novel may appear utopian to skeptical eyes. But they are mere reminders of the potential abundance that lives dormant in our doubting hearts. To entertain a dream embraces the possibility of living it.

The novelist, Enrique, creates the protagonist, Breogán: a mystic from Celtic Spain, who teaches the author how to enter the enigmatic *drift.* Their surreal discourse delves into the nature of love and evil, the enduring elements of relationships, our fear of death, and the mysterious stigmata, where the mind wounds the body. From the legendary regions of Galician Spain and the Highlands of Scotland, to the hermetic world of the Vatican, the dominions of science and spirit converge to argue the supremacy of courage and love, over fear and evil.

In an *incidental teaching* style, this fictional work enters a mystical domain with empirical grounding, to avoid the popular illusion that complex problems have simplistic answers. You, the seeker, are gradually exposed to a psychological space where unexpected events unfold, to challenge our biological limits and expand our transcendental beliefs. Although the magnitude of what happens to a priest in this novel within a novel could shake the foundation of Western theology and science, the Vatican's decision to keep it a guarded secret, reflects the complexity of disclosing truth to a skeptical world.

Just as love cannot be encompassed with words, there is no goal that can reach perfection. I believe our task, is to dance around beauty without disturbing its essence. *The Man from Autumn* invites us to explore the miracle of living with joy, rather than lamenting what cannot be helped. Only then, can we afford to face our transitions without fear, and the end of our journeys without greed.

To the *rightness of the moment,*

Mario E. Martinez
Autumn, 2004
Holy Cross Abbey, Ireland

Chapter 1

"I accept the challenge, and I will christen him…Breogán"

Returning to live and write in the Miami of his youth was haunting at best for Enrique Lugo. Coming home triggered memories of surfing with his friends by the dilapidated South Beach art deco neighborhood of his youth. There were no beautiful people prancing the ocean-side streets then. No, in those days the salty breeze carried the painful memories of elderly Jews who lived with shaming marks of inhumanity tattooed on their arms. Enrique's shame was different, and although miniscule compared to the crimes of Auschwitz, it seemed equally painful, to a twelve year-old, to be called a *spic* by kids he admired. Shame has no boundaries when it wounds the spirit early on the journey: it becomes an *Alpha Event.*

Now those valiant Jews were icons of honor, and the Spanish surfer was an anthropologist who addressed the ailments of a culture that had questioned his worthiness. Although the pseudo-compassion of our times has driven prejudice underground, hiding it out of sight only creates a collective illusion that it is out of mind. Enrique knew that sanitized dictums promoting sensitivity seldom reach the heart.

It was Saturday morning and Enrique opened the double doors and stepped unto his second story balcony facing Ocean Drive. The thought of Thomas Wolfe's admonition, *you can't go home again,* surfaced as he deliberated how to extract happiness from the fame and wealth his last two novels had brought him. It was alluring to contemplate the composition of joy. How much of joy is convincing self from evidence of prosperity and how much of it is inherently within? But Enrique already knew that symbols are more powerful than achievements. Those ethereal conceptions we call symbols can bring joy to the most humble experiences and hell to the peaks of accomplishment. So what is joy?

He remembered the time his dear uncle invited a beggar to come in from the streets and take a table at an elegant restaurant where they were having lunch. The beggar brought the taste of his social history, and ordered the simplest items on the menu. That day, Enrique learned the joy of witnessing compassion, and today while drinking his cup of jasmine tea he reminisced: *my uncle's benevolence lives on to honor him and comfort me*: thus, the endurance of symbols.

Tonight held a delightful anticipation. Enrique was dining with a woman of mystery and impressive beauty he met at an exclusive wine tasting two weeks earlier. There are two kinds of people who attend those functions: those who know wines, and those who know how to compress time with strangers. He was presently writing a novel that examined how the degree of intimacy we are willing to share, and the beliefs that guide our lives, are determined by what he called *cultural portals*. Enrique had been able to delineate cogently the dynamics of cultural boundaries, drawing from his expertise in psychological anthropology. He recalled how the conversation progressed that evening:

"Hi, my name is Enrique Lugo, and I noticed you were looking at me."

"Hello, Enrique, I am Kate Holland, and you amuse me with your assumption."

"Ah, I am in the presence of a sharp mind. But tell me Kate, can someone as beautiful as you remain humble?"

"There you go assuming again. Who says I am humble?"

"I guess it was wishful thinking on my part because I can only love the humble."

"Do you always love at first sight Enrique?"

"Oh, no, I only delight at first sight."

Kate smiled and, after a feisty conversation, gave him her mobile number. Enrique assured her that he would not fall in love with her until she learned humility.

He was taking her to an intimate restaurant in Coral Gables that specialized in Galician cuisine. Enrique was a preferred customer, because he spoke Galician like a native. His father was from Celtic Spain, and taught Enrique a language the boy tried to forget during the years of cultural bashing. Now, Enrique reclaimed his heritage with the honor of a medieval knight, and spoke Galician with the waiters when he dined at *Casa Xoán*.

As much as he tried, he could not stop thinking about Kate and how aloof she could remain from his attempts to charm her. He knew there are levels of detachment and layers of disclosure. He acknowledged his healthy regard for himself and made no excuses about it. That acceptance of self-valuation comes from transcending the ravages of prejudice, as one realizes that those who judge people by their ethnicity do so from a premise of cultural impotence. Yet, Kate was bright, tall and lithe, with a striking presence--a combination that could spell

Kryptonite for Enrique. He knew, perhaps for some primeval reason, that a woman like Kate could enter the portals of his most guarded secrets, rendering him vulnerable to her persona.

In his latest book, *The Anthropology of Self Esteem,* Enrique determined that, since the valuation of *Self* has contextual limitations, it was nearly impossible to feel emotionally worthy under all circumstances. But inability to recognize the worth of others precludes empathy, and resembles the dark pathology of a sociopath. Healthy self-esteem is more like a bamboo shoot than armor. Enrique argued that our concept of worthiness is shaped by the symbols of aesthetics, ethics, health and theology that we assimilate from our culture. Beauty has relative as well as transcendent traits that interact to accommodate the values of a culture. If thinness were a contributing cultural factor for example, some contexts could make thinness necessary but not sufficient to be beautiful.

At *Casa Xoán,* Enrique would dine with a woman who challenged his vulnerabilities, in an environment that represented his cultural strengths. He thought he had conquered his ghosts until Kate emerged to remind him of his surfing days, when ethnic insecurity was more draconian than the tallest wave he could ride. Miami Beach is not known for great surfing, but the waves Enrique feared and sought to defy were encountered during hurricane warning conditions, hours before the storm arrived. Was Kate a hurricane or a ghost? Of course, he also entertained a remote indulgence that she could be the partner he diligently sought, with little faith.

Brickell Ave. is lined with exclusive high-rise condominiums where the new wealth lives, but sprinkled between those monoliths facing Biscayne Bay are a few palatial homes that attest to the permanence only old money can achieve. As Enrique drove his Porsche Cabriolet while looking for Kate's address, he had no idea she was one of those immutable residents. He almost passed the property, not expecting it to be her residence. He drove up a winding cobblestone driveway surrounded by impeccable landscaping, at last revealing a Mediterranean mansion that competed with the magnificence of Vizcaya. Enrique smiled at his capacity to be impressed without jealousy. Kate opened the sculpted door, looking ravishing, paling his imagination and speeding his heartbeat.

"I was expecting Jeeves to answer the door and ask me to wait in the drawing room."

"Oh, we gave him the night off for good behavior."

"We?"

"Yes, *we.* I live with what others might call *domestic help,* and what I choose to view as my adopted family. By the way, your *Jeeves* is my *Frank*. He insisted on remaining with me after father passed, five years ago."

"How many *adopted family* members does it take to run this place?"

"Only four."

"How efficient of you. Kate, do you cook?"

"Like a Belgian chef."

"If you could only learn modesty, we could do great things together."

"That statement of attempting greatness seems far from modest to me."

Enrique was enjoying the sparkle of witnessing beauty with depth. *How could this woman be unattached? Or was she?* He mused.

As if she could read his thoughts, she responded. "You wonder if there's someone special in my life?"

"Not really. I was just guessing how long it took you to chose that fantastic mini you're wearing."

"Enrique, I'm pleased to notice that you don't lie very well."

"Kate, I am as pleased to confess that you're absolutely right."

They drove to *Casa Xoán*, where Felipe, the *maitre d'*, greeted them and conversed in Galician with Enrique as he led them to their table. Felipe elegantly prevented new customers from mispronouncing the name of the restaurant, by explaining that in the Middle Ages, the letter *x* was pronounced as *sh* and now as *h*. He was spared that chore with customers like Enrique.

"I didn't know you spoke Galician."

"Maybe you should make it a project to know me."

"Tell me, Enrique, have we established our comfort zones or shall we continue to banter?"

"What on earth do you mean?" Enrique asked with a staged sense of surprise and a roguish smile.

"You know quite well what I mean Dr. Lugo," she affirmed playfully with emphasis on the word *doctor*.

"Kate, I'll admit to you that, as worldly as I fancy myself to be, your brilliance and striking beauty keep me a bit off balance." Enrique responded in earnest to demonstrate he was not taking her lightly.

"I would not be wrong in assuming that, I am not the first learned blonde you have wined and dined?"

"No Kate, you're not, but you are the first woman in a long time who could reach a part of me that I thought was well protected."

"And that part would be...?"

"It's too early to disclose. We've just begun to compress time," he said in an attempt to regain emotional safety.

Before she could respond, Roi, the *sommelier*, arrived and Enrique ordered a bottle of *Bacvs Dei* '82.

"*Unha selección excelente. Benvidos ó Casa Xoán, Doctor Lugo.*"

"*Graças, Roi.*"

"Enrique, did you train the staff to rescue you so eloquently? Wait, don't answer! I guess I've asked a rhetorical question; so tell me about the wine you ordered instead."

Relieved by her graciousness, Enrique proceeded to explain like a proud professor.

"*Bacvs Dei* is a uniquely fruity and light wine with undertones of raspberries, made from the Mencía grape. Unfortunately, wines from Celtic Spain are underexposed. I dared to assume that you would allow me to choose Galician wines for the evening."

"Assume away, and we'll see how well you sail the vineyards."

The dinner and wines were superb, and the conversation was enriched with physical touches--to accentuate an occasional point. Magic ruled the evening. The topics ranged from his anthropological theory of love to her studies in Tibetan Buddhism. Enrique could not recall a finer evening and expressed his sentiment to Kate, who responded with a most engaging smile.

They drove back to her place in contented silence. As they walked to her door, she looked up to a lit window on the second floor, and instinctively down to Enrique's eyes. Their lips met with an anticipation that does not know tomorrow, but chooses to wait. He gently took her hands and kissed them with deliberate veneration.

"Kate, if this was not a dream, I want to see you soon."

"Dr. Lugo, this was definitely not a dream, and I want to see you sooner."

He drove home with a liveliness he had only experienced in transcendent states of meditation. In those deep levels of consciousness, personal horizons collapse and a sense of oneness suspends our mundane egos with indelible harmony.

Monday mornings are always difficult for a writer. Our culture designates that first day as a challenge to be productive for the working week. When confronted with the essence of beauty, whatever form of beauty, we encounter a symbol that can be sensed but never grasped. Poets are keenly aware of the elusiveness of beauty and craft words to explore its boundaries, rather than to attempt its definition. Now, Enrique had to draw from his acquired discipline to create a place for Kate that would not derail his productive energy. But what if his ingenuity could only be directed toward her? He was painfully aware that joy is a rich fuel that should be assimilated slowly, with grace.

That evening, Enrique was flying to New York for an interview on a leading television talk show that probed the effects of cultural trends on the quality of life. The show gained international recognition because of its appeal to discerning viewers, independent of geographic boundaries. The concept of reaching an international audience with an American talk show was considered impossible, until Eric Connery created *The Spin*. Given the stereotypical image of a successful television host, Mr. Connery was an unlikely candidate. He was erudite without arrogance, a debonair who adored women, a best-selling author with substance, and at the height of his creativity at sixty-seven. Even a prominent radical feminist conceded that, if she were to tolerate one man, Eric Connery would be her choice for his irreverent wit.

Enrique and Eric became instant friends after they met a year earlier to tape their first dialogue for the premier of *The Spin*. Enrique was a younger version of Eric in his savvy and good looks. Yet, they each enjoyed a marked uniqueness that brought admiration from the intellectually secure, and jealousy, masked as contempt, from the self-righteous. During their frequent dinners, they attempted to correct the ills of the world, seasoning their solutions with the best wines their favorite restaurants had to offer. Since Enrique lived in Miami and Eric in Manhattan, they alternated their dining encounters between the two cities. The author Trevanian has eloquently noted that *the excellence of restaurants in New York City is determined by the amount of abuse customers endure from their waiters*. But Enrique and Eric had a solution for that snobbery. They would order a sequence of wines that were not available, even in the best cellars, bringing pretentious *sommeliers* to their knees.

"Ladies and gentlemen, welcome to *The Spin*. This morning I am pleased to have as my special guest Dr. Enrique Lugo, a dear friend and colleague, who shares in my search for the elusive concept we call culture and how it affects our lives. I am especially pleased because today we will discuss Dr. Lugo's book-in-progress, *The Man from Autumn*. As our audience knows, Enrique Lugo is the best-selling author of *Portals of Evil* and *The Anthropology of Self Esteem*. One of the unique *spins* of our program is that we discuss books-in-progress from best-selling authors."

"Great to have you on again, Enrique."

"My pleasure to be here."

"Tell us, who is this ominous man from autumn?"

"Well, I am not so sure he's supposed to be ominous, but I guess with the trouble he's given me to imagine him, I would agree with your description." The audience laughed and began to relax. "My main character, who at this time has a provisional name, is a man for one season. During the autumns of his mystical life, he explores how culture influences our relationships and the charting of our personal journey."

"Can you expand on that?"

"Sure. This man sees autumn metaphorically different than most of us. Rather than the standard symbolism of preparing to emotionally welcome winter, my character...by the way Eric, why don't you name him on this show?" The audience applauded.

"Sensible idea, and thanks for putting me on the spot. Anyway, I accept the challenge and I shall christen him...*Breogán*." More applause from a receptive audience.

"Why Breogán?"

"Enrique, I ask the hard questions here."

"Fair enough," responded Enrique as he began to address the audience. "Well, by no coincidence, your learned host knows that Breogán is considered the mythological father of Galicia and, given that my novels involve some aspect of Celtic Spain, I could not imagine a more fitting name for my protagonist."

Eric smiled, responding to very enthusiastic applauds. "Now you see ladies and gentlemen, why Enrique is my most enjoyable guest?" More applause and laughter.

"In this novel, one of the themes our newly christened Breogán probes is the cultural variables that trigger bonding between two people, and how the personal histories they bring to their union compel them to evolve. I segment the process into *attracting, engaging* and *embracing*. To *attract* simply requires triggering inquisitive interest. *Engaging* goes farther and demands aesthetic compatibility. And *embracing* transcends the personal horizons of each participant and merges the best histories they assimilate from the collective wisdom of their respective cultures."

"Enrique, why did you develop your theory within a mystical theme?"

"Well, I was thinking of the modern mystics, who can expand the cultural horizons of fear that drain our power to accept joy as our intrinsic right. The fear of joy has many cultural masks, but it takes a mystic's probe into darkness to conquer it and show others the way."

Eric smiled with delight, as he realized Enrique had withheld this information from their dinner conversations to surprise him on this interview.

"In my research for this book, I studied people who defied the conventional cultural parameters so I could identify the more elusive, but enduring, rudiments of love, will, evil, and other fundamental forces that infuse the private journey of self."

"By *conventional* do you mean compliance with norms at the expense of joy?" Eric asked, to focus the audience on Enrique's train of thought.

"Precisely. By delineating what I call the *horizons of convention*, we can identify subtleties salient to those who defy the cultural constraints that affect their relationships, their worthiness and even their health. Our man Breogán views autumn as the allegorical foundation for his quest."

"Ladies and gentlemen, I can't wait to read Enrique's book. But without giving it all away, please expand on your unconventional sense of autumn."

"Eric, I think I can do that without losing probable sales." The audience applauded with laughter and anticipatory nods.

"Breogán is a man for one season, but by transcending the obvious interpretations our culture makes of autumn, he finds proclivities in the early stages of intimacy that affect the quality of relationships and longevity. As we grow older, we begin to acquiesce to the age horizons set by our culture. When you are thirty, your interpretations of what you confront in life and what you consider possible in your future are quite different than when you are sixty. Just as autumn is a season that can flavor our emotional experiences, growing older is affected by how we perceive stages of life that our culture partitions into yearly segments."

"Creative concept. Can you give us a practical example of your theory?"

"Certainly. Going back to the age factor, what happens if you drive a small sports car and your back hurts as you step out? A thirty year old may decide to take a yoga class to correct the problem, while a sixty year old may conclude that it's time for a bigger car. The attribution for the pain in the younger person leads to corrective action without giving up pleasure, whereas the decision to end the enjoyment of the sports car by the older person affects quality of life and precludes corrective action. I would even venture to say that the older person may not only get rid of the sports car, but perhaps also seek pain medication and muscle relaxants to endorse the limitation.

"You see, just as seasons affect our external behavior, cultures shape our internal beliefs. Cultural parameters of aging, aesthetics, and health influence the interpretations we make of our experiences in each of those areas. Those interpretations strongly impact the quality of our lives."

"Enrique, as you well know, although I am sixty-seven, I drive a *Ferrari Testarossa* and practice *Qi Gong*." The audience roared with laughter and Eric brought the show to an end with flawless timing.

The host and his friend drove to their usual *tapas* bar for a light lunch in the elegant Murray Hill neighborhood of East Manhattan. Eric wanted to discuss Enrique's attraction to Kate Holland.

"You know, Eric, at this time there is little to tell. A striking woman with a remarkable mind who lives with her *adopted family*, as she calls her domestic help, in a Brickell Avenue mansion, apparently without romance in her life. During dinner she told me she defended her doctoral thesis under Robert Kerman at Columbia University when she was twenty-five. Professor Kerman is an eminent scholar of Tibetan Buddhism and Tara Kerman's dad. Kate and Tara are friends, so you can just imagine the aesthetic energy that emanates when those two get together."

"The actress Tara Kerman?"

"None other."

"Enrique, you may recall your comment that Tara Kerman lives up to the beauty of her Tibetan goddess namesake, so when you speak of Kate as her equal I can imagine you must be in a state of euphoria."

"That's putting it mildly. In the short time that you and I have been friends you know more about my private self than most. I can tell you that although I have little faith in the benign outcome of relationships, I am smitten with Kate."

"In that case, how would your Breogán handle this quandary you've created? Before you answer; remember that, if you're not careful, you may become the man from autumn."

"Eric, you're a consummate smart ass."

The two friends laughed in unison as they walked out of the *tapas* bar, feeling the pleasing effects of the fine wines reaching their neural receptors. They parted with a Galician *abrazo* and Enrique left in a studio limo for La Guardia to catch a plane back to Miami.

Unable to shake Connery's words out of his mind, Enrique mused: *Eric might have a point. I could be living my own novel, so I have to be very careful not to sabotage the plot. The South Beach surfer is no longer a wounded child.*

A fiction writer should not project too much self into the main character, but Enrique thought that in the course of developing Breogán he could reach layers of his own psyche that would not be readily available through direct introspection. Exploring a character that appears to be separate from Self could bypass the usual defense mechanisms that block access to the *shadow*. The Swiss psychiatrist, Carl Jung, defined the *shadow* as a layer of Self so dreaded that it could only be brought to consciousness through archetypal interpretations.

"Good morning Kate, this is Enrique."

"Hi, I'm glad you called, because I am having lunch at this new *Café Ramah* restaurant. I'm told it serves excellent Indian food and I wondered if you'd like to join me?"

"Wonder no longer. You have astounding intuition. I was actually calling you for the same reason but without a restaurant in mind. *Café Ramah* sounds great. When shall I pick you up?"

"No, let's meet there instead. I have an Aikido class near by and it would be easier to go from there."

"You take Aikido?"

"Actually, I teach it."

"So I am having lunch with a martial arts diva?"

"Lucky you." Kate responded with a quick laugh and agreed to meet at 11:30 a.m.

Enrique arrived a few minutes early to clear his thoughts. He noticed how the ritualistic lunch crowd that makes or breaks a restaurant was beginning to fill the place.

Kate walked to the table wearing fitted jeans that accentuated her long, sculpted legs, and a lavender thin linen blouse that blended sensuality with fashion. Her hair was combed back, still wet from her shower, and her face expressed the triumphant glow of an athlete who had pushed her physical boundaries with great skill. Enrique greeted her with a kiss and immediately wondered if that level of intimacy was acceptable to her in public. She smiled and gently held his hand showing stylish approval.

"How's my *ninja*?"

"Your *ninja* is doing great. Although…as you know, *Dr. Lugo*, Ninjutsu, the style of ninjas, is different from Aikido," Kate explained with a playful smile.

"Of course I was aware of that, but I just love to see how delightful you look when you correct me. The *Dr. Lugo* part tells me I am about to be put in my place." They laughed and looked into each other's eyes with the same fascination they shared during their dinner at Casa Xoán.

"Tell me more about the theory of compression you're developing in your novel?"

"Ah, so the man from autumn is already competing for your attention. What if you like him more than me?" Enrique smiled and waited for her wit to unfold.

"If the man from autumn is the better man, how could I resist? I would have to follow him to the end of compressed time," Kate quipped with a playful grin.

"I don't want to entertain that possibility, but I would reluctantly congratulate Breogán for besting me."

As soon as Enrique finished his sentence, he sensed a surrealistic vestige of what Eric Connery had prophetically warned him could happen. For a brief moment, he actually felt jealousy toward the character he had created! Ironically, the *character* Breogán was conceived to transcend the limitations of the *author* Enrique. He realized how the piercing introspection needed to craft fiction obliges writers to walk a thin line between divine creativity and the shadows of hell.

They ordered the specialty of the house-- *masala dosa, sambhar* and hot *chai.* A typical Southern Indian meal of crepes with herbs, potatoes and onions, vegetable soup, and tea brewed with milk and spices.

"Kate, you've heard of Eric Connery's talk show, *The Spin?*"

"Of course, I saw him interview this very charming Spanish author."

"You saw the show? You're so stealth. Did Professor Kerman teach you that Eastern quality or was it your Aikido master?"

Kate smiled approvingly and continued, "Mr. Connery asked you some very insightful questions."

"Yes, Eric is a stellar interviewer. He takes the concept of Occam's razor to higher planes every time we discuss my theories. But getting back to your question, in my theory of time compression I argue that the degree of disclosure in intimate communication is determined by cultural predispositions. That alone is not such a novel concept. What I find most baffling is that, time can be compressed to disclose intimacy vertically or horizontally"

"What does that mean?"

"Horizontal compression involves instant intimacy with different people, without commitment to go deep with any one person. There is shallowness in the interaction -- indiscriminately sharing private behavior without bonding. The person disclosing appears to be very open when in fact the communication lacks exclusivity and depth. Intimate feelings are revealed without intention to invest in the relationship.

"In vertical compression, there is exclusivity, depth and commitment. Words have meaning and emotions have substance. I believe that authentic intimacy can only grow by going inward. I guess what I am saying is that horizontal compression focuses on quantity whereas vertical compression seeks quality."

"I am intrigued with your theory. No, let me rephrase that; I love it."

"Thank you, Kate. You're very kind." Enrique was pleasantly surprised by her reaction to his work.

"Enrique, I am going to ask you a personal question."

"Please do."

"I am very impressed with your views and I wonder if pain has been your teacher?"

"Fair enough, I'll answer your question. Pain is certainly one of the teachers I accept with as much grace as I can muster, but I am more interested in learning from joy. I'll admit that in my book I'm exploring the inspiring characteristics of joy but more importantly, I am investing in my own development. I find that pain teaches in order to understand and overcome suffering. Sometimes when I learn from a painful experience I sense a forlorn sweetness that can melt my heart. I believe that happens when we elevate our humanness in times of turbulence."

"And what happens when you learn from joy?"

"Ah, joy is more complicated because it compels us to encounter our fear of loss."

"Our fear of loss?" Kate asked with visible curiosity.

"Yes, when we have a learning occurrence where joy is our teacher, we feel very alive and exhilarated but at the same time this powerful emotion triggers a flash of our mortality and our need to invite others into a space that can only be witnessed from within. During joy we want to jump out of our skins and embrace what I call *unitive affiliation*: a need to bring those we love into that revered space. In that instance, we become painfully aware of our physical boundaries and the fleeting remnants of our bliss.

"For those reasons, joy is a very feared emotion. We're shaken from our illusion of separateness and yet when we taste oneness during unitive affiliation, we're confronted with our greatest fear."

Kate was transfixed – lost in a labyrinth Enrique had crafted with his words. She thought of Aristophanes' dictum *by words the mind is winged*. As if coming out of a vivid dream, she asked the next question with reluctant anticipation.

"And what is our greatest fear, Enrique?"

He took a deep breath, looked into her eyes, and spoke with the discomfort of a doctor giving a patient a bleak prognosis.

"Entering our divinity. Knowing that when we look with our physical eyes our oneness is limited by the boundaries of our bodies. Accepting that once we learn that our power lies within, we can no longer blame external hurdles for failure to live our dreams. Stepping into our divinity is the most decisive task of our journey. Yet, most of us never attempt it and few of us succeed when we try."

"Please forgive me for asking the obvious Enrique, but do you think the fear of accepting our personal power is greater than our need for joy?"

"That's a profound question I've pondered for years. I finally had to ask Breogán for his opinion," Enrique answered with a devilish smile that lifted the somber mood. "And... Breogán, being more evolved than I, explained it in a very haunting manner."

"Tell me what he said, Enrique, and I promise I'll resist his charm."

Kate had a remarkable ability to turn a conversation from existential heaviness to playful reflection. She danced the shift of moods with Enrique so flawlessly, he was able to sense how time could truly be compressed, and glimpses of glorious love experienced in defiance of conventional wisdom. Kate stirred him to live his theory.

"Ok, I'll tell you what Breogán had to say. Love is a universal force that we encapsulate within time and space. But since joy is the byproduct of love, we are seduced by the effect rather than the expression. Joy is the *consequence* of love and living our essence *is* love. The most intriguing part of our quest is that when we begin to feel the joy of love, we immediately fear losing the gift. When the fear emerges, it removes us from the process of loving and we experience the loss of something that is inherently ours. The loss is an illusion we create when we separate what we feel from what we are. That flaw in transcendental judgment happens when we try to hold on to what cannot be taken from us."

Enrique felt he was paraphrasing a close friend. As he explained his theory to Kate through Breogán, he was astonished at the clarity he could achieve by depersonalizing his own beliefs through a character that was becoming increasingly more vivid in his life.

Throughout their spirited conversation they hardly ate, but seemed nourished by the topic and several cups of hot *chai,* inconspicuously served by their Indian waiter. They left the restaurant and went for a walk without words on Ocean Drive. Perhaps experiencing *thoughts for food* as a fitting reversal of the better-known adage.

"Kate, did you know this is my neighborhood? Actually, we're half a block from my home."

"No, I didn't know you lived in Miami Beach."

"How can I invite you over for a glass of wine without you thinking this was planned?" Enrique asked, surprised by his genuine apprehension.

"You must remember, Enrique, that I chose the restaurant and I had no idea how close it was to your place. Therefore, in the words of the mystical Dr. Lugo, we *coauthored* this synchronistic event."

"We did all of that for a glass of wine?" Enrique asked teasingly, attempting to dissimulate the awesome tenderness that emerges when two people meet at their horizons of intimacy and, for a brief moment, become one. He fought the urge to share the emotional intensity that lived in the safety of his thoughts.

Abruptly, and typically of Florida's flash weather, thunderbolts exploded, followed by prancing cascades of heavy rain. Their drenched bodies felt the incongruous chill of tropical summer showers. But rather than hurriedly running for shelter, they held hands and, with a skipping reminiscent of *Singin' in the Rain,* reached Enrique's house.

"Do you have a *Jeeves* to greet us with a cup of hot chocolate?" she asked mischievously as Enrique opened the door.

"No, but you have me as your most devoted servant," he replied disarmingly.

"Let's go in and see how devoted you really are," said Kate, drenched from the cooling rain.

A dwelling is a reflection of self even when interior designers are given the freedom to interpret our personal aesthetics. Enrique's home décor tastefully melded the crispness of modern minimalism with the classical majesty of strategically placed antiques. He learned psychological principles of design as a child without realizing it, by listening to his father describe the distinctiveness of the period furniture he so artistically restored. Xosé Lugo had an exclusive antique shop, where Enrique spent time after school absorbing his dad's worldly philosophy.

Xosé believed that God periodically got bored, and created the vicissitudes of life to see how much power His children would exert to surmount them. Frequently, God was disappointed in the lack of faith His children accorded their own divinity. The conversations never lacked humor or underlying hope for the human condition. Enrique remembered his dad quoting Nietzsche and depicting him as a chronically depressed man with a notable compensatory wit. *God is a comedian performing for an audience who is afraid to laugh* was Enrique's prized Nietzschean sardonic dig. In those days philosophers had no antidepressants to quell their existential anguish.

Kate walked into the spacious living room and immediately felt at home. Oriental rugs delineated fashion islands to inspire conversation or promote serenity after a demanding day. The anthropologist's relics had a dominant presence in the room. Talismans of Amazonian shamans, Tibetan prayer wheels, and Masai warrior masks were but a few of the cultural artifacts that highlighted the décor.

"Enrique, I love your home. It affects me in a way I can't describe. What an odd feeling."

"Yes, cultural history speaks louder than words! But I've noticed you're trembling. You'll find towels and a warm robe in the master bathroom. Go to the end of the hallway and turn right."

Kate came back to the living room wearing his black terry cloth robe and he handed her a cup of hot chocolate. Her face lit up with appreciation and he smiled pleased with her response. In that brief exchange, he sensed the richness of offering primal comfort to someone who was beginning to enter his most intimate dimension.

While Enrique went to his bedroom to change clothes, Kate surveyed the space he called home. She allowed herself the fantasy of what it would be like to share his world. She realized that was the first time, since her father's passing, that she had thought up life plans without including her adopted family. She was rapidly brought back to the present when Enrique returned wearing a black kimono that underscored his engaging good looks.

"You know, Dr. Lugo, you're a very handsome lad."

"Well, thank you, Dr. Holland," replied Enrique, noting that, although said in jest, the formality masked their apprehension of flirting, their vulnerabilities. No amount of achievement can guarantee smooth sailing in matters of the heart.

The rain stopped as swiftly as it started, and they went to the balcony to witness how the sun returns to the ocean at the end of the day. Kate lamented how the majestic rituals of nature go unnoticed when we fail to celebrate the eternal present.

"Enrique, teach me how to compress intimacy," Kate blurted, to her surprise--and for the first time without the distinctive fear that erupted when she gambled with her emotional safety.

"Your openness to risk definitely moves me. You make it easier to admit that I may know the art of preaching compression, but I feel like a neophyte when I try to live it. In fact, I've only done it once and, although it enriched my literary inspiration, it ended a very desirable relationship. I learned how to describe the experience in my book, but I also found how the intensity of joy can scare some people away."

"How do you mean?" Kate asked, dreading what she might hear.

"This woman…" Enrique started to say, but took a deep breath before continuing, "was so afraid of vertical intimacy that she used dishonesty to sabotage our relationship."

"But Enrique, maybe she was just a dishonest person and chose not to engage in the forthrightness required."

"You know, Kate? You're very astute in pointing that out, because I've recently come to the conclusion that fear cannot justify deceit. It's impossible to create a *covenant of safety* without honesty."

"A covenant of safety? I love your terminology. Listen, I have a proposal," Kate said with enthusiasm in her voice, "let's create your *covenant of safety* by teaching each other how to expand our intimate boundaries with empathy."

"Kate, humble or not, your Buddhist mind is reaching my heart and I am falling in love with you."

"Enrique, your passion melts me."

Profound levels of disclosure, coupled with mutual physical magnetism, can make a powerful aphrodisiac. They both sensed that embracing the intoxication of the moment would prevent them from discerning between horizontal lust and vertical love. Without discussion, they chose compassion rather than passion and began their covenant of safety by tenderly holding each other throughout the night. The experience was analogous to delighting in the beauty of a Botticelli without having to take it home. Sex can be a confusing intruder when one is learning to honor the gift of intimacy. Yet, once sex is elevated to express love, two mortals can sample the eternal as one.

Enrique woke up to the first light of morning and saw Kate sitting full lotus on the floor, facing the ocean. The glow of golden hues that framed her face brought forth an image of an ethereal goddess. He marveled at how time ceases to pass through space when beauty elicits divinity.

"Good morning, *mi deliciosa.*" Enrique greeted Kate, as she came out of her deep meditation with a smile.

"Good morning to you... *mi delicioso,*" she responded, correctly using the masculine gender of the Galician word.

"But why are we calling each other delicious?"

"Because that's the word that comes to mind when I think of you. By the way, I thought you didn't speak Galician."

"I don't, but I am fluent in Spanish and I figured the word was the same in both languages."

"Kate, once again you figured wisely."

"So... according to your theory, how do we begin to compress intimacy?"

"We already started by creating a foundation for the covenant of safety," Enrique answered, enticed by the perimeter they committed to enter. "One of the most appealing aspects of vertical intimacy, is that we can reduce the time required to reach it, by delaying our primal desires as they emerge. A classical example is our decision to delay sexuality in our initial encounters. We didn't discuss the issue and yet, we intuitively knew that to allow those feelings to rule would have disturbed the covenant of safety."

"But Enrique, although I agree with what you're saying, I am certain there's much more to the covenant of safety than just preventing sexuality from becoming the sole motivation to achieve closeness."

"Yes, the covenant is complex. I believe what makes the exploration difficult is that, although we know there's more to intimacy than sexuality, our need for gratification gets confused with the purpose of our personal journey. You made an excellent suggestion to expand our boundaries of intimacy with empathy, because that's exactly what's needed to create safety. Rather than a guarantee to not hurt each other, the covenant is an agreement of honor to never engage in deceit. Ignorance, insensitivity or impulsivity can be resolved as long as the intention remains honest. The true enemy of emotional safety is deception."

"But *mi delicioso*, what I find so difficult to understand is how to genuinely forgive once we have been deceived in a relationship."

"Yes, I considered that same question through Breogán. Let me show you."

Enrique went to his study and brought back a manuscript. He quickly skimmed through it and handed Kate a page to read. She smiled, anticipating her first encounter with the words of the elusive Breogán. He wrote:

We cannot forgive without first acknowledging the love we experienced in a relationship. Closure requires releasing resentment and embracing gratitude. When we open our hearts enthusiastically, we assume that the loving bond will never end, and that disillusionment is not possible. But as we confront the pain of closing our hearts when a relationship fails, we attempt to heal by forgiving the pain we suffered, without appreciating the joy we received. We move from hurt to sadness; from anger to loneliness; and when we realize that we must forgive to relinquish bitterness, we forgive to end our pain, rather than to celebrate how we loved.

We must remember that forgiveness takes place in the soul rather than in the heart. When resentment shifts to appreciation, it replaces our quest for permanence with the serenity of our transcendence.

"This is magnificent, Enrique. It seems Breogán has experienced true forgiving."

Enrique looked at Kate and smiled, noticing how much he had shared and how grounded he felt with her. She was the sanctuary he needed to risk emotional abyss in the name of love. Now he could return to his writing, drawing from the inspiration that feeling loved ignited.

Chapter 2

"The multivariable meanings surface like an epiphany..."

Trinity College, Dublin

Lecture on The Intimate Language of Love

*"L*adies and gentlemen, we are pleased to introduce the Galician mystic and scholar Breogán, who will speak this evening about the intimate language of love." The audience applauded and cheered.

"Thank you very much for this opportunity to discuss a subject that has fascinated my mind and conquered my heart. I believe we come to this revolving sphere we call Earth to learn the intimate language of love and, we hope, to speak it fluently. Yet, most of us avoid this honorable quest, replacing it with a life of fear.

"I propose that love cannot be communicated intimately unless we're able to identify with the recipient as if we were one. Paradoxically, that oneness can only be achieved by taking an 'empathic leap' from Self, to feel as if we were the recipient of the love we are attempting to give. Let me explain what I mean by empathic leap. We spend much of our time interpreting, through our own personal reality, what we're communicating to others. This personal context is necessary to assess our own thoughts and feelings while we interact, but in order to assimilate the impact of our communication, we must jump out of our private Self and attempt to understand what we are contributing from the context of the recipient. To jump out of our private Self, and conceive what we are offering as if we were the receiver, is what I call the empathic leap. I caution that what commonly passes for empathy is nothing more than a projection of our own image, imposed on the recipient of our gift. True empathy requires leaping out of Self to feel as if we were the other person, rather than how we would feel under the predicament of the other person.

"I strongly contend that, in order to communicate the intimate language of love, two basic ingredients are required: The ability to experience the empathic leap, and the capacity to feel gratitude. With-

out the empathic leap, we are unable to connect with the oneness of our humanity, and without gratitude, we cannot accept the gift of love. We must offer with empathy and accept with appreciation, if we want to give our hearts a voice.

"Most of us know our limitations and how they make us feel help-less, but what fascinates me is how we can remain within the restraints of those limitations after we learn what we can do to liberate ourselves. Unfortunately, modern psychotherapy focuses on providing tools for change, rather than teaching how to access and steer the will. An alco-holic learns that abstinence requires changing lifestyle and patterns of thoughts. Yet, the recovery rate is discouraging, despite intellectual mastery of the tools required to change the behavior.

"I argue that our primary obstacle is that we don't seem to under-stand the origin of will. We say that will is all we need to achieve change, but this very intangible force remains a mystery when we at-tempt to assimilate it. Will is a commitment to reach a worthy objective in the face of adversity. When will is turned into action, the portentous evidence that predicts doom is replaced with faith in a providential outcome.

"So, if will is action that can free us from our surrender to help-lessness, what triggers the liberation? We can define will as existential strength, transcendental meaning, or with other labels that philoso-phers have debated for millennia. But this evening, I want us to move from attempting to define will toward identifying the conditions that support the action. Not an easy task, I assure you.

"We can agree that the adversities that call on an individual to ex-ercise whatever 'will' may be range from physical survival to preservation of personal values. Yet, that still does not tell us what promotes the organic process that frees the will to shift from intention to action. I invite you to consider that love is the foundation of will. The execution of will requires personal valuation in the case of self-preservation, or valuation of another person when the action is for the benefit of someone else.

"Will also surfaces to preserve symbols such as honor and truth. But neither symbol nor person can trigger the action of will without assigning worthiness to the intended recipient. If we value most what we love, then we can see that love is the fuel that feeds the will. It is very important at this point to identify the horizons of will. What contains it? What expands it?

"Since we have gone beyond attempting to define the will, we can begin to conceptualize how valuation takes place, and how the qualities that contain the action can be negotiated. To take action in the face of adversity requires an implicit acceptance that the risk is justified, be-

cause the objective preserves and validates our worthiness. We determine the valuation by concluding that the consequences of the risk we take are outweighed by the worthiness that we assign to self or others. Then, at that moment, we enter a dimension of symbols and begin to live them. In the case of asserting the will to speak against tyranny in a repressive regime, we must feel worthy of exercising freedom of expression, before we can embrace the symbol of freedom. This means that we must believe before we can act, and we must love before we can believe.

"Conceptualize the province of will having horizons that are activated by empathic leaps, and expanded by love. We jump out of private Self with empathy for the recipients, and we integrate them into our domain with love. Once the commitment is made to risk for a worthy objective, no amount of adversity can dissuade the will, and the most intense fear can be conquered by love."

As soon as Enrique finished typing the last word on his laptop, he felt as if he had just encountered a source of wisdom he could not attribute to anything from his own intellect. Skeptically, Enrique contemplated parapsychological phenomena as plausible explanations for the Breogán resource. Some mystics call the experience "entering the divine portals" or "riding *the drift.*" The quantum physicist, David Bohm, saw it as information from the *implicate order.* Enrique gave up trying to label the knowledge he had accessed and reasoned that, whatever it was, he needed to tap into it more than he cared to admit. At once he was enchanted and hesitant.

While he debated what to do, an idea surfaced: *what would happen if I could address this source of wisdom as if it were an entity?* Enrique asked himself while he positioned his fingers on the keyboard. He approached the screen on his laptop like a window into Breogán's world and began to type.

"Hello, Breogán. I know you're there, whether I created you or not." Enrique felt awkward typing to an unknown, but continued. He cleared his mind and began to think as if he were Breogán, allowing the empathic leap to take effect.

"*Hola, Quico.* Are you still afraid of others detecting your slight Spanish accent when you speak in class?" Enrique smiled and felt warm tears racing down his cheeks. *Quico* was the endearing diminutive his father called him. As for the light accent of his childhood, it was an apprehension he had never shared with anyone.

Enrique paused and allowed the excitement of his new discovery to take effect. The scientist in him wanted to see it as an exchange between his consciousness and a repressed compartment of Self, where all his personal history and accumulated wisdom resided waiting to surface into awareness. Perhaps he was accessing the collective intelligence that biologist Rupert Sheldrake calls *morphic resonance*. Sheldrake suggests that these resonating fields are an accumulation of information vital to the survival of each species. The *100 monkeys rule,* an example from comparative psychology, alludes to the feasibility of morphic resonance. It has been observed in monkeys, as well as other species, that when a critical mass of about 100 learn a task, all the other members of that species in the surrounding area tap into the information without having learned the behavior by observation.

A creative experiment was designed assuming that, if information accumulates in species-specific *resonating fields*, participants who worked a crossword puzzle in a newspaper the day after its publication` would do better than those who worked the puzzle the same day the newspaper was published: reasoning that the day after the publication, answers would be accessible from the resonating field. Indeed, that's what happened. Participants who worked the puzzle the day *after* the newspaper was published did significantly better than those who worked the puzzle the *same* day it was published.

"Tell me, Breogán, what do you think is my greatest fear?"

"Can you keep a secret?"

"Does that mean you know what I fear?"

"Enrique, this is your usual evasion, answering a question with another question. Remember, you've done that to Kate."

"Ah, so you know about Kate?" Enrique smiled immediately, noting Breogán knew him well. "Alright, you win. Yes, I can keep a secret. I guess I am a bit reluctant to hear your answer, because you may be a part of me I may not want to know."

"But what if I am not really you, and I am an *entity,* as you called me?"

"Well, whatever you are, I like your sense of humor. Then again, I may be complimenting myself."

Enrique stopped typing and began to feel foolish, wondering if he was bordering on delusional thinking. He followed his instincts and continued the dialogue.

"Let me answer your question Enrique. Yes, you fear going through life not knowing who believed in you unconditionally. We need at least one person in our lifetime to validate our worthiness. What I mean by that is that, if another person can truly reach your private Self and acknowledge your nobleness, even for a brief moment, then your despair dissipates, because someone has engaged your *transcendental humanity*. Yes, I know Enrique, you want me to explain."

"You're right. I do want you to explain. I can see now why Kate is so charmed by you." Enrique was enjoying this surrealistic exchange more than he had anticipated.

"Don't worry, Enrique, Kate loves you."

He sensed that Breogán was also having fun. It was as if a part of him was besting another part of him.

"My dear Dr. Lugo, as Kate refers to you, let me explain what I mean. Self-validation is vital to building a healthy personal identity, but we also seek emotional affiliation as social beings, and unison in the spiritual dimension. Although we connect emotionally in relationships to build existential safety, our transcendental fear remains. That's why most existentialists are stuck in despair. They, by definition, *exist* in the concreteness of their physical here and now. Without mysticism in their lives, they're unable to enter and chart *the drift*. Of course, Kierkegaard was an exception because he explored beyond the cognitive/emotional level, and explained how anxiety becomes despair when we face the infinite."

"Breogán, now I ask you with anticipation: what is *the drift*?"

"To answer your question, I need to continue with Kierkegaard. He wrote that anxiety and despair are symptoms that surface when the Self cannot find synthesis between the finite and the infinite. Anxiety is an alarm triggered when we reach the limits of our temporal embracement, but when private Self confronts the infinite, despair surfaces as a deeper alarm to announce the edge of our physical realm. When we delve into the spiritual, self-identity can no longer provide the grounding for the journey. At that time, we must take what Kierkegaard calls the *leap of faith*."

Enrique's excitement grew as he generated thoughts without ownership, caught up in the flow of dueling mentations he could not stop.

"Unfortunately, in his era Kierkegaard did not have quantum physics and chaos theory to speak with about non-locality and non-linearity. The former describes conditions without origin and the latter reflects patterns that have no predictable order.

"Arming ourselves with nineteenth-century Kierkegaard and twenty-first century cognitive science, we can engage *the drift* as modern mystics. Imagine the private journey of Self as a dance where the predictable and the chaotic interact with the physical and the transcendental. The reason we perceive order as the rule, and disorder as the exception, is that our brains select fragments of coherence from chaotic processes and modulate them to give us the illusion of origin and predictability in time and space. Although we feel like we weave in and out of *the drift*, we're always in it because chaos is intermittent in our minds, but constant in our world."

Enrique paused to assimilate what he was typing as Breogán and came to a disquieting awareness. He could not remember reading Kierkegaard, and his knowledge of quantum physics and chaos theory was elementary. He fought the impulse to label his experience with Breogán as something more abstruse than simply digging into his own subconscious.

"Tell me more about *the drift* and how it relates to mysticism."

As soon as Enrique typed his request, he drew a blank as to what the possible answer could be. He took a deep breath and looked at the screen without anticipating what he would write as Breogán.

"From an empirical perspective, *the drift* is a process where outcome cannot be predicted from segment to segment of physical reality, because the senses and the instruments of science are not able to chart simultaneity. We try to connect with our physical world to reduce existential anxiety, but we also seek unison in the spiritual dimension to resolve our despair. Within the finite, we validate our tangible humanity through love. But if we dare to approach the infinite, we can find our transcendental essence through faith. Love requires evidence to believe, whereas faith requires belief without evidence.

"To enter *the drift*, the need for predictability has to be surrendered in order to discover the *portals of synchronicity*. You noticed I said *discover* rather than *find*. The portals are discovered when you're already inside *the drift*, rather than noticing them before you enter. Finding and discovering have different cognitive registries. Finding requires searching for a known outcome, whereas discovering involves the unfolding of events that have meaning after they are encountered. When you're in the search mode you know what you're looking for, but when you're discovering, you don't know what you're seeking until you find it."

"Are you saying *the drift* has to be entered and traversed through the discovery mode?" Enrique asked, as if he were dialoguing in the Socratic method, where answers are reached through questions that test logical limits. The exchange was loaded with embedded acumen.

"I am certain, by now, you are aware that I can anticipate your thoughts. The question is whether you have full access to mine?"

"Breogán, you present complexities that remind me of Escher's prints."

"Excellent analogy. The print where the hand appears to be coming out of the paper to draw itself comes to mind."

"I am fascinated by your explanation of *the drift* and I am beginning to get hints of how it may unfold."

"What does that tell you Enrique?"

"Perhaps that I am embracing the portals?"

Enrique was now eminently aware of his answer-with-a-question style, but he didn't care to judge himself at that moment. He felt ambiguous in the role of Breogán, for the first time, not knowing whether to respond as he imagined Breogán would, or just let the information unfold. He chose to witness the void and let the exchange resume without preconceptions.

"Excellent Enrique! You chose to discover. If you had gone with your initial choice to preconceive my response, you would have disengaged *the drift*. Yes my friend, you entered a portal and discovered how it feels to cruise *the drift*. Once you enter the portals, occurrences that initially appeared improbable and without connection become meaningful in a multidimensional way. We are so disconnected from *the drift* that, when we encounter its inherent simultaneity, we view it as highly improbable but meaningful coincidences, and we call them synchronicities. Yet, within *the drift*, synchronicity is a frequent occurrence readily available in the discovery mode."

Enrique felt an overpowering sense of displaced compassion. It was like a strong connection void of connectors. Knowing he did not have to elaborate his next question, he simply typed the word *why*?

"I'll answer your *why*. The boundlessness you just experienced is what the Buddhists philosophers call witnessing without a witness. The boundaries that encapsulate the finite disappear and you transcend the illusion of separateness. Awareness that there is something beyond the end of our finite existence surfaces, and the sequence that we create to experience the illusion of movement through time and space vanishes. Without boundaries, there is no reference to ground our orientation. We lose self-image to find oneness beyond despair, no longer needing to be enclosed in a concrete identity. Self renounces despair in the face of the infinite when it realizes separation is an illusion we choose to live."

"Thank you Breogán. Until next time?"

Enrique had stayed up most of the night, but felt alert and refreshed. He never thought he would write a novel where the character would come out of the paper like Escher's hand. Where was he going with this experience? How could he continue the book with all the layers of reality it was generating? If he told his publisher what was going on, she would probably advise him to find a good shrink. Could he tell Kate? He would certainly never outlive it if he told Eric. That last thought made him grin, thinking how Eric would congratulate him--only after milking all the hilarity he could conjure from the Breogán encounters.

He had to tell Eric. Maybe there was synchronicity in Eric naming Breogán for him on the talk show. Enrique thought that if he was going to share *the drift* with Eric, he had to teach him how to enter the portals. But if he explained how to enter, he would be giving Eric a search mode rather than a discovery tool. His thoughts were spiraling, trying to understand how Breogán taught him to discover the portals without falling into the predictability trap.

Rehearsing in his mind how to teach Eric to enter *the drift*, Enrique recalled how he suspended predictability; took an empathic leap to expand the self-horizons; and allowed faith to approach the void through the discovery mode. The whole notion was incongruous, given that the portals unfold only when confirmation ceases and synchronicity replaces predictability, to register coincidence rather than consistency. Enrique slowly blurred his ruminations and fell into a heavy sleep.

The phone rang and Enrique turned slowly to see his publisher's name on the caller ID.

"Hello, Liliana, what a pleasant surprise."

"Enrique, you're being too formal with me. What are you up to?"

"I am not sure what you mean?"

"Please cut the bull and tell me."

"Ok, I'll tell you, but you need to contain that Italian fervor of yours."

"You like my intensity."

"Yes, I do, but now I need your calm understanding."

"What happened? Did you breakup with the goddess?"

"How did you know about Kate?"

"Dear one, I have friends in strategic places. Anyway, please tell me what's up."

"The book is taking a new turn, and I am not sure what I want to do with it."

"And what is that turn that distresses you?"

"Well...at first, I was clear on what I wanted to do. Then things started to happen."

"I knew that woman was going to derail you! I told your agent you should get away for a couple of weeks to clear your mind. Men just don't know how to handle gorgeous women with brains."

"Liliana, thanks for the compliment about Kate, but you're way off base. It has nothing to do with her."

"Then tell me what's wrong, so I can have anxiety issues to discuss with my shrink."

"You need a new psychiatrist. You've been going to that woman for two years and you're as stressed as when you started. Is she an angry feminist?"

"Enrique, sometimes you let your testosterone surges cloud your good judgment."

"Thank you Liliana, for that very deeply disguised compliment."

They both laughed without taking offense, as two friends do when they respect each other.

"Ok, *cara mia,* listen carefully and give me your opinion. This book has been the most difficult to write, because now I am more willing to confront my own insecurities as I progress with the story. My previous two books were more academic and I was able to detach from my own struggles. *The Man from Autumn* is very different in that I am truly looking for personal answers, rather than just giving insights to my readers."

"Darling, you're covering your insecurities quite well from what I saw in your interview with Eric Connery. That man is a handsome devil. Is he dating anyone worthy?"

"Liliana, you and Eric should get together. He told me he wants to tame that dominant side of yours."

"Did he really say that? He's too old for me. Well, maybe not, I've seen him with younger women. Tell him he can try to succeed where other deserving men have failed. Never mind; I'll tell him myself."

"Don't you dare discuss this conversation with him. It was just guy talk."

"Men are worse gossipers than women."

"Liliana, that's a well-kept secret that men will never acknowledge. But I will admit that I am worried about how to proceed with the book. Part of me wants to weave an exciting story, and the other needs to dissect my inner world through the main character."

"Enrique, I think you can succeed balancing both. Be the writer for your public, and the anthropologist of your inner world for you. I think this book could be a huge success. I've seen your resilience shine when you're conflicted. Remember *Portals of Evil*?"

"How can I forget? That book pushed my limits of compassion after interviewing all those serial killers and hit men."

"Yes, but you grasped the core of your topic, and the public loved it."

"Thanks Liliana. You're a dear friend."

"Yes I know. May I see a chapter or two?"

"Let me decide which way I am going first, and then you can have them."

"How far are you?"

"I am sure my optimistic agent told you I am practically finished, but I am progressing slowly."

"Well, good agents sometimes need to embellish the truth to publishers, but Michael never abuses it. That's why I like him. Ok, Enrique, remember, I am here if you need me. Let me know when you have something for me to read."

"I will, Liliana. Thanks for your support."

Enrique looked at the clock by his bed and noticed it was 9:00 am. It was time to face the world and its *daily gifts of discovery*, as Breogán would say.

He wanted to take a break from the book and enjoy an easy day. He went to the gym and had a thorough workout. Then, lunch at his favorite restaurant in Little Havana, where he ran into his Cuban friend Máximo Suarez. Like most of his compatriots, Máximo left Cuba after the revolution and was able to do quite well in Miami. He saved his money working two jobs for several years and made a fortune investing wisely in sugar futures. His family had owned several sugarcane mills in Cuba, and the principles of sugar commodities came natural to him, as he discovered in the early nineteen sixties.

Now, Máximo was quite wealthy and very lonely, because he never made time for a personal life and, after two bad marriages and no children, he was alone again. He was tall, with a full head of white hair and a distinguished air that no amount of hard times could diminish. He was seventy-three and professed that Viagra was for wimps.

Like Enrique, Máximo had strong Galician ancestry, and that was the initial match that brought both men together, despite their generational differences. When Máximo arrived in Miami penniless, he already had a doctorate in Iberian History, but never pursued academia from the teaching side. Instead, he managed to publish a book, and over a dozen professional articles in prestigious journals on Galician ancient history, while accumulating his considerable wealth. Enrique had recently picked Máximo's brain about the legendary Breogán and his place in Galician mysticism.

This time seeing Máximo at the Cuban restaurant had a different context. Although he had decided to give the book a rest, he interpreted running into Máximo as a potential synchronistic portal. In fact, after thinking about it, he never made plans to meet Máximo for lunch and yet, for years, they had enjoyed an unspoken luncheon ritual that just happened sporadically to sweeten their days. Enrique felt he entered a portal the instant he discovered the pattern he and Máximo had been coauthoring for more than ten years. He was hooked on Breogán's *drift* again. He felt he was beginning to learn the navigational parameters of discovery. Breogán was right. The multivariable meanings surface like an epiphany as soon as one engages *the drift*.

He went to Máximo's table and they hugged. Although Máximo had already ordered, Antonio, the waiter, took care of Enrique's standing fare of *langosta enchilada, arroz blanco* and *plátanos maduros fritos*. To drink, Antonio brought them their usual bottle of *Marquez de Riscal*. Unfortunately, the Cuban restaurant did not carry Enrique's beloved Galician wines.

"Máximo, have you ever noticed that we've been meeting for lunch all these years and we never plan it?"

"Yes, I have."

"What do you think about it?"

"I suspect you want to talk about Breogán again."

"Not so much Breogán, but rather what Galician mystics have to say about synchronicity in general."

"Well, I can tell you what Máximo the mystic has to say about it."

"You never told me you were a mystic."

"Enriquito, you never asked me," they both broke into a roaring laughter and toasted to synchronicity.

"Now, Máximo, you're not going to tell me you've been waiting all these years for me to reach my awakening, are you?"

"No, actually, I had given up on you until you asked me about Breogán after your interview with Mr. Connery."

"So then you know about *the drift*?"

"The drift?"

"Máximo, you're playing head games with me." Enrique smiled, waiting for an answer.

"As you know, Enriquito, the Galicians had no written language in the days of Breogán. Legend has it Breogán lived in the second century of the Common Era. He built a tall tower for his son to be able to see the green island across the ocean--what is now Ireland. His son was fascinated by the green island he saw from the tower and had to visit it. Sadly, soon after he landed, the Dannan Kings murdered him and that, inevitably, led to the invasion of Ireland.

"Why did they kill him?"

"They thought he was a spy trying to gather information for their enemies." Máximo answered, enjoying Enrique's interest in Galician ancient history. "Synchronicity is a modern concept, but in Breogán's time, they relied on the prophetic dreams of their mystics. These dreams brought past, present and future together, in a simultaneous manner that enabled them to find meaning in their chaos. The mystics taught that dreams provided clues to discover portals of power in daily experiences. So, in a way, the dreams of their mystics facilitated information to enter *the drift*. I am reminded of Carlito Castañeda's books on the teachings of Don Juan, where the Yaqui shaman explained how to travel the world of dreams."

"Máximo, why did you refer to Carlos Castañeda as *Carlito*?"

"That's what I always called him. Just like I call you Enriquito."

"You're telling me you knew Castañeda?"

"He contacted me many years ago to ask me about Galician mysticism, when he was working on one of his books. Although Carlito was born in Peru, he had Galician roots, and was looking for similarities between the Yaqui shamans of Mexico and the Galician mystics of Celtic Spain."

"Did you ever meet him in person? You know he was a consummate recluse who never permitted interviewers or photographers in his life."

"Yes, he was obsessed with maintaining a secret identity. We talked for years on the phone and we met once, outside Mexico City."

"You have to tell me what he looked like."

"He was short."

Enrique smiled and did not push the question further.

"Enriquito, one thing I can tell you is that, after researching mysticism in both Eastern and Western cultures, the premises are remarkably similar."

"I agree. The pivotal theme is *a calling* to an archetypal journey, with guides for those who seek the transcendental in their daily lives. I can't recall who said that *religion is a collective path to worship God, whereas mysticism is a personal quest to know God.* It seems to me that religion needs preachers and mysticism needs guides."

"Well spoken. The person you can't recall is Evelyn Underhill, who wrote a prolific book on the subject, appropriately titled *Mysticism.*"

"Máximo, tell me why mystics have such difficult lives? Teresa of Avila, John of the Cross and many others."

"I think that's a splendid question. When you look at the history of Western mystics, they lived considerably long but painful lives, whereas most of the Eastern mystics lived healthier, shorter lives. I think the reason is the difference in how they formulated their purpose. The Western medieval mystics thought the way to reach God was through suffering long and hard to be worthy of heaven. On the other hand, the ancient Eastern mystics did not believe in suffering as a way to reach God, but rather through paying their karmic debt. Once the debt was paid, they saw no need to remain on the mortal plane."

"Máximo, for an old Cuban you're very shrewd."

"Thank you Enriquito. I can also tell you, for a smart ass Galician, you've done quite well yourself."

Both men laughed and realized it was time to order *Larios 1866* for a perfect closure to a delightful luncheon. They loved that Spanish brandy, and were thankful this restaurant was one of the few places they could find such rare brand outside of Spain. Both men implicitly appreciated how each contributed to the quality of their lives. Enrique was beginning to recognize how these exquisite encounters nourished his literary voice. He wondered if his life could sustain its purpose without the joy he harvested from his writing.

Chapter 3

"I am curious to know why you chose autumn in particular."

Estaca de Bares, Galicia

After a successful lecture tour in Ireland and Scotland, Breogán returned to his home by the most spectacular beaches in the Coruña province of Galicia. The picturesque village of Estaca de Bares is in the most northern coast of Spain: a haven where Breogán windsurfed and wrote his books on the intimate language of love. Breogán lived with his wife who was impetuous and significantly younger than he. These attributes, that would assuredly lead to unsustainable turbulence, were harmonized with empathy and gratitude in a relationship that had outlived the worst predictions from the envious. According to Breogán, we enter relationships with archetypal wounds that are not only demanding, but also critical to the spiritual healing of two people who aspire to share their love.

Breogán argued, in his theory of intimacy, that relationships that are complacent from the beginning are doomed to a mundane existence. There must be initial storms to surpass, if we are to evolve beyond our tormenting egos. In a relationship, one cannot win and be happy at the same time, because the one who loses will live in resentment until a depleted image can be fed with another victory. This hopeless exchange at the expense of the other partner creates a vicious cycle of besting and being bested. Rather than compromising or struggling for control, successful partnerships learn the joy of entrusting the protection of their vulnerabilities to each other. Breogán and Sabela were a living tribute to his theory, not by the triumphs they shared, but by the personal demons they had conquered with their love. Emotional safety reigned in their world.

"Where's my dazzling woman? I am home."

"Your dazzling, and loving, woman is right behind you."

Whenever he arrived home from his lecture tours, they would play this game where he had to look for her all over the house, until she would sneak up on him with a hug.

"Did you bring me a present?"

"Yes, you're looking at him."

"I love my present. May I play with him?"

"I am your devoted toy."

They laughed and kissed running to the beach, tripping as they stripped naked, and jumped in the ocean. There was a naturalist area a few kilometers from their home, but their private beach gave them license to amuse the few neighbors who lived on that exclusive cove. One neighbor, who was not amused, gossiped about how this foolish couple was never going to stop playing childish games and settle down. At a recent cocktail party, Sabela suggested to this gossiping neighbor that she should consider finding a man who could make her feel like a playful girl again. The acerbic woman replied that she had never been playful in her life and had no interest in learning such useless behavior.

Sabela and Breogán swam until dark and returned to their beach chateau to shower together and dress for dinner. On his first night home, they would always dine at their favorite restaurant in the neighboring village of Porto do Barqueiro: he wearing black tie, and she wearing black mini. The villagers were grateful for the entertainment their renowned mystic and his too-young-for-him wife provided with their eccentricities.

Sabela was twenty-eight and looked twenty, and Breogán was fifty-five and appeared late thirties. Sabela's mother introduced them at one of his book signings. After a short courtship, Sabela married him, five years ago. Later, mom told Sabela that, although she thought Breogán was too old for her, he was simply irresistible. Of course, mom was only fifty-four.

"How's your dinner, Sabie?"

"Delightful, like you."

"While I was lecturing on the beauty of intimacy, I could not stop thinking about our love. I am thankful for your vivaciousness and the way you care."

"What about my gorgeous body?"

"That helps too." They laughed, truly enjoying each other's company, and the art of breaking bread with a partner for life.

"Sabela, I want to discuss something with you."

"You're leaving me for a younger woman?"

"No, something better than that."

"Breogán, I am going to punch that handsome face of yours."

Enrique drew a blank and stopped typing. What did Breogán want to tell her? He reflected on how his relationship with Kate differed from Breogán and Sabela's. He was enjoying how the characters were relating, and realized he wanted to share a similar companionship with Kate. Writing the novel versus dialoguing with Breogán had contributive differences to his creative processes. Enrique noticed he guided the characters in the novel when he was crafting Breogán's world, but when he engaged in the experimental dialogues, Breogán guided him. Enrique realized he was *authoring* experiences and projecting them to his characters, as well as *coauthoring* dialogues with his own projections. Although creative writers may engage both methods intuitively, Enrique sensed he was tapping into uncharted cognitive pathways, and returned to Breogán's mind with increased curiosity.

"Sabie, let me tell you my idea. How would you like to travel for a couple of months with me to research my new book?"

She let out a scream and jumped out of her chair to hug Breogán. They started to dance without music around their table. Instinctively, the other customers in the restaurant applauded, assuming they were witnessing laudable news from the outlandish couple. The owner was used to their outbursts of elation, and dutifully brought a bottle of champagne to each table, anticipating the couple's request. Breogán believed that joyful news should be celebrated with your surrounding audience, to bless the energy that triggered the event.

They left the restaurant singing old Galician songs and went home to share the delightful secrets of the night. In the morning they sat in their tall rattan chairs, facing a spectacular view of the ocean from their second-story sunroom. They drank their Ethiopian coffee with evaporated milk.

"My love, why do you want your adoring woman to research this particular book with you?"

Sabela had a natural ability to make Breogán feel vibrant with her words. Her synergy of tenderness and sensuality was his fountain of youth.

"You know, I believe autumn has mystical distinctiveness. In particular, I want to understand how this ethereal season affects the intimate language of love in legendary settings. As life partners we can learn its secrets."

"I am curious to know why you chose autumn in particular."

"Well Sabie, it's more like autumn chose me. When I looked for noteworthy events in my life, I found to my surprise that my momentous experiences mostly happened in autumn. But I also realized that, these unexpected circumstances, always surfaced in places known for their mystical legends."

"Then, what you're telling me makes me wonder how those patterns are affected when a partner enters your life?"

"Sabie, that's a marvelous question we can answer with evidence to support or debunk my theory."

"My mystical man, you scare me when you give me that pre-epiphany look of yours." Breogán broke out into a hearty laughter appreciating her depth.

"Ok, here we go...when did you have your first major exhibit?"

Sabela was an accomplished surrealist painter before she met Breogán. Soon after her eighteenth birthday, she was already showing her works at major galleries in Chicago and Barcelona. Sabela had extracted the best from Frida Kahlo and Roberto Matta to create a hybrid style that transcended the fervor and fluidity of both artists.

"Well, let me think...my first professional exhibit was in the winter. The reason I remember is because I froze my nubile ass on the way to the exhibit in windy Chicago. Then, I met you in the summer almost six years ago and we married in...Oh my God, we married in the highlands of Scotland in the autumn."

"Yes, my still nubile wife, we moved to Estaca de Bares the following autumn, and two autumns later, I won an award for my second book in Athens. The next autumn, Banco de España bought one of your best paintings in Santiago de Compostela, two days after we completed our pilgrimage to that city, in the middle of October. Should I go on?"

"Ok, my apprehension has now turned into excitement. You're an extraordinary man and I had the wisdom to find you."

"I never argue with beauty. Are you thinking what I am thinking?"

"Yes!"

They hugged and ran to their windsurf boards ready to sail the Cantabrian coast line, as they did when they shared exhilarating moments. Estaca de Bares has been described as the rugged, northernmost Galician peninsula that arrogantly divides the Atlantic Ocean and the Cantabrian Sea. The cove where Breogán and Sabela lived offered enough challenge to windsurf, without the ferocious waves that constantly pounded the ancient lighthouse a few kilometers away.

Enrique stopped typing and wondered if he also had an archetypal season. He made a mental note to discuss the topic with Breogán on one of their dialogues, almost feeling apologetic for intruding on the lives he was crafting. Yet, his curiosity outweighed surrealistic protocol, and he welcomed the joy of anticipating the next encounter with Breogán.

"Hello?"

"Hi, it's Kate. I'm in Scotland! Had to leave for Glasgow without much notice on a family matter. I just got to the hotel a few minutes ago and wanted to let you know I am okay."

"Hi, darling, thanks for calling. I had no idea you were out of the country. I called your house yesterday, and your hermetic butler told me you were *unavailable*. I already know you're not available."

Kate smiled and sensed Enrique needed her tender affirmation. "I am, without question, only available for you."

They had learned to identify the archetypal wounds that Breogán so eloquently described. More importantly, they knew how to promote healing when their haunting fears surfaced. Most serious conflicts in partnerships can be prevented if these primal wounds are addressed before they grow into panic disguised as neglect or duplicity. Breogán warned not to use the wounds to manipulate suffering like victims, but rather as opportunities to heal with empathy.

"Kate, your words confirm why I honor the way you love me."

"I just arrived and I am already missing you. Am I compressing time?"

"No, but your refreshing timing never ceases to amaze me."

"Enough mutual admiration. When can you catch a plane?"

"You want me to meet you in Glasgow?"

"Dr. Lugo, do I have to beg you in Galician to get you here?"

"No, *Dr. Deliciosa.* I am on my way. I'll call you with arrival time."

"Really?"

"Yes, really. By the way, does your suite have a small or large bed?"

"You'll have to see when you get here."

"Can't wait. Ciao, my love."

"My very words."

As he packed hastily, Enrique felt the excitement of meeting Kate in a foreign country. He was able to book a direct flight from Miami to Glasgow, at a price that airlines love to impose on travelers with first class urgencies or impulsivities. Kate was waiting for him at the airport looking more stunning than any of the arrival scenarios his mind had rehearsed during the lengthy flight. They ran toward each other sensing the ardor that grows in anticipation of the sublime.

"Kate, my love, you're mine."

"Bought and paid for." They laughed, affirming how the candor of their zeal, left nothing to regret. Their love ignored the fascist restrictions that political correctness imposes on intimate language.

In their hotel suite they managed to traverse their large bed with exhaustive mastery, as Spanish passion greeted Gaelic sensuality. Love and a bottle of *Veuve Clicquot* won the evening.

Enrique awoke to Kate's early morning meditation and savored witnessing her serenity. He was grateful for the cosmic chance that brought them together, and wondered how the charisma of love managed to transform mundane moments into inexplicable delights. But who was he to question the gods and their gifts to anointed mortals? He decided to accept and enjoy what some celestial power had granted them.

"Good morning. Welcome back from Buddhahood. Are you hungry?"

"Good morning to you, love. Yes, I am famished."

"Shall I order breakfast in bed for my princess?"

"Why don't we go for a walk, and discover a quaint café for a typical Scottish breakfast?"

"Kate, what's a typical Scottish breakfast?"

"Let's find out."

The day was sunny with a cerulean blue sky that begged for smiles from anyone who cared to acknowledge the vista. They walked around town and, as if ordained, they found a café near their hotel that exceeded the quaintness they imagined. They chose a table in a cobbled courtyard, facing a manicured garden with small fern trees and sprinkled begonias. Glasgow is known for its botanical gardens, with their rare orchids so famous that the World Orchid Conference of 1993 was held there.

The amiable waiter suggested local smoked salmon and dill in scrambled eggs, nutmeg potatoes, highland black pudding and a pot of hot tea. Kate wondered how long she could eat like that without working out. Enrique enjoyed the sumptuous breakfast wondering the same thing. He and Kate shared a healthy obsession with staying in shape.

"Kate, what brought you to Glasgow?"

"You, being an anthropologist with a mystical twist, are not going to believe the reason."

"I am listening."

"I never told you that my mother died when I was very young. Mom was from Scotland and was raised by an adoring uncle. She went to school in Edinburgh, and spent her summers at her uncle's estate in the Isle of Jura, which is one of several small islands on the western coast of Scotland. Jura is on the southernmost area of the Scottish Highlands, and is known for its mystical legends and the longevity of its hardy people. And I can tell you that my great uncle lived up to both claims. He was infatuated with the Highlander's myth of immortality, and he lived to be one hundred and two!

"But get this: he was killed two weeks ago in a hunting accident, when he fell off his horse chasing a wild boar. Records dating back to the seventeen hundreds show that there've been a number of centenarians in the Isle of Jura, despite a stark living environment. I got a call from uncle's solicitors asking me to meet them in Glasgow to execute his will. They informed me that great uncle Fergus Mac Alasdair left me his estate in Jura. A late eighteenth century manor, guest cottage and stables on two hundred acres of woodland. What am I going to do with all that?"

"Kate, that's wonderful news. A psychologist colleague who studies the cultural influences on aging called me a couple of months ago to talk about an article he had just published in the journal *Kybernetes* about how cultural parameters determine stages of the aging process. I was so taken with his theory, I downloaded the article from his website the next day."

"Tell me more about his theory."

"Well, after reading his article, *A Biocultural Model of Aging*, I found that he coined the word *biocognition* to conceptualize mind, body and historical culture as inseparable components of a unit greater than its parts. He argues that our cognition and our biology cannot be extracted from our cultural history. I do know from my own work in medical anthropology that cultural beliefs significantly affect health and longevity."

"Then I should tell you what my *highlander*, and almost immortal great uncle believed. We corresponded several times a year when I was a graduate student at Columbia, working on my dissertation. Great-uncle Fergus had the most elegant calligraphy and he sent me handwritten letters expounding his highlander myths. He had no use for computers, but now that I think about it, those arcane letters meant more to me then I realized." Kate cleared her throat to distract herself from impending tears and continued. "Anyway, back to his letters. According to Highlander legend, their people had a *second sight* called *taibhsearachd* that permitted them to see and hear ghosts, wraiths, and death sounds, as well as access to other visions not available to ordinary mortals. In those visions, they could see gates to a dimension of immortality. If you learned how to enter, you would gain the ability to travel at will between the mortal and immortal planes."

"Very creative legend. I guess your uncle never found the gates. Or maybe…" Enrique feigned a frightened expression to lighten the mood, "he came back from immortality."

"Well, smarty pants, I guess we'll never know. I do remember asking him if anyone returned from the immortal dimension, and he told me that some did because they could not live an eternity with the haunting memories of their losses. He was a true romantic like you, my dear."

"Kate, was your mom's maiden name Mac Alasdair as well?"

"Katherine Shannon Holland Mac Alasdair stands before you."

"Jesus! You can't get more Gaelic than that."

"You as well, can't be more Galician than Enrique Xosé Lugo Fraga."

"How do you say *touché* in Gaelic?

"I would rather answer with words of love, *Ta gra agam ort.*"

"Then, my delicious Kate, I will respond; *Eu te amo máis.* Can you imagine how making love in Gaelic would be like?"

"Why not in Galician?"

"I am sure we could relate to both."

"Sweetheart, I am running late for my meeting with Uncle's solicitors. I'll call you as soon as I finish, so we can make plans for the evening."

"Great. I'm going to do a little writing while you're gone."

The instant Kate left, Enrique experienced what Breogán called *portal flashes*: a sudden multi-meaning awareness of entering *the drift*. The portal flash brought to consciousness that Kate inherited an estate in the same legendary highlands where Breogán and Sabela married. Enrique estimated he had written that particular chapter a month earlier.

To Enrique's delight, these synchronistic experiences were happening with increasing frequency. If Breogán was just a writer's projection, then perhaps Enrique was either accessing *morphic resonance*, or some brain cybernetics that could be triggered by that type of introspection.

Enrique decided it was time to resume the Breogán dialogues. He went to his laptop and as the screen lit, he savoured the anticipation of encountering whatever Breogán was. Enrique started to type in a light-hearted mood.

"Greetings, Breogán. How's your windsurfing?" Enrique smiled and waited for the next move. After a few minutes of suspense, it started.

"*Hola* Enrique. I hope you realize I am leaving my captivating Sabela to chat with you."

"I appreciate it Breogán, and I'll repay your kindness with more creative adventures for your enjoyment. Perhaps a surprise ending?" Enrique thought levity, especially during these surrealistic exchanges, was crucial to humanize the experience.

"Let me save you some time, and begin to answer your questions."

"Breogán, I keep forgetting you can anticipate my thoughts."

"Well, my friend, I believe you want to know more about entering *the drift* and why it's happening so frequently. In order to address your concerns, I have to introduce some new terms. You see, just like your psychologist colleague had to coin the word *biocognitive* to encapsulate a new concept, I also had to develop a lexicon to convey *the drift*. I say *convey* because I am not teaching in a linear sense. As you know by now, predictability needs to be suppressed in order to experience the portal flashes that are becoming more familiar to you. So by conveying, I mean providing *internal precursors* that surface into multi-dimensional meaning when they match external events. That's why, when the two pathways meet, you feel the galvanizing of what I call *holographic knowing*. In your latest portal flash, the internal precursor was your choice of venue for my wedding, and the external event was Kate's inherited estate surfacing one month later. The organic succession that was growing within your mind-body exploded into consciousness when the external circumstances matched your internal creation. Synchronicity requires a *feedforward* condition that extracts *infolded* segments of information from future time-space, and sprinkles them into present time-space, initiating a *pending meaning effect*. Pre-meaning bundled in the present is suspended to be unpacked into meaning under propitious conditions in the future. Let me explain."

"Please do, Breogán. My head is spinning."

"Feedforward is information in the present that has coincidental relevance in the future. It's an experience with implicit wisdom in the present that unfolds into explicit meaning in the future. Synchronicity appears disjointed because the feedforward element is ignored."

"Breogán, if your feedforward theory is correct, then past, present and future are interrelated in time-space."

"Enrique, I need to go for now."

The fiction writer was in awe of his main character, and was very grateful for the conundrum gift. He knew, without being able to articulate it, why Breogán had to leave.

That evening, Enrique and Kate had dinner at a recommended Persian restaurant. She ordered lamb kabob in a mint glaze with sautéed okra, and he had saffron chicken stew with green rice. He decided not to discuss the Breogán experience for now, to avoid biasing the natural flow of *the drift*. It was better to let Kate follow her instinct and see where it would take them. She told Enrique all about her meeting with the solicitors and asked if he would visit the estate with her. He agreed to go and help her decide what to do with the property.

Kate had a difficult time separating her wishes from what her uncle wanted for her. Great uncle Fergus made it known in his Last Will & Testament that he hoped Kate would keep the property as a second home. Enrique was now an integral part of her life, and she felt he needed to be included in all decisions affecting the rhythm of the world they shared. That night, she knew he was her partner for life.

The estate in the Isle of Jura lived up to the mystical image Kate recounted from her highlander great uncle. The prim staff kept the residence and surrounding structures in pristine condition. The caretaker met them at the stable to show them five well-groomed horses, and assured them nothing had changed since the untimely accident. As if searching for answers, he told them of Mr. Mac Alisdair's mysterious absences. He would leave unannounced and return several months later without explanations. No one dared to ask, and the Master never offered.

Kate made the necessary arrangements for the staff to continue running the estate, and Enrique suggested returning for a more deliberate visit in the autumn. She agreed without questioning his choice of season. After all, autumn was only two months away. Enrique felt conspiratorial not sharing his motivation with her, and justified his decision by promising himself that he would explain everything at the appropriate time. They now owned two houses in Miami and another in the Highlands of Scotland, but one had to be chosen as their home. The flight back gave them pause to delight in how they were now returning to their daily lives as soul partners.

Chapter 4

"You've gone too deep to return to the world of vulgar eyes."

The pressure was on. Enrique had to keep his promise to write a surprise ending for Breogán. Why did he create those challenges? He smiled, reflecting he was perhaps making commitments to his own imagination.

It was time for a break from his internal chatter. That meant Máximo to the rescue. Enrique was not in the mood to chance *the drift*, so this time he called his old friend.

"Hello, Máximo."

"Enriquito? It's so good to hear from you. Are you losing faith in the drift? This is the first time you've called me in years." They both laughed and realized how few words were needed to communicate so precisely. "Well, my Galician friend, you will be pleased to know that the drift works despite your conscious intentions. I am cooking *caldo gallego,* which I never prepare for myself, so you must be the dinner guest I was expecting tonight."

"You can make *caldo gallego?"*

"My mother was Galician and, back in the dark ages when I was a kid, she taught my sister and I how to cook a *caldo gallego* that could win a culinary gold medal. By the way, I have a bottle of *Larios* to finish the meal."

"Máximo, you're a magician. What time?"

"Around nine-thirty. You know I hate to dine early, like peasants."

"Yes, Máximo, I know. This peasant will be there on time with a bottle of fine Galician wine."

Enrique called Kate and told her all about Máximo and his dinner invitation. She was glad to hear Enrique's excitement about his plans for the evening. He wanted Kate to meet Máximo, so she extended an invitation to cook one of her gourmand dinners the following weekend, for her sweetheart and his scholarly Cuban friend.

Máximo built his elaborate Mediterranean home in the opulent neighborhood of Coco Plum, before the real estate elite anointed the area. The well-placed antique furniture from Spain, and the exquisite sculptures from Italy, implied a classical European style. He retained ownership of this property through both divorces by claiming that he bought the land cheap because a Seminole shaman who, after white men murdered his wife, warned that no white woman would ever find peace on that land. The story gained some validity when Máximo reminded his ex-wives; the curse was to blame for his failure to make them happy. That, along with very ample settlements, allowed him to keep his only solace, after losing everything when he left Cuba.

Enrique arrived on time and was greeted at the door by Máximo's housekeeper, Celia. She served him a tall glass of *mojito,* mixed just the way Hemingway enjoyed it at *La Bodeguita del Medio* during his Cuban escapades.

"Enriquito, come to the kitchen so you can witness how I am slaving for you." Máximo posed a dramatic stance with his white apron, red scarf and chef's beret. His housekeeper reminded him all he had done was minor assembling, after *she* finished all the hard work. Celia had been Máximo's housekeeper for years, and he argued more with her than he ever did with both ex-wives.

"Dr. Suarez, no wonder you can't keep a wife. Who do you think would put up with your antics?"

"Well, Celia, I've kept you all these years."

"But thank God, not as your wife."

"Ah, so you want to be my wife?"

"Dr. Suarez, you need to stop dreaming." The intermittent bantering went on until she called the two men to the formal dining room, where she served the meal with flawless etiquette, and then disappeared.

"Enriquito, your wine goes very well with my exquisite cuisine."

"You're right Máximo, this is the most delicious *caldo gallego* I've ever had. And let's not forget your scrumptious sautéed calamari in white wine and capers. Thank you for the invitation."

"Let me tell you, my boy, I am modest about everything, except my cooking and my good looks."

As both men laughed, Enrique realized Máximo had an endearing affectation that reminded him of his father. Anytime Máximo said something humorous, he would wink and tilt his head in a way that compelled you to connect with his dignity.

"Alright, let's get serious. Tell me what ails you?"

Like all good mystics, Máximo could shift instantly from comedian to sage. Enrique told him about his experiences in Scotland and the portal flashes. Máximo listened attentively as he sipped the *Larios* brandy and puffed his *Cohiba Esplendido* Cuban cigar.

"Enriquito, now you can never go back. You've gone too deep to return to the world of vulgar eyes."

"What do you mean? That sounds gloomy."

"It could be, but it should be something to be accepted as a rare gift. Remember our conversation about the *calling* to an archetypal journey?"

"Yes I do, and I especially remember what you said about the different interpretations of the journey by Eastern and Western mystics."

"Well, you've answered the calling and you're on your way. Now, you're beginning to encounter your guides in unexpected ways. Some you meet externally and others appear within you. It really doesn't matter whether you identify them as your own reflections or as munificent entities. The ubiquitous wisdom is available to help you maneuver the synchronistic nature of your journey."

As Máximo explained the mystical path, he appeared increasingly more benevolent, perhaps, as a trusted confidant. The blue smoke from his cigar, melding with the whiteness of his hair, fashioned a luminous aura around his face that gave his words spellbinding credence.

"I should caution you that, although we're not living in medieval times, being Catholic makes us susceptible to the suffering model of learning we inherited from the theologians of that era."

"So how do we avoid falling into that trap?"

"Enriquito, I suggest you ask Breogán that enticing question."

"If that's your answer, then pour me another glass of *Larios* to soothe my curiosity and bring this terrific evening to a close. By the way, Kate and I would like to have you over for dinner next Saturday."

"Who's cooking?"

"Kate, of course."

"Then I graciously accept. *Salud,* my young friend."

"*Salud,* my dear friend."

Next morning, rather than engage the Breogán dialogues, Enrique decided to contact his old comparative theology professor from his graduate student days at Fordham University. Enrique recalled Father Jonas Simon's seminars on the Catholic mystics, and the many evenings they spent discussing the lives of St. Ignatius and Meister Eckhart at a trendy tavern near Lincoln Center in New York. Fr. Simon refused to retire, and was now a visiting scholar at Weston Jesuit School of Theology in Cambridge, Massachusetts.

Fr. Simon was quite pleased to hear from Enrique, and spent the next two hours on the phone addressing his former student's concerns. Hearing Fr. Simon's eloquent words, reminded Enrique of the excellence without arrogance, the Jesuits taught him to demand of himself.

"Jonas, I know you advocate Meister Eckhart's contention that the spirit honors the body as its physical temple, rather than St. Augustine's disdain for the flesh."

"Well, you know how I feel about that rascal, Augustine. Although there is no doubt his opus, *Confessions,* was among the first autobiographically probing literature, St. Augustine became quite self-righteous after all the carousing he did during his pagan days. He reminds me, God forgive me for saying this, of some of the contemporary fundamentalists, who want to monopolize morality after they had their fill of screwing around."

Enrique laughed enjoying, once again, Fr. Simon's scathing wit. Fr. Simon admired Meister Eckhart's spiritual optimism and argued that, if his beloved mystic had been born three hundred years later, he would have been a Jesuit rather than a Dominican. Enrique appreciated Fr. Simon's clear-cut preferences, and missed their discussions and toasting to theological insights with Guinness stout.

"Here's my question to you, as if you were my spiritual director," Enrique asked, apprehensive about his supposition.

"Enrique, I thought I *was* your spiritual director?" Fr. Simon responded with his customary cheerfulness before addressing a serious concern. But perhaps to remind Enrique that he could approach him at ease, after all those years without contact.

"You *are* my spiritual director, Fr. Simon."

"Thank you. Now, cut the formalities and ask away."

"Alright, as pre-Vatican II guilt-ridden Catholics, how do we avoid the trap of making suffering our teacher when we choose the mystical path?"

"Enrique, just look at me. Do I seem like a guilt-ridden Catholic to you?" Enrique laughed and agreed Fr. Simon was a superb example of joyful living. He was still teaching at close to eighty, eating good food and drinking choice wines, without giving up his love of swimming laps. He told Enrique he was still swimming a mile every other day, as his contemplative prayer, and continued. "Let your *bon vivant* spiritual director address the central question you're asking, because for the last three decades, I've noticed a surge of interest in mysticism, with little understanding of the need for balance."

"Jonas, I still remember your seminars on how we could apply the Buddhist *middle way* to the Christian mystical calling."

"You have a good memory. That's exactly what I still believe, with great conviction. I think that to approach the mystical life from a deprivation model is incorrect, but it's also as erroneous to follow the pop culture edicts that promise weekend epiphanies without living weekday compassion."

"I see how the middle way could balance the extremes of the journey, but why is the path so difficult? Did the Western medieval mystics view the challenges as prerequisite suffering to reach Christ? You see where I am going with this?"

"Yes, I do Enrique. But before addressing the core of your question, let's assess the common theme that mystics share across cultures, so we can find their archetype."

"Their archetype?"

When Enrique heard the word *archetype* coming from Fr. Simon, he wondered if it was a trigger for a portal flash. The word came up in his conversations with Máximo, and now with Fr. Simon, although it was a modern term not used in the mystical literature. Maybe the cross-cultural meaning of the word could be the key to what Fr. Simon was about to explain. Enrique withheld predictability and waited for the word to either ignite a precursor of synchronicity, or just be a false alarm.

"Enrique, let's assume that the mystical quest is an archetypal path sought because there is a basic dissatisfaction with the mundane world across cultures. Then, this yearning to satisfy more than the senses would facilitate receptiveness to the *calling*. But since suffering is inherent on the physical plane, then seekers may assume that it should also be experienced while engaging the transcendental dimension. Not due to any innate prerequisites to suffer, but because the implication of having to atone is superimposed on the mystical route." Fr. Simon took a moment to delight on the memories his explanations were eliciting. He continued, feeling years younger.

"So, the universal element that's shared across cultures dictates the cause and effect of atonement. One either has to suffer before reaching desired goals, or because of past conduct. It seems to me the Western mystics subscribed to the premise of suffering for future gains, whereas the Eastern mystics suffer for past karmic deeds. Of course, there are those who are so guilt-ridden, they subscribe to both modes of suffering."

"Jonas, would you call this tendency the *atonement archetype*?"

"Not me, but I believe you just did, exquisitely."

Enrique felt the warmth of his former professor's kindness. It reaffirmed his contention that, rather than looking for clay feet in our mentors when we no longer need them, we should appreciate their contributions that lead to our independence. He promised Fr. Simon he would stay in touch and thanked him for his judicious counsel.

The term *atonement archetype* kept circling Enrique's mind. His psychologist friend taught him that, when a spinning thought derails our stream of consciousness, we should give the rumination audience, rather than fight its perseverance. Enrique allowed the term to surface without resistance and, as it began to engulf his awareness, an unexpected progression began to unfold. He noticed the phrase was spinning faster and faster in his head, until it forked into two words that comprised the concept. The word *atonement* entered a space of medieval torture, where men in black robes were lashing their victims without mercy, whereas the word *archetype* mutated into a vision of benevolent entities dressed in white togas, dispensing wisdom without words. The bifurcation continued, with both images competing for dominance in his consciousness. Enrique experienced a sense of depersonalization similar to what people describe when they suffer a panic attack. It was a sense of suspended identity without reprieve that dared to threaten his sanity. His racing heartbeat and the cold perspiration on his forehead were his only physical grounding. He felt his awareness was hovering above his body, until the divergent images fused into physical exhaustion. Enrique collapsed on his bed, and went into a deep sleep.

The chimes of his programmed doorbell, playing *Penny Lane,* awakened him. He arose slowly, walked toward the sound of the Beatles, and opened the door.

"Enrique, I've been out here ringing your confounded bell for an eternity. You look terrible."

"Oh, good morning Michael. I overslept and completely forgot about our meeting. Come in and let's have an espresso."

His literary agent went to the spacious kitchen, knowing the request meant that *he* was to prepare the Cuban coffee. Enrique had an endearing helplessness about basic things that gave his close friends opportunities to reciprocate his generosity, when they took care of him. In this case, although Michael was Jewish, he made Cuban coffee like a native.

Michael brought two espresso cups to the balcony, where Enrique was waiting for his wakeup brew. He and Michael had a close friendship that did not require frequent contact. They met when needed, and enjoyed each other as two good friends conducting business.

"Michael, I wish I could make Cuban coffee like you."

"Stop lying. You know you have no intention of learning."

Enrique smiled, knowing there was nothing he could say.

"Ok, to business. Liliana called me in her Italian hysterics mode and insisted I pay you a visit. You know Enrique, that woman really knows how to dress. It's not just her choice of designers, but also her ability to accent her jewellery with..."

"Michael, I know Liliana has extraordinary taste, but please get to the point." Enrique interrupted him, amused at his friend's misdirected choice of profession. Michael was an imaginative and highly successful literary agent, but a frustrated fashion designer. He dressed with fastidious elegance, and had an effeminate demeanor he acquired growing up the only male around four doting aunts. Handsome gay men frequently approached him, assuming he shared their romantic predilections. It was hilarious to watch him deepen his voice, without changing his delicate mannerisms, when his sexual orientation was mistaken. It was also disheartening to see how society continues to judge people by how they appear, or the gender they choose to love, rather than by their capacity for compassion.

"I must say, Enrique, you're as rude as you are articulate."

"Thank you. Are you saying that I am fluently rude?" Enrique was trying to keep it light until he could recover from the emotional roller coaster he tried to sleep off the night before.

"Liliana is worried about you and, now that I see how you look, so am I.

"Michael, just how do I look?"

"Disheveled and exhausted. Is it that Kate woman?"

"Jesus, Michael, I happen to be in love with that *Kate woman,* and she has nothing to do with what's going on."

"Then, my dear Spaniard, what in heaven's name *is* going on?"

"Well, last night I had what mystics call an *unselfing* experience that scared the crap out of me."

"How does one *unself?*"

Enrique briefed Michael on what was happening with the book, his trip to Scotland, and gave him a detailed description of the horrifying episode he had the previous night. He also explained that, on the mystical excursion, these depersonalizing incidents were not uncommon, and at times necessary to shed the false grounding we have with our physical identity.

"Enrique, I think you have some exquisite material here. I am so tickled for you but... I think you're nuts!"

"Gee, thanks Michael. I am so pleased you enjoy my suffering." Although Enrique was jesting with his friend, he suddenly realized he was labeling his experiences as *suffering.* He immediately intuited that, the concept of suffering, rather than the atonement archetype, was the portal flash that triggered the holographic knowing Breogán had described in his dialogues. He was astounded at how *the drift* was always entered in stealth, and the integrative wisdom it provided never failed to produce a humbling effect. It all made sense. In his hellish episode, he had lived the dichotomy of punitive suffering vs. joyful wisdom.

"We can choose joy or suffering as our teacher, but our decision can lead us to a living heaven or hell," Enrique explained to Michael, as if he had been privy to the private thoughts that led to his conclusion.

"You know Enrique, sometimes I wish you were writing pulp fiction instead of your cerebral themes. Although, I will admit, there is a substantial audience out there who love your books. So, forget my advice and continue to be..." Michael rolled up his eyes, searching for the comical within him, "shall we say, *unusual*? By the way, do you have anything for me to read? Liliana is driving me insane."

"Michael, you'll be encouraged to know that I have the first four chapters ready for you."

"I love it. Please take better care of yourself. I have this spa I can recommend, that can be wondrous for people in your state of abandonment."

"My dear agent, take the chapters and go." They parted with an *abrazo* as Enrique did with all his friends. He had imposed his Iberian custom, a hug when you greet and when you part, on all his non-Hispanic friends, and they seemed to enjoy the sincerity of the ritual.

Chapter 5

"The drift was as real as each breath we take..."

"Susumu Tonegawa won the Nobel Prize in medicine in 1987, for his work in immunology. He found that genes in immune cells could rearrange themselves to produce diverse antibodies. Before Dr. Tonegawa's discovery, the scientific community believed genes were fixed from birth, without the flexibility to change their genetic endowment..."

Enrique had no idea where he was going with that topic, so he stopped reading the article he came across while searching for another subject on the Internet.

Breogán taught him to choose an unrelated topic that would win his attention while he was trying to find something else. Like looking up a word in the dictionary and finding a nearby word more interesting, then learning the meaning of the incidental word, and using it in a conversation. According to Breogán, this method of indirect seeking activated a *secondary intention* that could suspend predictability. It was one of the tools to navigate the drift, as well as a path to enter the discovery mode at will.

Breogán suggested that one had to visualize an interconnected universe endowed with *holographic wisdom,* to make sense of the secondary intention concept he was proposing. Meaning that, when our attention is focused on a goal, there are infinitely more interconnecting pathways leading to that goal than the one our attention selected initially. If we intentionally distract our *attention* from a chosen objective and scan the surrounding field of information for something to shift our *intention,* we can engage the interconnectivity of the pathways.

After pondering Breogán's theory, Enrique felt he had assimilated the secondary intention concept, but was still not clear on what the holographic wisdom entailed. He trusted his intuition to guide him and surmised that, since the work of Dr. Tonegawa caught his attention while searching for something else, it could be the secondary intention he needed to understand holographic wisdom.

Enrique recalled Breogán used the term *holographic knowing* to reflect a sense of multidimensional insights that we gain when we discover the interconnecting pathways of our journey. Enrique wondered what would happen if he could imagine a dialogue with the Nobel laureate:

"Dr. Tonegawa, what inspired your research?"

"I was interested in how immune cells managed to fight billions of viruses, bacteria and other micro-invaders with a fixed number of genes to design their antibodies. My suspicion was confirmed that genes required flexibility to reorganize, in order to meet a myriad of unanticipated foreign microorganisms. We found that the way genes are spaced in embryonic mice change as they develop into adulthood. The genes reassemble to produce custom-made antibodies that fight emerging biological and chemical enemies."

"I sense I am at the edge of grasping holographic wisdom by listening to your words, but I am not sure what else to ask you."

"Enrique, although I am not familiar with the type of wisdom you are seeking, based on my research in how memory is consolidated, I can suggest what you might want to try."

"Please do."

"It seems to me you have scattered bits of information that have not reached contextual meaning. If by the term holographic wisdom you are referring to multiple levels of understanding, then you might want to review the secondary intentions you experienced."

"Dr. Tonegawa, your suggestion gives me a hinting impression, but I can't get the full image to surface."

"Try to find a link between what you know of my work, and how you could associate it with the other secondary intentions you encountered around the time you found me. According to your theory of interconnectedness, I should be a piece of the puzzle. Good luck."

Enrique thought he was reaching a portal flash although he knew that, since by definition, the experience could not be predicted, to think about it would derail the process that causes it to happen. He closed his eyes and waited for an image to surface. A flash of another Escher print came to mind. This time it was the *House of Stairs,* where robotic worms climb and descend stairs that lead to circular labyrinths or unknown destinations. Enrique also remembered that Escher was not a painter. He meticulously chiselled woodblocks, and inked them by hand to create his prints. The artist designed some of his works on grids that could be twisted at different angles to give the illusion of warped space.

The idea from his reflections with Dr. Tonegawa, to review the secondary intentions, was beginning to make sense and Enrique permitted the experience to unfold. He recalled the images of the Nobel Prize winner's discovery, the subsequent imaginary dialogue with him, and Escher's surrealistic perceptual-looping designs. But these secondary intentions could have infinite associations, leading to endless conclusions. What was the potential *holographic wisdom,* in that chosen set of non-sequential events?

Then, when least expected and coming from nowhere, the portal flashes erupted into *holographic wisdom.* Just as a finite set of genes has the wisdom to create infinite defences to insure our survival, and just as works of art can illustrate our circular realities, so can we choose our paths, without fear of getting lost, when we accept the interconnectivity of our universe. The scientists and artists who dare to look beyond the boundaries of their peers reach the answers. *Holographic wisdom* is to know that *separation* is an illusion feeding our panic of never finding ourselves. Enrique felt the multidimensional insights were coming faster than his mind could assimilate, but somehow knew he could trust the outcome without having to dissect or analyse it into oblivion.

How could Enrique explain these findings to anyone? He considered calling the real Dr. Tonegawa, to discuss his experience and perhaps, thank him for his unwitting contribution, but decided to savour in silence the transcendental serenity he had gained.

In the process of writing his novel, Enrique was charting the navigational parameters of uncertainty. *The drift* was as real as each breath we take, and as elusive as how mind and body bring our breathing to consciousness. Enrique noticed this new sense of interconnectedness extended him to feel gratitude for his physical, as well as virtual sources of wisdom. Thinking of virtual wisdom, he wondered how the next Breogán dialogue would unfold, and smiled with curiosity.

Enrique wanted to understand how the reflective dialogues he was creating, provided access to insights that were not available through common introspection. He also noticed the inherent differences between his reflective dialogues with Breogán vs. Dr. Tonegawa. With Breogán, he felt an affinity, whereas with the Nobel laureate it was more like detached scholarship. Enrique smiled, imagining Breogán would explain the difference by asserting that Dr. Tonegawa was just a projection, whereas *he* was an esteemed friend.

That thought pleased Enrique immensely, and reminded him of how his psychologist friend explained the difference between the hallucinations of a psychotic and the visions of a mystic. His friend explained that, while the psychotic goes into a fragmented heaven or hell without knowing how to return or evolve from the experience, the mystic might enter that same space, knowing when to return, and how to grow more compassionate from the experience. The psychotic is brought back pharmacologically with disjointing suspicion, whereas the mystic returns at will, with unifying love. A split second could make a profound difference between a Charles Manson and a St. John of the Cross.

It was time to get some rest and take a break from all the subtleties between the mystical world and the mundane life. Sometimes Enrique wished he could lose his inquisitive originality and just find a regular job where he could climb some *corporate ladder,* or whatever the current cliché was. He was exhausted and wanted time alone. His psychologist friend explained it was called *empathic fatigue.* You spend so much time empathically leaping outside of self that, when you return to your personal identity, it feels depleted of nourishment. Perhaps that's why he felt so displaced.

Enrique wanted to give his quest for knowledge a cognitive vacation. He decided it was time to turn his mind off and just experience doing nothing. No more editors, no more agents, no more...

"Hello? Michael? What's up?" The phone call abruptly ended a restless sleep.

"Enrique, I loved your first four chapters! I can't wait to read chapter five... Enrique? Why are you laughing so hard? Just tell me what you're up to with chapter five? Your dear agent knows you're up to no good. Enrique, stop laughing and talk to me."

"Ok Michael, come over without questions, and I'll give you chapter five."

"If I were a fashion designer like Aunt Charlotte wanted me to be, I wouldn't have to deal with insane men like you. I'll be there shortly, but this boy is not making you Cuban coffee."

Chapter 6

*"The archetypal wounds transcend cultures and
reflect the three main infamies against our hearts."*

University of Santiago de Compostela, Galicia Psychology Department

Guardians of the Heart Lecture

"*I would like to take the rest of the time we have left to answer
questions.*"

*Immediately, about a dozen graduate students raised their hands
and Breogán pointed to a young lady in the third row.*

"*Breogán, I want to thank you for your insightful words. My question has to do with your concept of archetypal wounds. I read your
book on the subject but you only hinted on how to heal them.*"

"*Thank you for your compliment. You're right. I purposely did not
go into the healing aspect of my treatise because I was waiting for you
to ask the question.*" *The audience laughed and applauded in unison. It
was evident the students loved his work.*

"*But seriously, your question is vital because I don't want to
leave you with the impression that we're helpless victims. Instead,
we are wounded heroes seeking compassionate healing. I didn't expand on that part of my theory, because I wanted my readers to
identify their wounds without access to quick solutions. Now enough
time has passed that I can discuss the healing power of guardianship.*

"*As I mentioned at the beginning of this lecture, the archetypal
wounds transcend cultures, and reflect the three main infamies against
our hearts: shame, abandonment, and betrayal. Some wounds are the
result of our naïve interpretation of motives, rather than malicious intent. But the archetypal wounds are clearly inflicted by acts of reckless
ignorance or deliberate evil, before we possess the strength to cope
with their intensity. The genesis of these primal wounds resides in*

childhood and their resulting self-loathing is the element that preserves them until we enter a healing partnership to resolve them.

"Yes? The gentleman in the fist row," Breogán pointed to a young man with a goatee.

"What happens with those who choose celibacy or the contemplative life?"

"Which one are you considering?" The audience laughed, along with the student who asked the question.

"Oh, I was asking for this 'friend' of mine," the student answered with a wide grin, as the audience affirmed their enjoyment with more laughter.

"Well, you can assure that 'friend' of yours that the relationship does not have to be romantic, or with an actual person. Mystics do their best healing in isolation. The relationship is established with what I call healing fields, *which can include a partner, or not. Let me explain: callous action taken against innocence inflicts the archetypal wounds. Each cluster may vary across cultures, but the archetype remains the same. You can be shamed for failing to slay your first lion to satisfy the rites of passage in a Masai village in Kenya, or you can be shamed, as deleteriously, by a competitive dad in Madrid for failing to make the soccer team. Of course, if you learned to play soccer in Galicia, you have nothing to fear." The audience roared with approving cheers and applauds.*

"Let me tell you what I mean by healing fields. *Just as clusters of evil can inflict archetypal wounds, clusters of love can heal them. Each archetypal wound has a corresponding* healing field. *Shame is healed in a field of honor, abandonment in a field of commitment, and betrayal in a field of loyalty. A pledge to implement the conduct that promotes healing can be made alone within the corresponding field, or with a partner. If done with a partner, both parties agree to promote the conduct that defines the* healing field. *If done alone, the agreement to embrace the conduct is made with oneself.*

"The young lady with the ponytail has a question?"

"Hello Breogán. Please tell us more about your field *concept."*

"Yes, the field *is a psychological space committed to behaviors and conditions that facilitate the required healing. So for example, a field of loyalty includes all the permutations that support healing betrayal. That* field *would include behaving loyally as well as associating with others that support loyalty."*

"But Breogán, it seems like the contributions of the healing fields *are interdependent," the same student asked the question and remained standing waiting for a response.*

"I love to share my ideas with brilliant people. You have antici-pated my next point. Yes! You are absolutely correct. Not only are the qualities of the healing fields interdependent, but also they work syner-gistically, and one cannot stand alone without the other. Let me tell you why. They are the integral fabric of love. But just as important, the healing cannot take place without a covenant of safety. *And that is the first step of guardianship: to create a foundation of safety, by protect-ing your vulnerabilities and those of your partner within the corresponding healing field. If there is no partner, then you protect your own vulnerabilities, within the appropriate field. But let me be clear with what I mean by protection. Protection, in guardianship, means to risk with love in relative safety, rather than to build armor in fear.*

"Now, returning to the synergistic dynamics of the healing fields: *entering guardianship with a wound of shame, the covenant of safety would require the symbol of honor, with commitment and loyalty to that field. In the case of abandonment, the symbol of commitment would be chosen with honor and loyalty to that field. And a wound of betrayal would embrace the symbol of loyalty, with commitment and honor to that corresponding field.*

"So, you can see that, the healing fields *work in synergy with a primary symbol, supported by two subordinate symbols, based on the type of archetypal wound. I propose the symbols function as catalysts, converting haunting wounds into healing guides.*

"My dear friends, I need to stop. Thank you very much." Breogán heard disappointed grumbling, and granted one more question to a playful young lady.

"Breogán, I have a windsurfing question?" He was caught off guard, and the audience waited for his reaction, expecting to hear his lighter side.

"Go ahead."

"What should I do if I am tacking at the required forty-five degree angle, and the sail begins to dance?"

Breogán smiled and rubbed his chin with feigned perplexity. "I would suggest you engage the field of commitment, and take the mast forward to regulate the route, without letting the board get on to the wind."

The student began a slow cadence of applauds, joined by the audi-ence in a crescendo of cheers and laughter.

Breogán left the auditorium by a back stage exit, and met Sabela who was waiting in their olive green Hummer. He kissed her and they drove away for lunch at Don Gaiferos by the Plaza de La Quintana, in the an-cient part of the city. Santiago de Compostela dates back to the third century B.C. After St. James the Great was beheaded in the Holy Land in forty-four C.E., his disciples took his remains to Santiago. For centuries pilgrims have travelled from all over the world to visit the tomb of San Tiago, *as St. James is known in Spain. Alfonso III built a large basilica on the site of the tomb in eight hundred ninety-nine C.E. The Moors destroyed it when they invaded Santiago a century later, and it was rebuilt in the eleventh century. Architectural tenacity is one of the historical signatures of that legendary city where Sabela was born.*

They both ordered the savory langostinos with smoked mackerel and the house paté, with a bottle of Pazo de Xabaráns '97.

"Well done, my sweet docent, congratulations on your lecture."

"Were you there? I thought you went to the gallery?"

"Oh I did, but I came back for the best part at the end, when the cutie asked you that pertinent windsurfing question." Sabela liked to tease Breogán about his idolizing groupies.

"Sabie, that child was young enough to be my daughter," he tried to keep a straight face as he played along.

"And so am I. But I like the way you can call someone with that body a 'child'."

"Well, my love, it must be the food your generation eats."

"It must be. Alright, when are we starting our mystical search for the secrets of autumn?"

"I am glad you asked, because I've come up with another great idea for our expedition."

"Oh please tell me. No wait, let's order another bottle of wine, so we can toast to your marvellous idea."

"But Sabela, I haven't told you yet."

"Yes, but to use your own terminology, I have a feeling it's going to be a feedforward event."

Breogán laughed with abandonment, appreciating his wife's ability to bring out the best in him by just being the woman he adored. "Excellent prediction, Sabie. Ramon, please bring us another bottle of Pazo de Xabaráns. We're celebrating a future event."

Ramon had known Sabela since she was a child and, although he was her self-appointed protective uncle, he immediately liked Breogán when he met him. Ramón brought the bottle of wine and sat with the couple, as he usually did when they visited his restaurant.

"Breogán, what have you done to this child? She hardly drank before she met you, and look at her now. She's practically an alcoholic."

"Oh, uncle Ramón, you're so melodramatic. Pour me another glass, and let's toast to the joy of being Galician." Ramón did as his *adopted niece told him, and helped them consume the second bottle of that fine native wine. He kissed Sabela and Breogán, and went back to challenge his other customers with his separatist political views. Ramón was an icon in Santiago de Compostela after serving time in prison for defying Franco's dictatorial decrees. In those repressive days, the Galician language was prohibited in schools and public places.*

"Here's my idea, Sabie. Are you ready?"

"Yes! Yes! Stop torturing me and tell me."

"Our first legendary city to visit this coming autumn is going to be...Cabo Fisterra!"

"Oh Breogán, Holy Mother of God, the cape at the end of the world?"

"Correct, my artiste wife. You know your Galician history well. We're going to visit a town located in the most western point of Europe, where the Galician Queen Lupa refused the Christians permission to bury the body of St. James there, with a miraculous turn of events leading to the burial in Santiago de Compostela instead. Yes, the same Santiago, where my gracious wife and I are drinking this amusing wine, as we speak." Breogán enjoyed contributing to his wife's exuberance.

"Ramón, Ramón, my husband is taking me to Cabo Fisterra next month." Sabela declared to her adopted uncle, who was arguing politics three tables away. Ramón looked at the couple, smiled and lifted his glass to acknowledge his unusual protégé. Sabela had travelled worldwide, but knowing her Ramon figured that, although she could get excited about the most illogical things, there had to be something special in the historical Cabo Fisterra. His curiosity won, and he walked to their table and asked, *"Ok Sabela, what are you so excited about, this time?"*

"Dear uncle, we're going to Cabo Fisterra for a feedforward event." Ramón looked puzzled, but not surprised.

"Breogán, I know better than to ask you or your lunatic wife what she means, but why are the two of you so odd? What have you done to my little girl?" Sabela got up and, towering over Ramon, kissed his baldhead, securing a contented grin from the man who had taken the place of her departed father.

"By the way, give me the keys to your Hummer. You both have celebrated too much to drive," Ramón demanded with fondness that could not be refuted.

"Ok my sweet man, let's leave the Hummer with uncle, and we can take a taxi back to our hotel."

"Outstanding idea, my love."

Enrique pulled back from his laptop, wondering how the feedforward would unfold for the man from autumn. The author had no clue, but thought that, if he knew, it would simply be his preconceived creative writing, rather than an authentic *drift* occurrence. He decided to leave the search up to Breogán and Sabela so that both the author and his characters could be surprised.

It was time for the gym, and then to Kate's for dinner, with Máximo and his date. Yes, a couple of days after his invitation, Máximo had inquired, apologetically, if he could bring a *lady friend*. Enrique loved the request and asked him if the *friend* was a hot date: Máximo reacted with an anxious laugh. He and Kate could not wait to meet Máximo's Lady X, as Enrique called her, or as Kate preferred to say, *Lady X and her date coming for dinner*.

Enrique arrived early to watch Kate in culinary action. She was preparing everything herself, and the aroma of fine cuisine romanced his senses.

"Kate, I am very impressed."

"With my cooking?"

"No, with your exquisite legs."

"Thank you, my Neanderthal man."

"What do you think Lady X is going to be like?"

"I have no idea, but I am thankful you're excited about Máximo bringing a date."

"Yes, darling, especially because I know he has not socialized in quite a while. I take his decision to bring a guest as a compliment to us."

"Then if that's the case, I am flattered. We'll make them feel welcomed."

"Thank you Kate. Is your adopted family around?"

"All gone, with the exception of Silvia, who will be serving dinner."

"Are they gone for the evening?"

"Gone for the weekend."

"Really? What about Silvia?"

"She leaves as soon as she finishes serving dinner." Kate gave him a conspiratorial smile.

"Kate, there's a weather report predicting a snowstorm for tonight. Do you think I could stay over?"

"Of course my love. I know how devastating snow blizzards can be in Miami. Should we ask Lady X and Máximo to stay as well?" Kate asked, enjoying their little game. It was the first overnight at her place for Enrique.

"Oh no, not to worry. Máximo drives a Porsche Cayenne that can move on any terrain," Enrique retorted with his debonair grin.

"Well, it's settled then. Just the two of us tonight." Being with Kate was supreme. It was the best vertical love had to offer. In the short time they had known each other, the relationship had reached unprecedented depth.

The doorbell chimed on time, announcing the end of suspense. Kate and Enrique rushed to the door like inquisitive adolescents.

"Welcome to our home. I am Kate Holland. We're so glad you could come."

"Thank you Kate. Please let me present Claudia Weston to you, and to my dear friend Enriquito." Máximo had an old world charm that reminded Kate of her late father. That affectation won him immediate endearment with her. As for Lady X, the old rascal had exquisite taste in women. Claudia was an attractive woman in her sixties, with vibrant confidence and charm.

"Dr. Suarez, I must tell you, Enrique speaks very highly of you."

"Kate, you and Enriquito are very kind, but please call me Máximo. I should warn you though; Enriquito tends to exaggerate. Although… Claudia also tells me how special I am, so I may begin to believe it."

"I must say that, in the short time I've known Máximo, and I admit this is only our second date, he has thoroughly delighted me with his Cuban charm."

"Claudia, he's been teaching me some of that Cuban charm, and I am still waiting for a report from Kate." Enrique felt a sudden sense of family as he interacted with their guests. It was an alliance they were making, blind to generational differences.

After *hors d' oeuvres* and a few glasses of sherry, dinner was served. Claudia complimented Kate on the interior design of her home. Enrique agreed, noting the alluring sophistication of the place.

"Enrique, Máximo tells me you're working on a new book. I was impressed with your previous work, *Portals of Evil.* It brought a new perspective to the darker side of my work."

"Thank you Claudia. I am very familiar with the fine job you do as federal prosecutor. Specifically, the McNeal case you won, so persuasively."

"Well, I am grateful you followed the case."

"Claudia, if it's not an imposition, I would love to hear about that particular case. When I was a graduate student at Columbia, the McNeal case was discussed in one of our seminars on Tibetan Buddhist ethics, as an example of random violence." Kate felt an instant familiarity with Claudia, but was not able to identify the reason.

"Oh my Lord, you're Tara's friend! When you said Columbia, and Tibetan Buddhism, it all came to me. I remember seeing you with Tara, at one of Bob Kerman's parties, shortly after she divorced Gary Young. We didn't meet, but I remember Bob telling me you and Tara were close friends, and that you were one of his favorite graduate students. This is truly a coincidence."

Enrique and Máximo looked at each other, and resisted the urge to give the instance a mystical context. They smiled and continued to listen.

"Gentlemen, I am sure Kate knows what I am about to tell you, but Tara's mother was married briefly to LSD guru Timothy Irael, before she fell in love and married Bob Kerman. The surprising part is that Bob had been one of Irael's graduate students. You would not believe the stories Bob shared about Dr. Irael." Claudia was enjoying the rapport building with Kate.

"Well, I would believe anything about Timothy Irael. The man was raving mad," Máximo added, with deliberate theatrics.

"But getting back to your question Kate, I don't mind discussing the McNeal case, with the caveat that you don't let me go too long with it, or we'll be here all night. That case has haunted me all these years," Claudia admitted.

"I should tell you, Claudia, that although I didn't interview McNeal, I researched his background more than anyone one else for my book," Enrique interjected, as he recalled the most bewildering personal history he had ever encountered. McNeal was the personification of evil, without apparent cause.

"When I was asked to prosecute the McNeal case, I was very reluctant, because I had just lost my dearest nephew, who was tortured and killed by a terrorist group in Yemen. At that time, I was annulled of any compassion, and could only feel rage.

"McNeal was a serial killer, who tortured and murdered nine victims in three states. His ninth victim was an FBI agent who was close on his trail. After he tortured the agent, in ways that I will spare you, he sent pictures to the agent's children. When he was sentenced to death, he told the judge he was looking forward to continue his killings without mercy in prison, and that his only regret was that he was caught before he could murder another nine people." Claudia was visibly affected, but continued with resolve.

"Enrique can tell you, McNeal's psychological testing was well within normal, with unremarkable childhood and education. He was twenty-six when he was arrested. Had never married, and had maintained little contact with his parents. Every witness who knew him described him as an average person. No motives were ever established, other than his admission that he thoroughly enjoyed the power he had to make his victims suffer."

"Yes, I remember when I was researching his case for my book, how forensic psychologists and psychiatrists were baffled, looking for theories that could explain his inhumanity. Some even tried blaming social systems for failing to recognize *average children*, but McNeal continues to elude explanation." As Enrique spoke, he recalled his own conclusions about this bizarre case.

"Enrique, I read your book after the McNeal trial, but as a prosecuting attorney it helped me put the concept of evil in perspective. Can you give us your candid opinion on McNeal?"

"Claudia, you anticipated my question," Kate interjected, before Enrique could respond.

"Yes Enriquito, I am also very curious to hear your take," Máximo added to the increasing anticipation.

"I'll give you my honest opinion, but after I do, I want Kate to contribute her Tibetan Buddhist wisdom on the nature of evil." Enrique's request focused all the attention on Kate.

"Enrique, speaking of evil, I am going to torture you tonight for putting me on the spot." Kate instinctively brought forth humor, inviting everyone to lighten the somber mood.

"I am looking forward to your torture, my love. But seriously, one of the problems we have in our sanitized society is that we're afraid to admit there's evil out there, so we give psychosocial reasons for acts against humanity. With poor excuses for human beings like McNeal and the Osama Bin Ladens of the world, these apologetic theories result in explanations of diminishing returns. So what is evil to me, after researching the subject for years, and interviewing more than thirty perpetrators of the most brutal crimes? I'll answer that question with another question." Enrique thought Breogán would cringe hearing his statement, but felt he was leading everyone to a clarifying point, and continued.

"What does the perpetrator feel, during and after committing the crime, and how is the inflicted suffering justified within the perpetrator's reasoning? I asked the criminals I interviewed those questions, and based on their answers, they fell into two very disturbing categories. One set felt a sense of revenge for past injustices, with *an eye for an eye* justification, and the other set felt a sense of power over their victims, with *weakness as a flaw to exploit* justification. Perpetrators in both categories showed little remorse for their crimes and a history of major childhood abuse that turned into generalized rage. Both categories had a cause and effect quality that could give some credibility to the psychosocial explanation for crimes against humanity, but there were a few like McNeal that didn't fit either category. No history of childhood trauma, no signs of conventional psychopathology, and no neuropsychological disorders: *nothing* to justify their criminal behavior.

"In the two *cause-and-effect* categories, I saw rage, born out of fear, turning to evil. Although the criminals who did not fit those two categories could be described as having inner turmoil we can't measure or understand, I believe this type of perpetrators are agents of evil in the purest sense. It's possible to be evil with cause, as well as to be evil without cause. Both cases choose contempt for the option to love."

Enrique left the others absorbed in their private thoughts, until Máximo broke the spell, reminding Kate it was time for her Tibetan Buddhist perspective.

"Well, before I jump into this ethical swamp, let's have Silvia bring dessert and coffee. And of course, *Larios,* for Máximo and Enrique."

"Máximo and Claudia, now can you see why I adore this woman? Darling, where did you find the *Larios?*" Enrique was touched by Kate's commitment to please him.

"*Enriquito*, as Máximo calls you, I have my ways," Kate responded, with a winning smile.

"From the joy I see in you men, I want some of that *Larios* as well," Claudia said, to the delight of all. "By the way Kate, your lobster thermidor was heavenly. I implore you to share your secret."

"Hear, hear," Máximo's kudos for Kate's cuisine were echoed by Claudia and Enrique.

"Ok, my first non-Buddhist secret is that you have to steam the lobster using a *Mersault* white burgundy, but I'll share the recipe with you Claudia, and then perhaps you can let us savor your version."

"It's a done deal. The next dinner, is at my home," Claudia offered, with pleasure.

"Now, I can give you a Tibetan Buddhist perspective: God, how I'd love to have Professor Kerman come to my rescue," Kate lamented. "But anyway, according to Tibetan Buddhist philosophy, good and evil evolve from the dualistic world we conceive, and as a consequence, we choose to reincarnate when we refuse to learn compassion in our lifetime. The concept of *karma* is misunderstood in the West, because we see it as a system that rewards or punishes us based on our conduct in past lives. Instead, we are the authors of our actions, and those actions are intrinsically punishing or rewarding to Self. So instead of *karma* being a device of cause and effect, it's what Buddha called *cetana*, which means intention, volition, will. Acts of evil remove us from compassion, and thus we punish ourselves in the process. While the

West conceives evil as malevolent action against another, Tibetan Buddhists believe evil is malevolent action against self. That conduct lacks *inclusive compassion*."

"Kate, I am fascinated by your comments, and I guess the attorney in me begs the question: if evil is action against self, then are we justified with our intervention to protect others who would be hurt from the evil action? In other words, even if murder is an act of evil against self, there is also a victim who is murdered," Claudia asked with genuine interest.

"Indeed, the Tibetan Buddhists use the term *grandmother compassion*, to describe the lack of action that permits violence to take place. His Holiness the Dalai Lama suggests that *defensive action to prevent violence is non-violent action*. That makes preventive action against violence justified. Now I'll leave it to Claudia's legal mind to discern what willful action against compassion should be deemed criminal," Kate concluded, as she smiled and turned to Claudia.

"My dear, you've discoursed, brilliantly, the quintessence of evil. But for now, I won't touch that subject with a legal ten foot pole." Claudia lifted her glass and toasted to the beginning of a treasured friendship. "You and Enrique have given substantive Eastern and Western perspectives to a very dark subject. Thank you very much."

"Claudia, I told you these kids are gems," Máximo asserted, with the grin of an approving parent.

The evening came to an end with warm *abrazos* and an agreement to meet again at Claudia's in the near future, for her rendition of Kate's lobster thermidor. The snowstorm never materialized that night, but Enrique and Kate remained impervious to the weather in their state of bliss.

Chapter 7

"Slowly, that inner force that propelled you to
savor invincibility begins to weaken…"

*E*ric Connery was flying to Miami to visit Enrique, for what they called periodic *image tune-ups*. He phoned Enrique early in the morning to tell him he had good news to share. Enrique was aware that if he showed curiosity, Eric would only give him tantalizing fragments, playing with his compulsive need to know. They had ways of testing their respective limits in areas that few dared to risk. Although at times these experiences can be unsettling, when the pushing is done with devotion, they have a humbling effect that invites one to reconsider priorities and change course. These *image adjustments* are vital for people with power who can insulate their egos from truth. The deleterious effects of neglecting self-probing to keep vanity alive are apparent in the rich and famous who rely on sycophants to gauge their conduct.

Eric was an avid fan of *Jai Alai,* and Miami has the oldest *fronton* in the nation. The Basque game is played in a three-walled court, where a speeding hard ball is propelled and scooped with a long weaved basket attached to the hand of the player. The hand-made basket is called a *chistera,* and after attempts to reproduce them industrially with synthetic substitutes failed to match the endurance of the natural materials, *cesteros* continue to make them by hand using a precise combination of hard wood and soft reed.

Jai Alai is the fastest game on earth, with the *pelote,* as the hard ball is called, reaching speeds of up to 188 miles per hour.

Enrique was taking Eric to the Jai Alai fronton, and then dinner at Casa Xoán. Eric commented that, if it weren't for the colorful Cuban accents in Miami, going to a Basque Jai Alai match and later dining at a Galician restaurant would feel like an evening in Spain. The two friends arrived at Casa Xoán, after watching world-class Jai Alai, at the famed Miami fronton. Although Eric seldom gambled, he tried his luck with pari-mutuel wagering on the second match of the night, and won five hundred dollars. He was in splendid mood, and could not think of a better friend than Enrique to celebrate the gifts of a charmed life.

Felipe, the *maitre'd,* brought them their *Lustao* sherry, from *Jerez de la Frontera* in southern Spain, to start the evening. The word *sherry* is an English bastardising of the Spanish name of the region, *Jerez*. The distillation of wine to sherry was invented by the Chinese and brought to Europe by the Moorish invaders, who occupied Spain for seven hundred years.

"Eric, have you toyed enough with my patience to share the good news?" Enrique had been waiting for Eric to volunteer the information, but invariably, his friend was better at withholding, than he at delaying rewards.

"Yes, I am ready to capitulate. You're one of the first to know what I am about to tell you. Your good buddy is madly in love! My gallivanting days are over; with my blessings."

"You dog! When did this happen? Why did you hold out on me? My sincere congratulations." Enrique was visibly excited for his friend.

"Thank you Enrique."

"Who's the fortunate lion tamer?"

"Julietta Sabatini," Eric uttered the name, expecting Enrique to recognize it.

"Exotic name."

"Well?" Eric asked continuing to expect recognition.

"Should I know this woman?"

"Enrique, Julietta is Liliana's older sister. You know, your dear publisher, Liliana?"

"No way! How did that happen? Liliana talked about a sister who lives in Italy, but she never mentioned her name. Is that her?"

"Yes, she moved to New York three months ago, and we met at a cocktail party. We hit it off instantly, and when she told me Liliana was her sister, I wanted to call you, and blow your mind."

"Well Eric, let me blow your mind. I had a recent conversation with Liliana, which I was not planning to tell you, and she joked about daring you to tame her, after I told her your macho comments about her. Thank God, you fell in love with her older sister."

"Why are you thanking God?"

"Because, still jokingly, Liliana said she liked you, but thought she was too young for you."

Eric started to laugh uncontrollably, until he stopped and looked at Enrique with tears of hilarity. "Enrique, Julietta is only a year older than Liliana." Both men laughed contagiously, and padded each other's shoulders.

"Eric, has Julietta told Liliana? Enrique asked with concern in his voice."

"We made the sibling association the other night when were having drinks at the Flatiron Lounge. Julietta called her sister immediately to tell her, and they started speaking rapid Italian and laughing hysterically. Liliana got me on the phone, threatening to castrate me if I hurt her big sister, then she called me a dirty old man and congratulated me in Italian. I am encouraged to tell you that Julietta is a tad less emotional than Liliana."

"Eric, a *tad less* emotional does not seem very comforting, knowing Liliana the way we do."

"A sobering thought," Eric pronounced with a grin, as they toasted again to the joyful news.

"Eric, your bedroom at my place awaits you, as always."

"Well, you see..." Eric's face, turned uncharacteristically red.

"Is she in town?" Enrique interjected with exaggerated surprise, delighting in Eric's rare moment of modesty.

"Well, yes she is. We booked *separate* suites at the Delano in South Beach," he stated with a sheepish smile.

"Eric why separate suites? I am sure Liliana would give you permission to share a suite, if you promised to behave with her sister." Enrique was enjoying teasing his friend. Eric ignored him and went on.

"Can you imagine when the gossip columnists get ahold of the news? Especially the scorned gossip columnists."

"Eric, I am sure you've scorned a few."

"Yes, Lori James comes to mind."

"You devil. I had no idea you *scorned* Ms. James."

"Enrique, I think you're enjoying my predicament too damn much."

"Yes I am. By the way, what does Julietta do for a living?"

"She's a shrink, but she's never practiced."

"Why not?"

"Mega wealth. She went to medical school in Italy, and did her psychiatry residency at Johns Hopkins, but only to please her dad, who was an eminent psychiatrist in Rome. After completing her residency, she went back to Italy and shortly afterward, her dad passed away; so I guess she was freed of the commitment to practice."

"Eric, she's going to analyze your inner demons," Enrique said mockingly.

"You better prepare for my revenge. You've enjoyed yourself without mercy at my expense but... I wouldn't have it any other way. On a serious note, I do want to discuss some concerns." Eric's solemn mood signalled he was ready to enter a private moment.

"Ever since you were on my show, I've been captivated, by your *horizons of convention* idea. I guess we don't think much about cultural influences when we're busy living our lives. Then your heart is invited to love when you're reaching your sixty-eighth birthday, and these cultural conventions surface with brutal clarity."

"Happy birthday, my friend. I am so pleased you made time to visit." Enrique was moved by his friend's candid disclosure.

"Thanks Enrique. I do want you to tell me more about how we fall prey to these cultural admonishments."

"Admonishment is exactly what we encounter. Our culture, and not exclusively our genes, determines the affinity for partnering, the limitations of aging, and by implication, how long we hang out on planet Earth. I'm convinced that at the time we enter one of these cultural portals, let's say retirement at sixty-five, all aspects of the culture collude to inculcate the way of thinking set for that portal. You will then be inundated with media enticements and advice from so-called *experts* for medication, living styles, vehicles, treatment of illnesses, and anything else the culture deems characteristic for that stage of life. Slowly, that *inner force* that propelled you to savor invincibility begins to weaken from the constant cultural demands to subdue your hopes, and surrender your dreams."

"Well, Enrique, I'll be damned if I am going to trade in my Ferrari for a van."

"That's the Eric I love. Julietta is a very lucky woman."

"Thank you, friend. I needed to hear what I already suspected."

Enrique drove Eric to the Delano hotel in South Beach, and thanked him for sharing such happy news. Their friendship was solid, and they were grateful for the mutual support they enjoyed.

During the short drive from the hotel to his home on Ocean Drive, Enrique decided he needed to learn more about how mystics approached the cultural portals, and how to retain the *inner force* he was beginning to identify. He smiled, comparing his introspections with how children gain abstractive proficiency, by dialoging with their imaginary characters. Perhaps Breogán could help him advance to the next level of insight. Yes, his man from autumn would be the first order of business, early next morning.

Chapter 8

"My interest in this riveting topic is psychological rather than theological."

Pontifical University of the Holy Cross, Rome
School of Theology

The Stigmata Lecture

"St. Francis of Assisi received the stigmata, or wounds of Christ, in twelve twenty-four A.D., after fasting for forty days on Mt. Alverno. Although it was the first recorded account of this mysterious phenomenon, some scholars suggest that St. Paul's allusion, 'I bear in my body the marks of the Lord Jesus', in Galatians 6:17, may qualify him as the first stigmatic, if his statement is taken literally. I should also note that, two years before the St. Francis incident, a monk in Oxford claiming to be the redeemer of mankind proclaimed his five crucifixion wounds were the work of God, but after his arrest for blasphemy, he confessed they were self-inflicted. Some speculate that torture was employed to persuade him. Since the time of St. Francis, there have been more than three hundred and fifty cases recorded.

"The position of the Church has remained, 'leave the interpretation of whether the stigmata is the result of divine intervention or self-initiated to each individual's belief.' It's also my understanding that, subsequent to the time of the Apostles, the Church does not recognize extraordinary occurrences as divine intervention. Perhaps there are scores of theologians arguing the point as we speak." Breogán heard a few restrained laughs from the audience and continued.

"My interest in this riveting topic is psychological, rather than theological, and I presume that's why I was asked to lecture here today. There's substantial evidence in the scientific literature that our beliefs affect our immune system and ultimately our health. Observing acts of compassion can increase antibodies that fight upper respiratory infections. Placebos can have the same pain-relieving effect as narcotics, and nocebo injections can constrict or dilate the bronchial airways,

69

depending on the expectation presented to the subject, despite the injections being nothing more than saline. Confession, some here will be glad to learn, decreases blood pressure, heart rate and stress hormones like cortisol, while increasing immune function.

"So, if we exclude divine intervention and self-infliction, what can be said about these crucifixion-like wounds, in light of evidence that they resist infection, and the affected do not develop anemia despite daily loss of blood? Padre Pio, who was recently canonized not for his stigmata but for his devotional deeds, is said to have bled a cup of blood a day for nearly fifty years without deleterious effects.

"But before discussing the psychology, or I should say the biopsychology of stigmata, let me bring up another perplexing characteristic that merits consideration. The medieval artists depicted Christ on the cross with the wounds on the palms of His hands. Forensic scientists have inferred the Romans knew that if the palms were nailed, they would not be able to bear the weight of the body. Thus they nailed the wrists instead. The Shroud of Turin, as well as other evidence, confirmed the forensic supposition.

"There is no more compelling evidence that our biology conforms to our beliefs than the fact that, before the scientific evidence about the anatomy of crucifixion was available, stigmatics manifested their wounds on their palms, whereas contemporary cases have their wounds appearing on their wrists. I will also mention that attempts to produce the wounds under hypnosis have failed.

"Then, given the information I've shared so far, what is the biopsychology of stigmata? I suggest that, in order to begin to understand the motivational components of stigmata, we need to examine the medieval model of suffering. In those days, suffering was the vehicle to identify with Christ. The tormented lives of the Catholic mystics of that era provide ample evidence to support the penance model. So if suffering were the way to identify with Christ, certainly to replicate his wounds would be the ultimate compliment. Reading the personal accounts of how some stigmatics prayed for their wounds sustains the contention that suffering was a desired state."

Breogán scanned his audience and noticed half were clergy. He was pleased that the other half was secular youth. He wondered how many adhered to the model of suffering, and how their choice would be influenced by theology and age.

"The apparent power that the mind-body process has to manifest suffering in the flesh could have momentous implications. Consider that, if belief can injure tissue when one identifies with the suffering of Christ, to identify with the love of Christ could have powerful healing

effects. If stigmatics can bypass the harmful physical consequences of their wounds, possibly by creating a super-immune state, then we can only imagine what could be achieved if we investigate the biology of love.

"I submit to you that science has advanced to a level where the consequences of prayer, faith and love can be measured and funneled to accomplish healing, rather than promote suffering. Research is presently underway to study changes in the molecular structure of water that has been blessed, the effects of compassionate imagery on the growth rate of malignant cells, and the role of faith in spontaneous healing.

"Thank you very much for the time you have afforded me to respectfully suggest, science and theology need not continue to exist within the dualistic model that has kept them in conflict."

Breogán was treated to a standing ovation from an audience known for their conservative Opus Dei tradition.

After the lecture, the Vice Dean of the school of theology, Rev. Liestra, greeted Breogán and accompanied him to a private reception where they met other faculty members and several diplomats from the Holy See. The Vatican is recognized as a sovereign government within the Republic of Italy and has its own diplomatic corps. Most countries have ambassadors representing their diplomatic missions at the Vatican.

"Signore Breogán, let me introduce myself. I am Fr. Carlo Fellini. I teach psychology at the Catholic University of Milano. I was very gratified by your comments on the biopsychology of beliefs. Mesmerizing subject."

"Thank you, Father. You're very kind."

Father Fellini was a short man in his early fifties with a balding pattern reminiscent of a medieval monk. His face reflected a lifetime of inquisitive compassion. Breogán felt an instant kinship with the priest.

"Well, tell me Fr. Fellini, how's psychology faring at Milan's finest?"

"In great shape after a very painful liberation from fundamental Church dogma and Freud's views on religion."

"Now father, will you burn at the stake for such heresy?" Fr. Fellini responded with a deep laughter that personified joy.

"I can tell you, signore Breogán--sadly, such inhibitions still exist at other universities that will remain unnamed. But let me ask you a question that crossed my mind as you were speaking about the pattern of suffering. I see people so debilitated by their learned helplessness that they cannot move beyond their suffering. They seem to invest their

energy in learning how to be more proficient with their pain. How do you contrast such behavior to the medieval mind you discussed in your lecture?"

Breogán's first thought was to tell Fr. Fellini the 'signore' was not necessary to address him, but since it sounded endearing rather than formal, he decided to enjoy it a bit longer and went on to consider the question. Before he could answer, another priest introduced himself to compliment him on his lecture and moved on to discuss Church politics with one of the Vatican diplomats standing by the buffet table. These pleasant interruptions made Breogán wonder if he needed to mingle, but concluded he wanted to befriend Fr. Fellini and resumed the chat instead.

"Father Fellini..."

"Oh please, call me Carlo."

"I will, if you call me Breogán, although I love the sound of the Italian word for mister."

"You've got yourself a deal, signore." Both men laughed and shook hands to validate their agreement.

"Now, to answer your question, I believe there's a fundamental difference between the two forms of suffering. Learned helplessness does not appear to be a conscious act of will but rather a surrendering to impotence, whereas the medieval suffering was an act of volition to identify with Christ.

"Admirable clarification, Breogán. To carry your postulate a step further, with the medieval mindset there is a force propelling the will even though it is misguided. But sadly, learned helplessness is a state of disowning whatever power we may have to choose our destiny."

"Carlo, I think this is the beginning of a lovely friendship."

"May the Lord hear you." They exchanged cards and agreed to stay in touch via email.

Breogán continued to socialize graciously and, although he made several other favorable acquaintances, he felt Carlo was the prize of the evening.

Enrique stopped typing, concluding the morning had been productive. He planned to dialogue with Breogán and instead, *the drift* led him to the subject of stigmata. It was time for lunch with Andrés Vitón, to discuss fees for a series of lectures based on his second book, *The Anthropology of Self Esteem,* that Enrique had agreed to present. He was meeting Andrés at a small Argentinean restaurant a few blocks away. It was their preferred place to eat because its ambiance could take the edge off an unpleasant side of business that prices artists for the market.

Enrique had a formula to choose restaurants: equal measures of a delectable specialty, servers who enjoyed their work, and an atmosphere that could compliment the personalities of the guests he invited to break bread.

Andrés was a superb booking agent who promoted best-selling authors with something more to offer than reading their own works to cable audiences. He was from Argentina and proudly announced his distaste for *tango*. Andrés was not aware that his slick black hair and tapered double-breasted suits were too much temptation for Hispanics not to associate him with tango idol Carlos Gardel.

Enrique loved to walk from his home to the Argentinean restaurant during the busy hours where ethnic dramas unfold in multi-cultural neighborhoods. The short distance from Ocean Drive to the restaurant on Lincoln Road displayed, with equal vividness, the fortunes of the eccentric and the misfortunes of the weird. He lamented how the power of wealth can euphemize human tragedy.

"How's my dear *gaucho*?"

"Doing well, my dear *torero*."

Enrique was aware that *gauchos* have not roamed the Argentinean Pampas since they were massacred and exiled from their lands in the eighteen hundreds by a series of segregationist governments, and Andrés knew that *toreros* are not from the Galician region of Spain where Enrique's family called home. But both men loved to pretend cultural ignorance to tease each other.

"Before I sell you like a slave to your adoring public, I need a glass of wine," Andrés warned after hugging Enrique and kissing him on the cheek, as Argentinean men do when they greet all their friends.

"Andrés, why are you wearing a suit in this sauna weather?"

"Because, unlike boorish authors, I am a proper gentleman."

"But this boorish author is buying you lunch."

"Well, you could have told me earlier to spare insult to your self-esteem."

"*Don Andrés*, what an awful transition to the topic of our luncheon."

"You're right; my wife tells me I am getting more banal with age. But what does she know; she's a foreigner." Although Andrés' wife was American, anyone who was not from Argentina was a foreigner to him.

"Ok, Enrique, listen carefully so we can conclude our business before the food arrives. You know I hate to negotiate while I am savoring a good meal." When Andrés pontificated, he would rock from side to side like a hen settling on her nest and adjust his double-breasted jacket to emphasize his points.

"All right Andrés, I am ready."

As Enrique prepared to listen, Breogán's conversation with Fr. Fellini flashed in his mind without warning. He remembered something felt unfinished when he stopped writing to meet Andrés for lunch, and then it came to him: Fr. Fellini used the word *force* when he was elaborating Breogán's description of the two types of suffering. That was it! Enrique found a link between the *inner force* that he wanted to discuss with Breogán and Fr. Fellini's use of the word *force*. He decided to withhold predictability and perhaps discover a feedforward event in his conversation with Andrés. He wanted to conclude the business side of the meeting so he could test the interconnectedness with Andrés.

"Enrique, you're tuning out on me with that absent look of yours. Were you fantasizing one of your chapters instead of trying to make some money? Artists are all the same. They need astute businessmen like myself to protect them."

"Sorry Andrés, I had too many thoughts running in my head. Tell me about the deal."

"Ok, five lectures between January and April of next year. All expenses paid with expected first-class flights, hotels and meals. Each lecture will last three hours with book signings afterward. *Magellan Seminars* will do all the promotion, scheduling, etc. and after my commission is extracted, you will pocket fifteen thousand per lecture."

"Ok," Enrique responded nonchalantly.

"Ok, what?"

"Ok, I agree."

"Enrique, you take all the joy out of my work. I love to negotiate and get excited. What if you could demand more? What if that amount was just a beginning offer?"

"Andrés, I trust you and I know that when you come to me with figures, you've already kicked someone else's ass on my behalf. True?"

"Of course it's true, but you take all the fun out of it. Let me tell you," Andrés did his hen rocking ritual and continued, "those cheapskates at Magellan started with fees that would insult even a naïve business person like you. But your *gaucho* friend negotiated soundly and persuaded them to capitulate. Ah… I can smell the *churrasco* coming."

Churrasco is a sumptuously grilled skirt steak of Argentinean fame, served with a *chimichurri* sauce made of minced fresh parsley, onions, garlic, oregano, basil, thyme, lemon and olive oil. The synergy of flavors from the first morsel complemented the *Bianchi* wine from the Mendoza region in Argentina. Although Enrique did not usually eat red meat, there were occasions that would feel like dire deprivation if he did not indulge.

"I'll send you the contract with all the details by the end of the week. Now tell me what you really wanted to discuss. It's never about money with you."

"You know me well, Andrés. Yes, I do want to discuss something about my theory with you. What drives you to go on when you feel defeated?"

Andrés looked pensive, and surprisingly, was taking the question seriously. The negotiator turned to introspection and dropped his guard.

"The love for my children drives me. That's the first thing that came to mind. Why did you ask me that question?"

"Because that's a topic I am researching for my book. Can you tell me more about what drives you under dismal times?"

"I am going to disclose something very personal, because as much as I mock you about your puzzling ways, I have great respect for your integrity." Perhaps to access the strength he was trying to describe, Andrés picked up his wine glass and slowly swirled it in a dance with the sunlight that was gently warming their table. He took a deep breath and continued. "I believe when you love someone completely, it liberates you to accept your end with dignity. You love so much, you can leave this earth at any moment without regrets. Enrique, we fear death when we have not truly embraced the depth of love."

"Andres, you've shown me your wisdom with inspiring sensitivity. But why do you talk about death?"

"Actually, it didn't dawn on me until now, but I am going to be fifty-one next month and my father died at that age. Then, last weekend I met with my financial planner who insisted I am not preparing well for my retirement."

"I have the cure for that. You, Eric Connery and I need to have dinner soon. Let me tell you what's happening: your *biocultural portals* are pounding you to conform."

"And my treasured *amigo*… what the hell does that mean?"

"Andrés, I am going to send you an article a psychologist friend of mine wrote on how our culture can kill us faster than our genes. But I want to thank you for sharing that private side of you. I am truly honored," Enrique felt words could not match his appreciation.

"Enrique, to be honest, I don't know where those pearls of wisdom came from, but I was also impressed." They both laughed at how immodesty can incongruently suggest humility when expressed without ego. Enrique wondered if that invigorating form of boasting happens when we question the origin of our wisdom. Like an awareness that the brilliance we're exhibiting was *coauthored* with a higher entity.

"Ok, pay for lunch and let's go back to the salt mines." Andrés had reached his limit for accolades.

"My pleasure. Please give that *foreign* wife of yours a kiss for me."

"Thank you, I will, *torero*."

On his walk back home Enrique took a different route so he could pass by a small antique shop that reminded him of his father. The elderly shopkeeper looked nothing like Enrique's dad, yet he was a private source of sweet reminiscence. When Enrique peeked inside, he always felt like hugging the little man without saying a word. The journey offers sustaining gifts for those who care to look.

Chapter 9

"Faustus can only influence what already exists within you."

If the *drift* were given human attributes, like programmers do with their computers, *chance* could be the mother that provides its potential, and *will* the father that perseveres through its erratic space. Then, when our choices and our tenacity are welcomed as benign teachers, we can learn priceless lessons rather than lament our lives away.

Slowly, Enrique was charting his unpredictable space with increasing competence. The gradual mastery reminded him of his surfing days when he was recognizing that, although patterns of waves are predictable, every wave has a chaotic probability that can unfold without the slightest warning.

Will and *chance* were collaborating with Enrique when he heard his book *Portals of Evil* was mentioned in a blockbuster movie that tamed *Silence of the Lambs* with its darkness. The Interpol agent in the film, played by Oscar winner Hollie Berings, used Enrique's theory of evil throughout the film as her guide, to help her catch the satanic character named *Faustus,* who was flawlessly played by Randall Caine. That fortunate occurrence brought Enrique's book back to the bestseller lists and numerous invitations for interviews from the social inquisitors of late night shows.

Typical of the capricious nature of *the drift*, the publicity generated for *Portals of Evil* by the *Faustus* film paled when compared with the soaring popularity *The Man from Autumn* gained from one scene in the film, where the Interpol agent consulted a mystic to learn how to battle the shamanic powers that the evil Faustus was using to lure his victims. A talk show celebrity, citing Enrique's appearance on Eric Connery's show, asked Hollie Berings if Breogán was the mystic who advised her character in the film. She was pleased with the question and responded ambiguously to increase the suspense. Hollywood loves mysteries and it turned an inadvertent incident into a formidable publicity stunt. *Faustus* became a cult film before its time because it delved into the dimension of evil archetypes. Since the evolvement of consciousness, the quest for esoteric forces to protect us from the dark side has not ceased to entice our heroes.

The insatiable questions about the mysterious Breogán were a source of amusement for Ms. Berings. As the unplanned publicity mounted, she asked Liliana to arrange a meeting with Enrique to discuss his Breogán character. Liliana tactfully promised to try but cautioned her it was highly unlikely that Enrique would agree to meet before the book was completed. A competing publisher made an offer for a sequel to *The Man from Autumn*, without seeing the unfinished manuscript that was several months away from publication. The anticipation of excellence creates its own momentum.

In a *Good Morning America* interview, Randall Caine was asked if his portrayal of Faustus was influenced by Enrique's book. Mr. Caine responded with his characteristic British charm: "I read *Portals of Evil,* but I am looking forward to learning more about the mystical ways of this *Breogán* chap, so I can protect myself from bad reviews."

What else was there for Enrique to do, but consult Breogán? It was comforting to know his creation was only a keyboard away.

"Breogán, what have you done to me?"

"Hi Enrique, are you enjoying my notoriety?"

"To be honest, I am approaching it with caution."

"Author of my days, what happened to your sense of adventure?"

"Well, my enigmatic friend, that's easy for you to say while you're enjoying windsurfing in Galicia with your talented wife."

Enrique knew the inspired dyad was always triggered by the frivolity of the exchange. It seemed the lighthearted spar brought down walls of self-consciousness that limited what his personal reality could accommodate.

"Of course, I know what you're thinking. You wonder how you, or actually how *I,* can make good after all the publicity about my ephemeral identity."

"Precisely. So how are *you* going to deliver?"

"Enrique, you already know the answer. We must trust *the drift*."

"You know, Breogán? That's the first time you've used the word *we*. That pleases me greatly."

"That was my intention."

Reading Breogán's response, Enrique wished he could bring to life this charismatic character. And yet, it was already happening at a level he had never imagined, given the publicity his unfinished fictional work was gaining. A popular television comedian remarked that he was looking forward to asking Breogán what he really thought of Enrique.

"Enrique, have you seen the *Faustus* film?

"Why do you ask if you already know I haven't?" Enrique thought of typing a clever response as Breogán, but decided to pause instead. After staring at the screen for a moment, he took a deep breath and felt connected again.

"Very good Enrique. You're a fast learner."

"Well, I am calling Kate and taking her to the movies tonight."

"By the way Enrique, I've seen the film and you'll be impressed with the insights you'll gain."

"Now Breogán, you know *Faustus* is not showing in your *Estaca de Bares* paradise." Enrique imagined Breogán smiling at his response.

"I propose we chat again after you see the film. Kate will be the key to your portal flash."

"Very well Breogán. I'll let you know."

Enrique realized the reflective dialogues were generating intellectual challenges to test *the drift*. If everything *were* interconnected, then any present action would have a corresponding *feedforward event* to unfold in the future. He also wondered if one could find future meaning in *any* present event by simply pushing the limits of associations. If that were the case, what would qualify as a synchronistic moment?

The logical progression he was following brought him back to the question of mysticism versus insanity. Delusional thinking generates a *word salad* that has no consensual coherence. A schizophrenic can have elaborate conversations completely void of cogent associations. Interestingly, Carl Jung studied the disjointed language of psychotic patients, and even their degree of incoherence had some archetypal symbolism that suggested a deeper level of associations. So it seems nothing can be interjected completely free of interconnections.

Enrique turned off his internal query until he could see the film. He was looking forward to watching Randall Caine in a role that was already competing with the malevolence of Hannibal Lecter. But what really caught his attention was the character Nailah Grant, played by Hollie Berings. Rather than the usual FBI agent formula, Nailah was an enigmatic Egyptian-American beauty who, after completing her graduate studies in international criminology at Sheffield University, was recruited by a covert unit of Interpol that investigated international heinous crimes committed by individuals with paranormal abilities. The undercover outfit was formed after law enforcement agencies from several countries shared data that suggested criminals with psychic abilities were using their gifts to commit atrocities. Nailah, which means *successful* in Egyptian, was trained as a forensic scientist and had no interest in parapsychology, but after several months of special training and studying classified archives at the U.S. Interpol Bureau in Washington, she was willing to probe how the power of mind can serve evil.

The film began with Faustus in a strange ritual, harnessing an energy around him that apparently compelled his victim to commit suicide at a distant location. His first *remote murder* victim was an Albanian retired government official, who was driven by this malevolent energy to grab a gun and shoot himself in the head. Faustus was committing *telekinesis* crimes where all the physical evidence led to death by suicide.

Nailah was able to connect the ostensive suicides to Faustus when she was studying the classified cases where parapsychological abilities were used to commit murder. She learned that Faustus had done research for the KGB applying patterns of *remote viewing* to inflict tissue damage on prisoner subjects at a distance. The CIA dismissed Faustus's work as science fiction when he suddenly disappeared from the espionage research scene. Nailah had a hunch that, although her fellow agents saw it as naïve inventiveness, paid off when she noted that Faustus's wife and three of his colleagues had "committed suicide" shortly after he dropped out of the KGB project.

Remote viewing, in which a person can perceive the shape of objects at a distance without physically seeing them, has been a topic of interest to parapsychologists for decades. The military applications of remote viewing have been researched by the CIA at Stanford University and by the former KGB at Odessa University with very promising results, showing that individuals trained in remote viewing techniques can describe and draw the layouts of military installations located many miles away. On the malevolent side, there is declassified evidence now that the KGB conducted experiments with political prisoners to test the effects of highly charged electromagnetic fields on remote viewing. They found that extrasensory perception increased at the expense of brain damage.

In the *Faustus* film, Hollywood embellished the KGB research to create a plausible story resulting in the most chilling psychological thriller of the decade. Faustus had learned to use the energy involved in remote viewing to influence the thoughts and emotions of his victims. As Nailah got closer to finding Faustus, she began to have terrifying suicidal thoughts that confirmed she was on the right trail and that Faustus knew she was coming. To preserve her sanity, Nailah consulted a mystic with training in forensic psychology to help her battle an opponent far beyond her psychic capabilities.

Her private meetings with the mystic always took place in his dimly lit library surrounded by tomes of cryptic wisdom. The mystic explained that we experience our thoughts and emotions within a living field of information where benign and malignant energy could intrude. But that energy could only intensify the beliefs that already existed in the personal field rather than change them.

When Nailah told the mystic about her recent suicidal thoughts, he warned her about the looming danger of continuing her pursuit. After she persisted with her intention to catch Faustus they had the following conversation:

Nailah: *Sir, I must continue. He is pure evil.*

Mystic: *You may lose your life trying.*

Nailah: *I know sir, but there's no turning back, not now that Faustus knows I've uncovered his diabolical scheme. I have no protection.*

Mystic: *You offer a persuasive argument. It bounds me to help you.*

Nailah: *Thank you. I'm ready.*

Mystic: *Faustus can only influence what already exists within you. He takes the self-destructive propensity that lives in the concealed awareness of his victims and feeds it with his evil energy. You see? In a very ironic way, he is merely giving power to the self-punishing susceptibility of his victims and they do the rest.*

Nailah: *What can I do?*

Mystic: *You must find your 'tormenting burden' and confront it.*

Nailah: *What do you mean sir?*

Mystic: *We all carry a burden that haunts us. Who shamed you or demeaned you when your heart was very young? What is your secret burden?*

Nailah: *The instant you asked those questions I felt out of breath.*

Mystic: *Go back to the first time you had that sensation.*

She took a deep breath and closed her eyes before answering.

Nailah: *This is going to be very hard to reveal. I thought I was over it, and when you asked me to remember my burden, I wanted to cry.*

Mystic: *Bring it out my dear. Your life may depend on it.*

Nailah: *When I was around nine my family moved from Cairo to a small town in the States. One day on my way home from school, this angry man came up to me and asked: 'what's a little nigger girl like you doing on this part of town?' I didn't know what the word meant so I responded: 'sir, I am not nigger. I am Egyptian'. He laughed and answered: 'nigger, Egyptian, it's all the same shit'. I ran home crying, hardly able to breathe. I never told anyone, but I looked up the word nigger and I felt very sad for that man's hatred.*

She tried to hold back her tears but the mystic came up to her and whispered something in her ear. She thanked him as she cried and laughed in his arms.

Mystic: *You were a brave little girl then. And look at you now: a very courageous woman.*

As Enrique watched, he was not aware of his sobbing until Kate turned to look at him. Unable to contain her own tears, she gently held his hand and told him how much she loved him. He wanted to walk out of the theater, but instead, he bit his lower lip like he did many years back when he was confronting a menacing wave.

The mystic explained that the suicidal thoughts came when Faustus sent his energy to give impetus to her shame. For protection, he taught her a powerful ritual and made her promise that she would never abuse it. When she felt the self-destructive urge coming, she should sit quietly and begin to breathe anger in and breathe fear out until she regained control. Next, she should breathe love in and breathe anger out visualizing herself gradually surrounded by a beneficent light. He told her the ritual would change her living informational field from shamed little girl to honorable woman, allowing the pure light of love to function like a mirror that would reflect the negative energy back to its evil source.

The film continued with spellbound progression coming to an ominous ending: Nailah had a dream where she felt an intense self-destructive urge to stab herself with a kitchen knife. She woke up in a panic, but managed to start the protective ritual. While she was following the breathing procedure, she had a *remote viewing* experience where she saw the place Faustus was hiding and sending his dark energy from a few miles away. She continued the protective sequence until she exuded a white light that radiated in all directions. When the luminosity subsided, she drove frantically to the place she had visualized, broke down the door, ran to a small study and found a bloodied knife on the floor. She ordered fingerprints and DNA workup on the knife and blood. The following evening, when she downloaded the results from the Interpol database, a picture of Faustus emerged on her computer screen.

After the movie, Kate and Enrique went to a night owl's coffee shop in Coral Gables for *latte* and *biscotti*.

"Kate, *Faustus* is one of the most disturbing films I've seen," Enrique said as his thoughts circled around Breogán's suggestion that she would provide a key insight from the story line of the movie.

"I was terrified. But Enrique, how did they match the DNA? Faustus had never been caught."

"Great question. Remember at the beginning of the film, when they showed Faustus working in the KGB lab?" Enrique asked trying to anticipate Kate's response, but he willed himself to cease judgment.

"Yes, I do now!" Kate responded with enthusiasm in her voice. "They were collecting hair samples from each scientist without any explanation. It was ingeniously left to the audience to conclude they were establishing a DNA database that later gave Interpol access to the declassified KGB files."

"You own the mind of a sleuth. Do you have any other great deductions?"

"That's all for now, love. I don't know about you, but I am exhausted. Shall we go home?"

"Yes, *mi deliciosa*. Are you staying with me tonight?" Enrique asked, wishing she wanted his company that night as much he longed for hers. *Faustus* had stirred a ghost he was going to be battling soon.

"I better stay with you tonight. They're predicting a snowstorm around Brickell Avenue."

Enrique smiled and hugged her with gratitude. They were beginning to understand how love requires a language that can read essential needs between the lines of trepidation.

In the morning, Kate left early to teach her Aikido class, and Enrique decided to mingle with the tourists and go for a swim. Although the beach on Ocean Drive was like a stage for exhibitionist hard bodies and oblivious soft ones, Enrique could still swim out to find serenity, looking at his home and the moving crowd while he floated, seeing it all from a distance.

"Hello, Kate? This is Claudia."

"Oh hi Claudia, what a nice surprise."

"I was calling you to thank you for the email with your lobster thermidor recipe. I'm going to do a trial run to refine my culinary skills before I have the gang over."

"No need for that, Claudia. We're looking forward to a great meal whenever you're ready."

"I also called you because I saw a most disturbing movie that reminded me of our conversation about evil. Have you seen *Faustus*?"

"Yes, we just did last night, and Enrique and I were truly shaken."

"My God, Hollie Berings should win another Oscar for her performance. But I wanted to ask you about a scene that I just can't turn off."

"Claudia, I can't turn off the whole film. Which scene were you thinking about?"

"Do you remember when they alluded the first victim was an Albanian ex-government official?"

"Yes I do, and it was never mentioned again. I wondered why Albania of all places?" As Kate was recalling that scene it bothered her in a most peculiar way.

"Kate, I know Enrique is getting all this tremendous publicity from the film and I wondered if they consulted him for the script?"

"No, it was a startling twist. Nailah just kept referring to his theory of evil in the film and that's how it took off. Enrique was taken by surprise and obviously his publisher was overjoyed."

"I can imagine. I read a review of the film and it mentioned the director hired a psychologist as technical adviser, who is an authority in what they call *incidental learning*."

"Claudia, is that like subliminal advertising?"

"No, I actually learned the difference from the article. It said subliminal methods introduce a visual image faster than it can register consciously to influence you without your awareness. But incidental learning involves presenting information that teaches you something indirectly related to the subject you are ostensibly learning. The article discussed tasks where children learned a particular behavior by practicing another. It gave an example of using video games to help children who have eye-hand coordination problems."

Kate mentioned the DNA to Claudia and they ended the phone chat with more questions about the film than when they started. Kate could not stop thinking about the elderly, Albanian retired official in the film. She felt a disturbing lack of closure.

As soon as she finished her conversation with Claudia, the association hit her like an artic storm. Frank, her butler, was from Albania! She rushed to the kitchen where Frank was sitting drinking his afternoon hot chocolate.

"Hi Frank. How are you today?"

"Katie, I am doing quite well, but you on the other hand seem troubled."

"Why do you say that?"

"Because ever since you were a little girl, your voice goes up an octave when you're worried."

"Christ, am I that transparent?"

"No, I just know you that well. Remember when you used to get in trouble with Mr. Holland and you'd come to me so I could intercede?"

"How can I forget?"

"Well, that's the same voice I just heard."

Kate went up to him and hugged him as she had done all her life, and he pretended not to like it, as he always did. Frank was the surrogate father who was always there, and she was the daughter he never had.

"Frank, tell me about Albania."

"It used to be part of the former Soviet Union."

"Mr. Frank!" She always called him that when he evaded her questions.

"Alright, what do you want to know about those communist peasants?"

Frank's father was murdered by the Albanian secret police and his family's farm was confiscated and given to the workers his dad had always sheltered. Frank and his sister escaped to America in the late forties, running from one of the most brutal dictatorships in the Soviet Block.

"What happened to the Albanian government when the communists took over?"

"Those who resisted were imprisoned or executed and the rest were given bureaucratic jobs. Why this sudden interest in Albania?"

Kate explained the scene in the *Faustus* film where the elderly Albanian committed suicide without any explanations. Frank told her that, although he had not seen *Faustus*, according to an article in an Albanian newspaper, a number of high government officials committed suicide after the collapse of their dictatorial regime. "Either guilt or fear of reprisal for their abuses led them to take their lives," Frank said concluding from the article he read.

"Thank you dear."

"I don't know what I did to help, but you're welcome Katie."

"Mr. Frank, one more question." She also used the *mister* before a question, when she was afraid of the answer he might give her. "What do you think of Enrique?"

"He seems worthy of your love," Frank responded with smiling eyes.

After discussing the concept of *incidental learning* with Claudia, Kate wondered if the unexplained scene with the Albanian former official was another hint for the audience, similar to the hair samples clue given at the beginning of the film, to make sense of the DNA match at the end. Whatever was going on, Kate thought the film's consulting psychologist had done a commendable job keeping everyone baffled, in addition to terrifying them with the chilling story.

Silvia prepared a hot bath for Kate, anticipating her wishes. Kate's extended family could read her needs with unfailing accuracy. They pampered her with love rather than the adulation wealthy employers negotiate with their hired help. She melted her stress in her Roman marble bathtub surrounded by candles and the scent of burning *Edessa* incense. Her eyes closed with contentment and she thought of how Enrique had nourished her life.

Some parapsychologists suggest that being in a calm state while submerged in soothing water can increase the conductivity of thoughts between two people who share a harmonious union. Apparently that's what happened when Kate picked up the phone next to her bathtub to call Enrique, and he was on the line before she dialed.

"Enrique? I was just about to call you, and you were there. Did your phone ring?"

"No, you picked up right after I dialed. Welcome to synchronicity."

"My very thoughts."

Kate told Enrique about her chat with Frank and the association she made with the Albanian scene. Enrique wanted to pursue the theme to see if it was the precursor he needed from Kate.

"Enrique, this may be irrelevant, but do you remember when the elderly Albanian was picking up the gun from his desk to shoot himself?"

"Yes I do. What about it?"

"The camera briefly scanned the desk and it showed a framed photograph of a distinguished looking man." Kate wanted Enrique to recognize the photo to confirm her suspicion of who she thought it was, without biasing it with her guess.

"Yes, you're right," Enrique said as he replayed the scene from memory. "To me, it looked like the Duke of Windsor. But what would a photo of British royalty be doing on the desk of an elderly communist bureaucrat?"

"I asked myself that same question, but I also thought it was the Duke of Windsor," Kate responded with satisfaction from validating her suspicion.

Edward VIII, King of Britain and Ireland, later known as the *Duke of Windsor*, gave up his reign in the name of love when he abdicated in 1936 to marry American divorcée Wallis Simpson. Or at least that's the romanticized version presented for public consumption. Since nothing is simple in love and politics, after Edward's death in 1972, some biographers have considered more sinister motivations.

There is intermittent speculation that both the Duke and Duchess of Windsor were sympathizers of the Third Reich at best, and may have engaged in espionage at worse. Soon after Edward abdicated the throne, he and Ms. Simpson married in France at the home of a suspected Nazi spy. Their sympathies with Fascist regimes were confirmed by wedding gifts of an inscribed solid gold box from Adolf Hitler, and one hundred carnations from Benito Mussolini.

"Alright, let's follow the cues from the photograph and see where it takes us," Enrique proposed, excited about the hidden implications they could uncover. "Do you remember anything that could establish a pattern with the other victims?"

"Enrique, that film never ceases to impress me. There *was* a pattern now that I think about it. All the victims were elderly Europeans and…" Kate stopped to push her memory expecting a major clue to erupt in her train of thought. "Yes, of course, there were two other *suicides* where the camera scanned the room, hinting a photograph to the audience. The third victim had a framed photo of the Spanish dictator Francisco Franco and the fifth or sixth victim had one photo of …"

"Errol Flynn, the swashbuckling actor of the nineteen forties!" Enrique blurted before Kate could finish.

"I am glad you know your black and white movie stars because I was going to say Cary Grant."

"Yes dear one, they were way before your time," Enrique said, affecting the tone of a wise elder.

"So, we have the Duke of Windsor, Francisco Franco and Errol Flynn. What can you make out of that unlikely trio? Could my *ancient* man enlighten us?" Kate posed the questions with the mischievous posture that Enrique had come to adore.

He was beginning to sense the brewing of precursors as he prepared his thoughts to respond. It was like pressure mounting, veiled messages begging for meaning. He wanted to tell Kate how Breogán had predicted she would provide a key ingredient to the portal flash, but decided to hold off and allow *the drift* to take its course. The *holographic wisdom* would come loaded with its inherent multidimensional meanings. All he had to do was allow his awareness to abandon control and let the progression take place. Then, the fragmented memories found contextual relevance and the disjointed time-space converged to significance.

"Kate, it's all coming together. What an ingenious way to make movies! Here's the plot," Enrique could hardly contain his excitement and paused to breathe before continuing, "according to one of his biographies, in 1937 Errol Flynn sailed the *Queen Mary* to Europe, carrying a bank draft for $1.5 million donated by Hollywood's pro-Communist sympathizers to help the loyalist side of the Spanish civil war. The money never reached its intended destination and, with Errol Flynn's pro-Fascist leanings, it most likely went to Franco's revolutionary forces instead."

"Darling, where do you come up with these obscure facts?" Kate asked, with the look of a proud mother praising her child for unexpected achievement.

"Oh, but there's more, and you'll see when I finish, that it was *you* who provided the key to the riddle. Several months later, Errol Flynn traveled extensively through France and areas of Spain controlled by Franco's forces. All that time he was followed by British MI5 agents who suspected he was aiding both the Spanish Fascists and the Third Reich. The suspicions proved accurate when Flynn was followed to the *Hotel Meurice* in Paris, where he met none other than the infamous Nazi heavyweights Martin Borman and Rudolf Hess. And according to historian Martin Allen, it was the Duke of Windsor who greeted the three gentlemen and invited them to his suite for a secret meeting. But I must emphasize, some academicians have criticized Mr. Allen's biography of the Duke of Windsor, arguing the book is tainted with antimonarchy bias and extrapolations rather than indisputable evidence.

"Good Lord, Enrique, you sound like the narrator of *Unsolved Mysteries*!" Kate always made him laugh at the most opportune times.

"Well, I think recalling Allen's book, coupled with your Albanian scene, triggered the connection. You know, although the film may have presented clues based on Allen's book about the Duke of Windsor, I don't believe a man who gave up his kingdom for love would betray his country. But I do believe you're the brains in this family."

Kate smiled hearing him refer to her as *family* for the first time.

"Well, here comes the big question," Enrique looked at Kate to gather his thoughts before continuing, "why did Faustus go after these elderly gentlemen?"

"Always follow the money, my good man!"

"So you think it was the money Errol Flynn never delivered to the loyalist Spaniards?" Enrique asked as he ran possible schemes in his head.

"Yes, and let me tell you why. You may recall that when Faustus left the KGB he seemed very upset reading a document in Spanish that looked like a bank account summary, and right after that scene they showed his next victim slashing his wrist with Franco's photograph nearby. The elderly men knew where the money went and when Faustus found out about it, he had to silence them. So the film very effectively mixed facts with fiction, leaving it up to obsessive people like you and me to sift the evidence and keep the story alive," Kate concluded triumphantly.

"Kate, you have a radiant mind."

"Thank you darling. We make an unbeatable duo in many ways. Oh! I just realized I am meeting Claudia for lunch in an hour. She's taking me to a restaurant on Fisher Island that she rates first class. If it lives up to her claims, I'll treat you to dinner there next weekend," Kate said, as she ended her bath to dress and leave.

"I love taking the ferry to Fisher Island, so I am looking forward to being your kept man for that evening. Ok love, enjoy your lunch and say hi to Claudia for me."

Sitting on his balcony, facing the ocean, Enrique returned to the Faustus film. He thought there were more unanswered questions that could be pursued indefinitely, but he realized the *portal entrance* was always incidental and unpredictable. As soon as he thought he was entering the portal, the flow would always redirect itself to expand his humility horizons. And this time was no exception. Just when he assumed he had the Faustus enigma neatly wrapped, the flash arrived with uncanny revelation.

Enrique was taken back to a conversation he had with his father on the way home from a fishing trip. He was ten and his father looked invincible, reassuring the boy. Dad would always be there to protect him.

"*Quico*, do you remember the story I told you about the Spanish civil war?"

"About your dad fighting with Franco?"

"Yes, he fought on Francos's side, thinking he was defending Spain from the pro-Communist loyalists. But after Franco took power, he ruled Spain with an iron hand, and your grandfather opposed him when he realized the country had been saved from the Communists, but not from oppression."

"*Papá*, why did they kill grandfather?"

"*Quico*, I wanted to wait until you were older to tell you what really happened. Your grandfather was an honorable man and, when he turned against Franco, they framed him to look like he had stolen money from the bank he headed in *Santiago de Compostela*. Although he was innocent, he resigned his position immediately, but was unable to live with that stigma. Because of his pride he did something very sad."

"What did he do?" Enrique remembered asking his father with the apprehension of a boy who did not yet understand the ways of evil.

"He wrote a letter to the editor of the newspaper *O Correo Galego,* swearing his innocence and denouncing the perfidy committed against him. Sadly, the paper never published the letter, but I still have a carbon copy. He then committed an act against his faith that risked eternal damnation."

Enrique recalled feeling too afraid to ask his father what action could risk *eternal damnation,* and he repressed the details of that conversation until now. His grandfather was compelled by shame to commit suicide. He was unable to live with his *tormenting burden.*

Chapter 10

"... but if life passed without her, the mountains would weep for him."

Cabo Fisterra, Galicia

*C*ape Fisterra has some of the most treacherous reefs in the world. The infamous Petoncino and Centola rocks outlining the coast have claimed countless shipwrecks, dating back to the earliest Galician maritime history. Extending out as the most western point of Europe, Cape Fisterra was considered the end of the world in the Middle Ages. The Roman general Decimus Brutus, known as the Galician, was horrified when he first witnessed from the Cape how the sun disappears into the vast ocean.

Although Santiago de Compostela claims the sepulchre of St. James, it appears the drift was at work, judging by how Christ's disciple was first taken to Fisterra as the intended resting place. According to Galician folklore, a boat without helm was guided through a labyrinth of reefs, to land safely on a small beach in Fisterra. Sheltered by the darkness of night, four men disembarked carrying the body of St. James wrapped in white sheets. The men were looking for a suitable place to bury the Apostle and requested an audience with Queen Lupa. They were taken to the castle in the land's end only to be imprisoned by the Galician Queen, who did not believe their mission.

As the Christian servants of St. James prayed for guidance from their jail cell, a shining light broke their chains and allowed them to escape. The Queen's soldiers were killed crossing a bridge that collapsed when they pursued the Christians. As an act of faith, the Christians revisited the Queen and asked her for a cart and two oxen to take their master's body for burial elsewhere. The Queen, still obstinate, gave the Christians a couple of wild bulls instead, but when she observed how the fierce animals responded with gentleness toward them, bewildered by the miracles she had witnessed, she demolished her Celtic pagan temples and converted to Christianity.

Breogán and Sabela arrived in the town of Fisterra mid October to learn the mysteries of autumn in a place of legends, as alchemists did *from secret formulas to transform base metals to gold. The couple rented a small cottage by the ocean with furnishings so well appointed they immediately felt at home. Breogán insisted on a house with a fireplace, which was not difficult to locate in that picturesque fishing village where wood was still the fuel to burn against the chilly winds of the Fisterra seashore.*

Breogán was especially pleased to find a stone fireplace in their snug bedroom, in addition to one in their panelled living room. The cottage had a protective ambience conducive to delving into his forbidden inner dimension. Perfect for an inquiring mystic and his muse.

Before visiting an area, Breogán researched its local culture and what he called its living historians: the residents who remained, through the vicissitudes of their hometowns, to tell the stories. That night, they were dining at the Hostal Mariquito to see one of the living historians. The hostel had regional artists perform after dinner, so the couple's first night in Fisterra was given to hearing folksinger Paulo Zas. This minstrel became a Galician icon for the surrealistic imagery of his lyrics and the eerie melodies he could conjure with his guitar. Paulo interpreted the sounds of the ancient Galician bagpipe with a style reminiscent of early Bob Dylan. His music had a naïve finesse that could be surmised best as supplicant arrogance. *Paulo traded fame for purity and, at fifty, continued to resist being discovered outside of Spain.*

"Oh yes, here it is. Reservations for two at ten under Mr. Breogán," the host at Hostal Mariquito confirmed as he led Sabela and Breogán to their table.

"Breogán, I am so excited to be here with you. My mother and I adore the music of Paulo Zas, and he's performing tonight. You're so good to me," Sabela said, with her contagious affection.

Gratitude is a prime gift in a loving union. It's often confused with indebtedness when interpreting the motive is left to the ego. It's next to impossible to accept from others what we disown about ourselves. Accordingly, before we can offer the gift of gratitude to others, we have to learn to accept our own worthiness gracefully. Sabela was a master at expressing her gratitude because she was at peace with her own radiance.

"Sabie, why don't you order the wines for the evening and I'll order the courses to compliment your choice of vineyards. Agree?"

"I agree," Sabela affirmed, as their waiter stood by their table ready to assess her taste in Galician wines. "My good man," she addressed the waiter, who was old enough to be her grandfather, "we'll start the evening with a bottle of Terras Gauda 1998."

The elderly waiter was amused by her youthful audacity and pleased with her choice of white wine. "Wise selection, madam," the waiter complimented her and smiled, wishing he had a granddaughter like her.

"Oh Breogán, please tell me how proud you are of how much I am learning about Galician wines."

"My sweet friend, I am more than proud, I am ecstatic," Breogán added, knowing how much he truly loved this woman who could flavor any utterance with glee. He had learned from Sabela that life could be a celebration at any age when love is honored through the eyes of compassion.

Sometimes their rejoicing was so prevailing that outsiders concluded such attainment of merriment could not be authentic. But skeptics never learn from love. It was quite simple. Breogán and Sabela were dedicated to guarding each other's hearts, healing each other's wounds, and validating each other's worthiness.

The bottle of Terras Gauda was pleasantly matched with the first course of Vieiras a la Galega, consisting of baked scallops sprinkled with minced onions and breadcrumbs marinated in white wine, olive oil and vinegar. The famed Coquille St. Jacques, literally from the French: scallops of St. James, gained their culinary name after the shell of scallops became the symbol of pilgrims journeying to the tomb of San Tiago in Compostela.

For the second course, Breogán ordered bacallao en leite: a salted Galician codfish browned in olive oil, battered and slowly cooked in milk with toasted saffron. To complement the bacallao, Sabela chose a bottle of Monterrei Verdello, for its light and aromatic enticement. Finally, coffee and brandies were served and the lights dimmed to introduce the artist.

"Ladies and gentlemen, tonight we are very pleased to bring you a rare treat. No preambles are needed to present a living legend: Paulo Zas." The owner of the hostel was visibly moved as he made the introduction.

The dining audience stood and applauded vigorously to welcome a man dressed in black with longish graying hair and beard. His face carried grace and pain: someone who had paid a high price for his rebellion without remorse or need for pity. He spoke in Galician with a sonorous voice. Paulo could be performing at Carnegie Hall, but he chose a select group of compatriots and cultured tourists to share that evening.

His songs spoke of our quest to be understood although we can't begin to understand ourselves. How he was growing old unwilling to compromise his vision of a mate who could sense his loneliness from a smile and read tenacity from his fatigue. If she could only love him, he would move mountains, but if life passed without her, the mountains would weep for him.

The audience was awestruck by this aging titan. He transposed the room to a stage where each member could perform their secret dramas with the ideal lover or loyal friend they never had.

The last verse of his closing song perhaps heralded an impending feedforward:

"I sail melodies that roam my head,
Reaching earth's flaming bottom.
What's the path my life has led?
With every turn I end in autumn."

The spotlight faded and Paulo waved to a cheering audience while he walked toward Breogán's table. He addressed the couple in Galician:

"Hello Breogán, I am elated to see you and Sabela here tonight."

"Thank you Paulo. Would you join us for a brandy?" Breogán made the invitation, looking at Sabela. "I am sure you're wondering how Paulo knows your name, so I should let him explain." Breogán observed Sabela's perplexed expression.

"I was not aware you knew each other. Darling, you're full of surprises," Sabela added as she turned to Paulo.

"Please let me clarify. Your husband and I have been friends for years and I have admired your work at several of your exhibits. In fact, last month I bought one of your paintings at a gallery in A Coruña," Paulo was enjoying Sabela's amazement, "but I can tell you that I did not know you and Breogán were in town, so I was very surprised as well."

"Yes, it was quite a coincidence that Paulo was performing here tonight because when I made reservations for dinner, I had no idea," Breogán confided to Sabela.

"Mr. Zas, I am so pleased you like my work. I am speechless."

"Paulo, for Sabela to be speechless is the ultimate compliment."

They all laughed and ordered brandies to commemorate their serendipitous encounter.

"What brings you to the end of the world?" Paulo had a presence that gave eminence to his questions.

Sabela waited for Breogán to answer wondering how he would approach the subject and how much depth he would share.

Enrique paused to read the last page he had just written and noticed his fluidity had reached an impasse. Paulo was a consuming character and Enrique was having difficulties integrating him into the story. He began to search his own apprehensions rather than continue to write aimlessly. As soon as he gave his restrained creativeness audience, clarity began to ascend. Artists know, when admonitions are ignored, the noise grows louder until it derails the flow.

In this case, Enrique found the culprits were two competing premises that remained dormant until one had to dominate. Should Paulo come in as a friend or as an incidental foe? To ride *the drift*, Enrique had to release his inventiveness without restrictions. But to achieve that goal, he had to face his own emotional objections. He intuited he had identified too much with Breogán, and perhaps was trying to protect him. But protect him from what? Was Paulo a threat to Breogán or was he a threat to Enrique? Then without warning, tears brought a covert lesion to light.

Enrique felt an uninhibited progression of sadness to rage when the memory of infidelity externalized. He recalled discussing briefly the painful incident with Kate, but he never told her how that woman had wounded his soul when she defiled him with one of his close friends. Now he was projecting his fear of betrayal to Breogán and wanted to protect him from Paulo. It was revealing to note that Enrique was developing Paulo as someone who had not found love. Was it because of fate or flaw of character? Although Enrique had not felt vigilant with Kate, his unresolved dread of betrayal subconsciously gained a voice as Breogán's protector. It was safer for Enrique to question Sabela's vulnerabilities in a space detached from his own demons, than to distrust Kate in his own life. Now he had to move forward in the vicarious place he was crafting without contaminating, with his own bitterness, the potential wisdom he could gain from a character he distrusted. Due to the interconnectedness factor, a writer can only minimize personal projections, because unfulfilled dreams and unconquered fears constantly vie to pervade the work. Once again, Enrique chose to trust *the drift* and continued.

Before answering Paulo's question, Breogán knew that whatever he selected to share would set the stage for the part each player could contribute to the drift. This time, he thought the most appropriate strategy was to respond with his own question.

"Paulo, I was particularly drawn to the last verse of your closing song, so I was hoping you could tell me what inspired the lyrics?"

Sabela smiled, consorting with Breogán's approach. She had also picked up on Paulo's use of the word autumn *when he was singing, but*

decided she should let it pass. Sabela was becoming a formidable stu-
dent of the drift, *and valued how much she had learned from Breogán*
by trusting his flawless intuition.

"Yes, I am very fond of the meaning that song has for me. What
part affected you the most?" Paulo responded, not knowing what
Breogán wanted specifically.

"Oh, I thought the lyrics had powerful imagery and I wondered
what you meant by 'sailing the sounds that roam your head', and
where those sounds end?"

Breogán was sensitive to how the drift *needs to be attained without*
telegraphing our expectations to potential portal guides. It's like put-
ting out a morsel, and waiting to see how it's going to be consumed.

Paulo gazed at Sabela, and then down toward his glass of brandy
before answering, "The uncharted melodies I integrate with my guitar
and voice are the ocean that my words can sail. And when I get lost, I
feel a restlessness that pleads to be interpreted, but as I disembark to
find my grounding, I confront the fires of hell," Paulo stopped and
waited for Breogán and Sabela to take in his allegory.

"Mr. Zas, I think your imagery is alarmingly beautiful," Sabela in-
terjected, and asked the next question knowing it was the right moment.
"Why does your quest end in autumn?"

Breogán and Sabela avoided looking at each other to keep Paulo's
response pristine.

"Ah, so autumn is of interest to you?" Paulo was delaying his answer.

"Your reasoning is what is most interesting, Mr. Zas." To
Breogán's delight, Sabela continued to minimize the biasing cues with
her prudence.

"Well, to be very candid with you, I did not completely appreciate
that part of my lyrics until you asked me to unravel the surrealistic fab-
ric of that song. I think to me, autumn represents the penultimate
chance to reach the earthly delights and avoid the fires of hell. Autumn
is the season before our wintering end. As long as there is one more
chance before the music is over, we can dream and we can sail with
hope."

"Paulo, did autumn have that specific meaning when you wrote the
lyrics?" Breogán asked trying to grasp how the latency of feedforward
converges with the uncertainty of the drift. *If feedforward is a coinci-*
dence with delayed meaning in time and space, how is the implicate
information orchestrated in the present to divulge its meaning in the
future?

"Not exactly, it was akin to knowing that it had to be a part of my
expression without access to the purpose. At the time, I knew the word

had to be integrated in the rhythm of my lyrics only because its absence would leave an indelible vacuum. In a very imprecise manner, the word 'autumn' had prominence by how its exclusion would disrupt the allegory I was weaving." Paulo was honing in on the inconspicuous rendering of the drift. *True to his artistic talent, he could converse fluently at the edge of semantics.*

"Mr. Zas, if you envision autumn as a symbol representing a next-to-the-last chance to reach your aspirations, do you approach it with joy or fear?" Sabela asked from a different perspective, intuitively complementing Breogán's frame of inquiry.

"Sabela, your question raises the issue of motives. Breogán, I pray that some day I may find a companion as connected as yours," Paulo nodded as he looked admiringly at the couple.

Breogán and Sabela expressed their gratitude with a smile.

"Historically, motives have eluded me in my work and perhaps to my detriment. But as I search now to respond to you, it seems to me I am living in repetitive cycles to defy hell, and doing everything possible to avoid joy." Paulo sighed and looked at Breogán before asking a question that pleaded honorably with his friend.

"What do you make of my paradox, Breogán?"

Breogán held his wife's hand in a gesture of solidarity for what he was going to offer his friend. "Paulo, you're an incomparable human being who deserves the best of love. Sabela and I have weathered storms you can't begin to fathom, but we believe the transparency of our motives has been our salvation."

Without the slightest disruption, Sabela picked up on Breogán's pause and continued for him from her parallel perspective, with tears in her eyes. "Mr. Zas, my husband couldn't be more accurate in what he's disclosing to you. As young and existentially lacking as I may be, I can tell you that dissecting my intimate motives has been both liberating and terrifying. I've been blessed having Breogán as my guide, but I can also tell you that it has been equally difficult for him, despite his attainments on the subject we're discussing." Sabela squeezed Breogán's hand, affirming her gratefulness.

"Sabela, please tell me you have a twin sister." Paulo's sincere timing broke the somber spell and brought needed laughter to the trio.

"Thank you Paulo, we all needed a good laugh," Breogán said, as he lifted his glass of brandy to praise the mood. *He looked pensive as he prepared to elaborate on his theme. "I believe, or actually, Sabela and I have concluded, that motives can be structured only from fear or love. If their inception comes from fear, they*

simply lead to protecting self and doubting others, whereas if they are grounded in love, they foster caring for self as well as trusting and caring for others. The danger in acting without identifying the genesis of our motives is that fear is pervasive and can consequently corrupt our natural proclivity to love."

"Mr. Zas, now you can see why I am so in love with this man. And to answer your question, if I had a twin sister, I would be delighted for you to meet her," Sabela glowed with generosity.

The penultimate season: next-to-the-last chance to redeem our joy and discard our dread. The feedforward had unfolded. Paulo's contribution to the numinous code of autumn was priceless. Three mortals, sharing a table in a quaint little restaurant at the end of the world, had just entered the drift.

Breogán and Sabela knew there was no need to remain in Fisterra. They had planned to stay longer, assuming the hidden meaning would be related to the myths that lived at the land's end. The drift taught them that legends were only fertile ground to enter the mystical portals: always in the most unexpected manner, with unanticipated guides, leading to unforeseen wisdom.

Breogán and Sabela hugged and kissed Paulo and thanked him for his gift. Before parting, they taught him a mystical ritual to disengage the destructive cycles that were inhibiting his joy. Breogán called it severing the blinding loops.

The couple drove their Hummer to the tip of the peninsula, and that dawn, they witnessed how the sun rises from the vast ocean at the end of the world.

Rather than writing a story, Enrique felt he was watching a movie about untainted knowledge. Stopping to inspect his fears had unleashed his blocked creativity, or perhaps to use Breogán's term, *severed his blinding loops.* Paulo had turned out to be an honorable man and, in a virtual sense, Enrique felt he owed him an apology. More accurately, he owed the trio an apology for different reasons. His fear of betrayal had maligned Paulo, doubted Sabela's integrity and, by implication, construed Breogán as a potential cuckold. These remarkable insights brought him his own holographic wisdom about the dynamics of archetypal wounds.

Enrique marveled at how we retain our unresolved fears deeply coded in our intimate space, ready to ascribe their features to those we permit conditional entry. When a potential lover gains entrance with *predetermined scripts,* it can only lead to fulfilling the prophecy forewarned by the fear. With an archetypal wound of betrayal, the afflicted embraces a state of suspicion, and attributes traits of disloyalty to the potential lover. This untenable collusion keeps the wounded safe from having to risk the *leap of faith.*

The coded fears can also be projected beyond Self and the potential lover. In Enrique's case, he extended his *predetermined scripts* to the fictional characters he was permitting to enter his intimate space. We seem to play out our wounds, reluctant to sever the blinding loops that sustain our anguish when love comes our way. Enrique and his characters were learning that *the drift* could only provide a *chance* for liberation, leaving *will* as the agent of change.

Chapter 11

"The confrontation of our fear triad is the foremost milestone of our journey."

Enrique was up early that morning and decided it was time to learn more about Biocognitive theory. He turned on the CD his psychologist friend had just published. As he began to listen on his balcony, the *beautiful people* were prancing Ocean Drive.

"There is an invigorating force ready to propel us out of disillusionment when we choose to learn from our anguish. Some welcome the chance to abandon misery, while others retain their disparaging formulas and seem surprised when the obvious pain remains. Those who wallow in their toxic reruns are cognizant of their position and can be very incisive about what enslaves them while somehow remaining stuck. The reluctance to give up self-destructive patterns ranging from addictions to abusive relationships has been attributed to unworthiness, passive control, masochism and other counterproductive devices.

"Although these defeatist behaviors are certainly identifiable in those who live in misery, they only reflect distractions rather than causes. Just like obsessions and compulsions are strategies to avoid anxiety-producing thoughts and emotions, self-destructive behaviors are paradoxical efforts to deny our mortality. Every act of self-destructiveness is a futile attempt to defy the inevitable end we dread: a choice of piecemeal dying to circumvent the realization that the Grim Reaper does not make appointments. All phobias can be reduced to a fear of death, and all underlying motives to maintain the phobic status quo are the product of living a fatalistic life.

"But if someone fears dying, how can they engage in acts that can hasten death? The heavy smoker and the cocaine abuser are certainly aware they are shortening the lives they fear losing. So there has to be a surreptitious logic operating these self-defeating codes.

"There are three implicit distracters born in fear that maintain the motivation to unwittingly self-destruct. This *fear triad* serves to avoid confronting death-anxiety, to engage in behaviors that challenge death, and to choose the manner in which death will arrive. The smoker uses nicotine to distract from death-anxiety; to challenge the limitations of lung function; and to choose cancer as the most likely way to end life. Similarly, the battered spouse colludes with the abuser to be distracted from the same death-anxiety; to challenge the limits of how much trauma the body can take; and to choose fatal injury as the destructive end. The self-defeating codes remain hidden, but their respective distractions reach consciousness as masked causes. The fear triad offers avoidance, defiance and choice: a dismal misuse of the noble mind-body-spirit at the service of dread..."

Enrique paused the CD to watch skaters zigzag through the Ocean Drive traffic. He wondered if the skaters were performing one of their fear triads as modern *toreros* defying vehicles. The fear triad model could be a tool to explain Breogán's blinding loops. The concept could begin to explain why people are fixed hopelessly on their symptoms, rather than facing the causes of their pain. Enrique's psychologist friend compared such misguided awareness to a driver stopping for gas when the oil light goes on. He put on his earphones and turned the CD back on.

"... But, if the practitioner of misery could access existential backbone, the real enemy would materialize to be defeated by reckoning that the solution is choosing *how* to live rather than *when* to die. Trusting that the end of our physical existence is the beginning of another phase on the eternal journey of our soul. Although these propositions may be construed as comforting platitudes, the choice to make peace with our mortality liberates us to exult one abundant life, rather than to die a thousand deaths before our time on earth is over. The confrontation of our fear triad is the foremost milestone of our journey. We can ignore it with our demands for evidence and live in terror, or we can let faith guide us to trust what we cannot verify with our puny senses.

"The fear triad is a colossal deception, and the self-defeating codes that support it can be exposed for what they are. The avoidance serves to maintain distance from reconciling our mortality. The defiance encourages action to test our mortality, and the choice determines how we hasten our mortality. Given that fear is the most primitive of our emotions, it can only yield infantile solutions for our existential predicaments. But if we are reminded that compassion is the supreme expression of love, it can give us impetus to address complexity with refinement.

"When we devote the wisdom of compassion to confronting our death-anxiety; to trusting the power of our resilience; and to relinquishing the obsession to know our end, it can deliver us from a life of terror."

Part one ended and Enrique switched to the second CD titled *A Biocognitive Antidote to Dread*. He was captivated by the artwork on the cover. It showed Picasso's *The Blindman's Meal*, painted during his blue period. It portrayed a thin blind man wearing a beret, sitting at his sparse dining table with an empty plate. And with an expression of despair, holding a piece of bread in his left hand and groping for a jug with his other hand. Enrique wanted to learn more about the painting and went to his study to select a Picasso illustrated biography from his bookshelves. He smiled as he read the work was reminiscent of *El Greco,* painted in Barcelona in the *autumn* of 1903.

He could see from his balcony an attractive young woman in a white bikini listening with great interest to a local Don Juan. Although science cautions us not to generalize from single observations, Enrique could distill from a distance that the tentative body language of the woman was contemplating romance, whereas the smooth predatory routine of the con man was ready to degrade her gift. Enrique settled on his recliner and started the second CD.

"Before advancing to the practical applications of my theory, I will delineate the psychology of our existential struggle. We are given a period of time and space to live with the knowledge that there is an end. And the dread of this awareness of being mortal comes from the dilemma that it poses. We have to surrender a body that we have dedicated our lives to nourishing, we have to leave those we chose to love, and we have to question whether we end in nothingness or transcend to *somethingness*. So, there are two basic predicaments: to disengage and to confront.

"Disengaging from Self and others requires a farewell to love, whereas confronting a beyond-life dimension summons mystery. Two psychological directives are operating here: releasing the known, and facing the unknown. When we struggle to let go of what ails us and welcome what is best for us, we can judge others and ourselves with greater compassion if we consider the roots of our dread. Those ostensibly simple decisions can be overwhelming, because their solutions involve milder versions of the transcendental disengaging and confronting that we dread to death.

"One of the greatest obstacles to resolving our transcendental dread is our categorical aversion to living our loves and our lives. When we avoid, defy, and choose our death, we apply the same dreadful criteria to loving others and ourselves. This proposition, however, begs the question: if we accept love unconditionally, does it not make it more difficult to let it go when our end arrives? But that line of reasoning assumes love is to be owned rather than to be lived. We mourn the absence of what we possess, not what we live. To live love is more than to exist it, but when we approach love as a possession, we fear losing it.

"Just as we cannot possess love, we cannot own our existence. The illusion of ownership enslaves us with dread, but living love and life rather than existing them liberates us from the fear triad. We no longer have to avoid, defy, or choose what does not belong to us. In Biocognitive theory, the grossly misunderstood Eastern concept of attachment is contrasted with the Western version of ownership. In particular, Buddhist philosophers impart attachment as the root of suffering. They teach that attachment encompasses craving, ignorance, and avoidance. Attachment endorses craving the delusion of permanence, perfection and substance in the world. It promotes ignoring or not seeing the direct experience of reality by interpreting the world as illusions that conform to our personal beliefs. And it facilitates avoiding our pain by giving hatred power. Buddha taught that hatred was synonymous with clinging, because it gives our causes of pain substance and permanence.

"To parallel ancient Eastern wisdom, our Western model of suffering should introduce the element of control. We can make the infamous claim that our Western culture has contributed the illusion of control, masked with ownership, as the modern cause of suffering. Thus, Biocognitive theory equates Eastern attachment to Western ownership. The differences are subtle but culturally significant. The East has emphasized spirit at the expense of the physical, while the West has sacrificed the transcendental for material gains. Both approaches beg convergence. As members of the human community we cannot afford to meditate our lives away while children die of hunger and illnesses. But just as significantly, we cannot accumulate abundance without spiritual wealth.

"The operational advances of Western cognitive science can enhance the philosophical depth of Eastern thought on the topic of suffering. With this ambitious claim, we can begin to demystify transcendental dread and hopefully find its antidote.

"Our beliefs are the most powerful cognitive tool we have, and if we exercise our free will we can choose to believe whatever empowers us to counter our existential and transcendental challenges. Since love is the most advanced emotion we have been able to produce as a species, we can choose to believe that love is the antidote to our greatest fear. And let us assume that we have secret dreams waiting to be discovered by love. Although we cannot take attachments or ownerships beyond our end, we can choose to wake up from that deceptive nightmare, and begin to live our abandoned inspirations while we discover the power of love.

"In Biocognitive theory we redefine the course to confronting our dread and the obstacles to its resolution. More central than fearing our end is lamenting how we lived our lives. There is substantial evidence from research in hospices to support the notion that lamenting is the most prevalent impediment in the process of dying. We have evolutionary mechanisms to transition us from breathing embryonic fluid to breathing air when we are born, as well as turning off our breathing when we expire.

"We cry when we are born not out of anguish, but to inhale our first breath of air. Yet we give our first life-enhancing mechanism a sinister interpretation. And this same tainting of a natural mechanism is applied to our end when we cease to breathe. While these breathing transitions are inherent and involuntary, we have no biological equivalent to execute free will. Our biocognitive codes provide coping devices to begin and end our lives without our consent, but our design does not include contingencies for actions triggered by our will.

"Biocognition is a theory of hope based on prudent science and cogent philosophies rather than wishful thinking. Instead of interpreting our first cry with anguish and our last breath with terror, we can grow existential backbone by recruiting our most evolved emotions to investigate our transcendental dread. Without denying the Eastern ingredients of attachment and the Western craving for control, the key to finding the antidote to our transcendental dread lies in our lamenting what did not occur while we lived, rather than in our fear of the unknown when we die. If rather than seeking answers to resolve our fear of dying we empower our passions, we can diminish our lamenting and learn how to face our end gracefully. The existential shift alleviates transcendental dread in several ways: we can move from avoiding death, to approaching our neglected dreams; from defying death, to accepting our joy; and from trying to control how we die, to choosing how we live. Then, we no longer need to crave the elusion of permanence; avoid with hatred; or remain ignorant of the reality we could live. Fear is our venom and love is our antidote."

The silence marking the end of the CD brought Enrique back from an existential reverie. He instantly contrasted the experience with the time he depersonalized after discussing the atonement archetype with

Fr. Simon. That chat triggered a mystical *unselfing*, and now he felt the CD had transported him to a counterpart dimension. An image of naming the other side of a coin brought the word *selfing* to mind. Another piece of the puzzle was revealed: the mystical journey was like a pendulum shifting from *unselfing* in transcendental groundlessness to *selfing* on existential ground.

Aromas from the corner Italian bistro reminded Enrique it was time for lunch. He accepted the invitation to follow the enticing scent of pesto. Breogán taught him these simple sensory cues bring the mystical journey to life if we discern signal from noise. At times, these allurements were nothing more than residuals of local disharmony to be ignored. But when fractals of *the drift* arrived, we could always tell by the *rightness of the moment*. The navigational chart was allegorical and the instruments to maneuver the streams were intuitive. But the mystical journey can be enslaving for those who want to approach it with rigid rules. One could go hungry waiting for the right aroma.

Enrique sipped his glass of Barolo and was ready to order the pesto until the waiter announced that the special was his favorite bay scallops *calzone*. The server added in a conspiratorial whisper that the chef insisted on preparing the dish that day after complaining it had not been featured for months. *The drift* is divinity teaching us with a cosmic sense of humor.

Enrique scanned the customers around him, wondering who among them were living their passions. It was certainly not the frazzled young man in the dark corporate suit who had taken his laptop to a rushed meal. The man's emaciated frame did not restrain him from ordering a diet cola and small salad for lunch. Would this cubicle warrior lament or fear a most likely boutique illness compelling him to early retirement? Enrique knew that if he alerted others about the bleak existence they were weaving, their blinding loops would prevent them from responding with gratitude. He decided to take his critique inward and ask what passions were eluding his own life.

Lunch hit the spot because it was in harmony with the rightness of the moment. Enrique walked to the Cuban kiosk next door and ordered a *cortadito con leche evaporada*. He loved the combination of steaming espresso with evaporated milk, and wished he could enjoy a good cigar with his *cortadito* as his father did. But after realizing at sixteen that smoking was something his lungs would never accept, he determined to find a better way to be *cool* than having to master the art of welcoming emphysema. He decided to postpone his rescue of latent dreams until he could discuss them with Kate.

Chapter 12

"Of all the gin joints in all the towns…"

Máximo and Claudia visited a foreboding neighborhood in the evening. They had heard of a most unusual place in Little Haiti where tales of *Voodoo* and black magic thrived. Ethnic migrations enhance communities with their exotic cuisine, art, religion and enriching ways of life. But they also bring their own brand of evil, expressed in their cultural crimes. Little Haiti is certainly no exception in its contributions to the edification and detriment of Miami's multi-ethnic fabric.

Claudia persuaded Máximo to attend a lecture at the home of Jude Fouché, a *Voodoo* priest who gained notoriety after a series of articles in the *Miami Herald* about his obscure exploits. *Voodoo* is a religion practiced in Haiti, with ancient roots in Africa. *Voodoo* (also spelled *Voudu* in an attempt to shed its stigma) has been recognized recently by the Haitian government as an ancestral religion, after a long struggle to coexist with that country's predominantly Catholic population. Claudia learned from the article that there are two primary forces in the *Voodoo* pantheon: *Rada* is the good *loa* or spirit, and *Congo* is the wrathful *loa* responsible for the death curses, zombies and wild sexual orgies associated with black magic. The article cheered a recent action of Jude's—apparently, three Haitian thugs stole ceremonial valuables from the priest's home, but after weeks of agonizing dreams about tortuous damnation, the thieves recovered the items they had fenced, returned them to their owner and confessed their crimes to the police.

Although Jude alleged he was a *Rada* practitioner of the peaceful *loa,* he did not hide his past as a notorious *Congo* priest feared for his potent black magic. Jude claimed that in a hellish vision similar to the dreams described by the repenting thugs, he saw Rada pulling him out of an eternal fire and selecting him to work for the immaculate light. Since that revelation, he had applied his *Congo* expertise to protect others from evil curses. The article compared Jude to a brilliant computer hacker who opted to design anti-virus software for non-profit organizations after a similar apocalyptic vision.

What caught Claudia's attention about Jude's mode of practice was the confrontational style of defense he offered his clients. He not only provided protection, but also retaliatory action that would dissuade future curses, by rendering the perpetrators insomniacs from terrifying dreams he could disseminate. Jude thought these *near-death warnings* were more benevolent than other underworld curses that terminated a believer's life leaving no trace for forensic pathologists to determine the cause of death.

The parallels between Jude's manipulation of dreams and the remote murder of the *Faustus* film did not go unnoticed by Claudia and Máximo as they prepared to meet Jude that evening. The *Herald* article disclosed that Jude's lectures were also attended by *Congo* priests who sought relief from their counter-curse nightmares or who attempted to challenge his powers. On more than one occasion attendees reported seeing someone in the audience go into epileptic convulsions requiring emergency medical attention. After the paramedics removed the insolent contender, Jude would resume his lecture, lamenting the presumptuous tenacity of those who defied the immaculate light.

Little Haiti, like most neighborhoods low on the socioeconomic scale, has sectors that cope with their learned helplessness by turning to drugs, prostitution or a life of crime. But there are many others like Jude, who convert their anguish into productive faith and become healers or liberate themselves from their enslavement with education and hard work. Although the power of prayer has no limits, begging solace vs. imploring resources will yield disparagingly different results.

Máximo and Claudia arrived a few minutes early. As they stepped out of the Porsche Cayenne, they noticed the universal signature of power. While all the dwellings around were worn cottages with security windows and doors, Jude's home had the presence of a Normandy chateau protected solely by the energy of respect. His lectures were by invitation only and limited to small groups, never exceeding twenty-two. A hostess dressed all in white greeted the guests at the door and directed them to a living room furnished in a gaudy version of Louis XV, where tea and sipping rum were being served. Cigar smoking was permitted, but not cigarettes. Máximo appreciated the mood that could be summoned in men by an atmosphere of aged rum and fine tobacco. When he shared his observation with Claudia, she reassured him that his *machismo* had a charming effect on her. He kissed her hand to seal the image she had encouraged.

Another hostess dressed in white announced the guests should move to a large family room that had been converted to a comfortable lecture area. The lights were subdued and the seating was arranged in a semi-circle facing a large stuffed chair with a table and small banker's lamp to the side. The audience, of about eighteen, was a mixture of

Haitians and outsiders: some experiencing anticipatory curiosity and others conspicuous apprehension.

The hostess went to the front of the room and spoke, first in a Haitian Creole called *Patua,* and then in an accented English that added to the enchantment of the evening.

"We welcome you to the home of our *Gro Houngan* Jude and wish you a peaceful stay."

Claudia whispered to Máximo that priests were called *houngan* and priestesses *mambo.* Máximo grinned and held her hand gently.

Jude came out from behind a thick burgundy curtain and extended his arms out with palms up to the audience and smiled elegantly. He had a small frame and white hair in a horseshoe balding pattern. At first glance his power was not apparent, but as his rich voice came alive and his face illuminated, he commanded a wisdom that could shield believers from any looming doom.

"Welcome to my home. I hope to make your evening most pleasant and rewarding. There is mounting interest in our religion and way of life, and an equal amount of misconceptions about our Haitian culture and beliefs. Tonight, I will bring you to my realm, but those of you who do not wish to partake are welcomed to leave now with my blessings."

Claudia recalled from the *Herald* article how Jude dissuaded those in the audience who came to do him harm by politely asking them to leave at the beginning of his lectures. If they stayed, it was at their own peril. She was beginning to see Jude as a guardian angel whose work was the antithesis of *Faustus.*

"I see that no one is getting up to leave, so I will continue joyfully." The group laughed and looked around to see if anyone had not participated in the casualness of the moment.

"When Haiti was under French rule," Jude continued, "slaves were forbidden to practice their *Voodoo* religion, but its prohibition did not succeed in eradicating our faith. When we gained our independence in 1804, all whites were exiled from our country and sadly some, including Catholic priests, were killed. This prompted the Vatican to break relations with Haiti that year lasting until 1860. During those fifty-six years our *houngans* and *mambos* worked hard to restore the religion, and in the process, created a most unusual mixture of *Voodoo* and Catholicism. The animosity between our faith rooted in Africa and our Catholic inheritance from the French subsided in the 1950's and now *Voodoo* drums and music are incorporated to the Catholic Church services.

"You must understand: like every other religion, *Voodoo* has forces of good and evil. Our priests work through good spirits like

Rada to heal, perform religious ceremonies, interpret dreams, cast spells and make potions for good purposes. Then there are those who consort with evil spirits like *Congo,* also known as *Petro,* to make *zombies,* and to cast death curses. Although the tales you hear about black magic are quite real, fortunately its radical practice is relatively limited."

Jude paused to look around the audience, as if scanning for the evil spirits he was describing. Suddenly, he spoke in rapid *Patua* to one of his assistants, who rushed to the corner of the room searching for something that alarmed Jude. She reported back in *Patua* and he smiled with relief.

"Please forgive me for this interruption that I will explain," Jude resumed. "While I was lecturing, one of the participants got up and went to the corner of the room before he walked out. My assistant tells me he left an amulet of *Kalfu* on the small altar in the corner. *Kalfu* is the dangerous spirit of the night and the moon is his symbol. But the talisman is only a feeble attempt by the man who left it to announce he is plotting against me. Ignorance has no end, but be confident that our intruder will need psychiatric services within days. Most definitely, modern science has no cure for that type of crisis."

There were laughs of comic relief followed by spontaneous applauds. Jude was pleased with the audience's reaction and extended his arms out in gratitude. Máximo commented to Claudia that he had noticed a man getting up during the lecture, but since the room was dimly lit he was unable to see what he was doing. Claudia was thrilled with the spectacle she was witnessing.

"My dear guests, let me demonstrate what I mean by the two forces." Jude transformed his presence from lecturer to sorcerer in a flash. He seemed to grow in stature and his soft persuasive voice turned to imminent authority. Collectively, the audience could palpate the energy that was building in the room and complied with Jude's request to relax and let him guide the presence they were sensing.

"I want you to close your eyes and relax. I will summon a peaceful spirit to bring you love." Jude spoke in *Patua* as candles were lit at the four corners of the room. After a few minutes of incantations in his native language, he returned to English and addressed the audience again.

"You will notice the energy that was scattered around the room is gently settling on your right shoulders with the weight of a kind hand. Enjoy it and welcome it as a loving gift by letting it travel to your heart." There were several exclaiming sighs from the audience, confirming the movement that Jude was guiding through their bodies.

"Please exhale, emitting a sound of comfort. Keep your eyes closed and now prepare for the next visit." Jude made his request with distinct caution in his voice. The energy changed abruptly from settling to disquieting. There was a thumping sound as Jude spoke in *Patua* again, but this time he sounded more vigorous.

"Now you will notice a heavy weight on your left shoulder that is traveling to your throat." His mention of the word *throat* set off a series of coughs and choking sounds from the audience perhaps responding to mass hypnosis or something worse. Some had to get up and move around to catch their breath. There was panic in the air. Máximo and Claudia managed to keep their eyes closed, holding hands to stay connected.

Jude spoke forcefully and although it was in *Patua,* the group could discern he was petitioning the force to desist. The coughing stopped and the group was asked to open their eyes, stand up and shake their shoulders to clear any residual negative energy. The group followed his instructions and felt comforted as Jude's two assistants circled the room burning incense and chanting in *Patua.*

Jude stood from his chair and went around the group hugging and kissing on both cheeks each participant to conclude the session. The incense carried the bouquet of an ancient wisdom where science remained a stranger.

Claudia and Máximo thanked Jude and asked if they could meet in the near future to learn more about his ways of battling the dark side. He was appreciative for their request and promised to invite them over for a private session. On the drive home, they wanted to compare their impressions of the two forces, but were afraid that words would vanish what was apprehended that evening. They decided to wait for the sanctity of morning to discuss their encounter with *Voodoo.*

After driving Claudia home, Máximo stopped at Versailles for a Cuban espresso. That restaurant in Little Havana stays open until four a.m. on Saturdays. It was one of the reassuring landmarks that could appease Máximo when he missed the *real* Havana of his youth. At three in the morning, he presumed other elderly Cubans were home dreaming of their lost motherland. But a burst of laughter almost spilled his hot espresso, when he thought about the elderly bladders of those Cubans, awakening them to reality several times a night. Máximo did not subscribe to the cultural portals that compel biology to diminish function with age. His doctor was always amazed to see how Máximo's physiology defied the clichés of growing older. He went home to sleep away his melancholic memories feeling good about his life.

He woke up at 11 a.m. well-rested from the Haitian experience, and decided to call Enrique for a hardy lunch at their favorite restaurant on *calle ocho*. He met his protégé at 1 pm. and they ordered their usual *Marquez de Riscal* wine to start the meal.

"Enriquito, you're not going to believe what Claudia and I did last night."

"Máximo, at your age you can do anything you want and I won't judge you. Did she please you?" Enrique loved to play with his friend's generational taboos.

"My boy, it's nothing like that. Get your mind out of the gutter." Máximo allowed Enrique to enter a personal space forbidden to others. It was like a son amusing his father with his precociousness.

"Ok, I am listening. Tell me what happened last night."

Máximo briefed Enrique as if describing a novel highlighting how Jude guided the group through diametrically opposed conditions. He wanted Enrique's opinion on the parallels with the *Faustus* theme from an anthropologist's perspective.

"Máximo, this Jude fellow seems to have tremendous command of his craft. I agree with the similarities you found with the remote viewing in the *Faustus* film. I can tell you that *Voodoo* priests are confirming the feasibility of distant mind control for both good and nefarious purposes. There's credible medical evidence about the efficacy of prayer to promote healing on unsuspecting subjects. So if benevolent intention can be transmitted with our thoughts to produce physiological benefits, then our minds may be capable of doing harm at a distance as well. You can find in most ancient cultures the concept of *evil eye* doing harm and the shaman's rituals to counteract its effects."

"My boy, your comments brought back a childhood memory that I had completely forgotten. When I was around six, I remember my mother talking about *mal de ojo*, the evil eye idea that you mentioned. She would pin a small onyx amulet on the inside of my shirts and one day when the stone cracked, she told me it meant someone had sent me *mal de ojo* and the onyx broke to absorb the hit. I remember wearing these little black stones until I was a teenager," Máximo reminisced with nostalgia in his voice.

"Of course, your story is an example of the contributions African slaves made to Cuban folklore. Also, on a lighter note, let me add the mambo of Perez Prado."

"Yes, thank God for that," Máximo said with his unique wink. "Come to think of it Enriquito, you brought up Perez Prado out of thin air not realizing how coincidental it was."

"How do you mean?" Enrique asked trying to figure the link.

"Well, Perez Prado and Israel "Cachao" Lopez invented the famous mambo rhythm and, being a fan of these two Cuban musical prodigies, I know they were strongly influenced by the Afro-Cuban version of *Voodoo* called *Santeria,* in which the word *mambo* also means *priestess.* In fact, I recall reading an article where Perez Prado explained his interest in *Santeria* and how he purposely chose the word *mambo* to give his music special magic. I can't believe I am remembering all this trivia."

"My dear historian, this is the interconnectedness theory that I expounded with Breogán."

"Enriquito, I am beginning to worry about how you refer to your main character as if he were a colleague. Do I need to find you a shrink?" Now it was Máximo's turn to jest about his friend's creative license.

"You know Máximo, Eric Connery expressed the same concern. Are you guys plotting against me?" They laughed in unison relishing the timing of humor.

"But tell me Enriquito, as an anthropologist what do you make of *Voodoo* priests summoning spirits to do good and evil?"

"Well, many ancient cultures converse with spirits, but what we tend to forget with our modern arrogance is that all faiths commune with some facet of spirit. All religions by definition worship a deity that is spiritual in nature, whether it's Buddha, Mohammed or Christ. I think what differentiates the so-called *primitive* religions is that they have not given up what theologians call *revelations*: a public or private witnessing of spirit. For example, the Catholic Church maintains that *public revelations* ended with the close of the apostolic age, proclaiming anything else a private incident. So, even the visions of Joan of Arc and other luminaries are deemed *private revelations*. Other contemporary religions deny the option of divine intervention by dismissing any form of revelation as hysterical rumblings."

"What about the question of evil spirits?" Máximo asked, with increasing interest.

"Think about how the universal theme of malevolent forces is evident from the Satan of Christian scriptures to the evil spirits noted in Buddhist sacred scrolls. And whether these forces are a product of our own creation or not, they could be manipulated by those who are initiated to its secrets. So as an anthropologist I am mainly interested in how primal cultural beliefs can affect our biology."

"Do you believe evil comes from a supernatural source?" Máximo asked, knowing he had mixed expectations.

"My friend, I am the disciple when it comes to our relationship, but

I will give you my personal opinion. I don't believe in evil spirits or a supernatural dark side. But I do believe there is evil action and, like any other form of *subtle energy*, it can be accumulated and transposed to do harm. So as it relates to your evening with Jude, I would say he has learned to harness and maneuver, at will, ambient positive and negative energies. In his particular culture they attribute it to consorting with spirits, but in ours we may explain the effects as mass hypnosis or accessing some *subtle energy* fields. Independent of the interpretation, I am inspired by the power of the mind and its endeavor to balance hatred with love."

"Thank you, Enriquito. I am proud of you, son." Máximo's compliment watered their eyes, leaving nothing to be said with words.

Máximo went to Claudia's unannounced, and she welcomed him to a precious evening saying little and understanding much. Romance is ageless when we stop counting our existence and begin to live our life.

Enrique had not seen Kate in several days. She had been busy with an international Aikido competition held in Miami, but left him a message to call her as soon as he got home. Enrique had a phone installed in his Porsche, purposely limiting accessibility to travel time. He felt these electronic shackles were technology's endeavor to intrude on meals and solitude.

"Hello *mi deliciosa.* How are you?"

"Hi honey, your *ninja* needs to be rescued from the martial arts scene."

"And I am just the man to do it. I tried your cell earlier, but it was turned off."

"Yes darling, we're required to leave our cell phones in the lockers when we're competing."

"Did my luscious fighter kick some butt today?"

"Yes I did, repeatedly. You'll be proud to know that I won second place in my division."

"Well, you're in first place with me."

"Enrique, why is it that Spaniards can get away with such deliberate charm?"

"Because this Spaniard is taking you to dinner tonight to celebrate his woman's triumph."

"Dr. Lugo, does it please you to boast that I am *your woman*?"

"Oh my love, if women only knew how little it takes to wrap an *empathic macho* around their little fingers. Manliness can coexist with empathy."

"Honey, what is this *empathic* twist you've given primitive man?"

Enrique loved the bonding mirth they shared. Her emotional integrity gave him passage, without apologies, to the bounty of her femininity.

"You will hear this evening how I propose to elevate the *empathic macho* to a level of honor," Enrique teased to feed her curiosity.

"Where are we celebrating tonight?" Kate asked with a flirtatious tone.

"I am not telling."

"So be it. You know my Buddhist training can detach me from speculations, but *you* on the other hand, will not be able to resist wondering what I am going to wear for you tonight."

"Kate, it serves me right for tempting an *avatar*. Now I'll obsess about it all day, but such is the price to pay for loving a goddess."

"You're too kind, my prince. See you at eight."

Enrique could bring out a sweet vulnerability Kate had only felt with her dad. Although she had been selective with her intimacy, she had socialized with enough men to conclude that most had an implied agenda to either control or be controlled. She found both instances very distasteful. Yet, Enrique's mixture of susceptibility and strength invited her to differentiate between being with a man versus being possessed by a man.

Kate's Ivy League education had acquainted her with the best minds in academia. But her father's warning about the utopian intolerance promoted by self-anointed professors of correctness was beginning to ring true. While she was unimpressed with men who wore their testosterone as a badge used for conquering, she had little tolerance for those who feminized themselves to ingratiate confident women. Kate had never known men like Enrique and Máximo, whose reverence for the honor and wisdom of women made their distinctive manliness entrancing rather than offensive. It amused her to imagine how Enrique would rehabilitate *machismo* at dinner that night.

Kate liked to take long, hot showers to clear her mind and test new conceptual grounds. She had learned a Tibetan Buddhist ritual to shake up the rigidity of assumptions. A statement that expressed the concept to be expanded was repeated like a mantra, while observing the body reactions and flow of meanings that the repetition would produce. She closed her eyes and under the steaming shower began to verbalize: *I am Enrique's woman, I am Enrique's woman, I am Enrique's woman...*

With the first few repetitions, she noticed her body recoiling like an object without value. Anger erupted and her stomach tensed. She released the tightness gradually and began to feel weak and exposed. She witnessed with great effort the frail edge of self and the paradoxes that restrained her joy. The mantra became entangled with the circularity: *to conquer an avoidance one has to enter what is being avoided.* She surrendered to the moment, and saw how her fear of domination escalated, until it was transformed by empathy to a feeling of *participatory belongingness.*

Kate succeeded with equal freedom to verbalize and resolve the balancing side of the mantra: *Enrique is my man.* She grasped a new sense of *affiliation* as she experienced a transition from sole ownership to mutual stewardship. She felt cleansed, sensuous and centered. Kate knew something fundamental had transpired. Gratitude replaced defensiveness and she could look forward to opening other semantic cloisters that had limited her potential to be loved. Since words reflect our personal reality, modifying the semantic space where words reside can change our collective reality.

On his way to pick up Kate for dinner, Enrique thought of how he felt the first time he drove to her house, and how the interpretation of space changes with intimacy. This time, the driveway looked smaller and more inviting. He noticed more details in the landscaping and on the facade of the house. His mind had altered the emotional valence of that physical setting from apprehensive anticipation to joyful familiarity.

He walked to her door and rang the bell, wondering what Kate had decided to wear for him. Frank opened the door, prolonging Enrique's guessing game.

"Good evening, Dr. Lugo. Please come in. Ms. Holland will be down directly."

Enrique was always amused by Frank's formality, and greeted him warmly to reduce the ceremonious quality of the moment. The evenings Enrique spent alone with Kate when the extended family was gone gave him license to roam her house with total freedom. Now the norms of protocol dictated he assume the role of visitor, waiting in the study for the proprietress of the residence. Since we interpret time and space unwittingly through social rituals, we don't realize we can step out of our own creations.

The expectancy was well rewarded when he saw Kate come into the room. Images of splendor, paling words of poets, raced through his mind. She wore a minimalist dress of darkest blue silk that gently draped her sculpted body. Kate was a luscious apparition that he feared would vanish if he affirmed her presence.

"Enrique, you're not saying anything. What do you think?" Her voice brought him back from the similes she had cast.

"My love, it's not so much what I think as what I feel. You have outdone yourself in touching my heart."

"Do you like?" she asked as she swirled in a hypnotic waltz.

"Kate, thank you for reading my wishes better than I could ever do."

"Oh my, I detect the beginning of an enchanting evening." Kate was in a generous mood, clearly wishing to please the man she had chosen to trust.

Enrique's Porsche had the top down, ready to welcome the Miami summer night. When he took the MacArthur Causeway, Kate began to narrow the location of the dining surprise to Miami Beach. But as soon as they reached the end of the causeway, he turned around and headed back to Miami. Enrique was impishly doing his best to keep her confused.

"Enrique, you're such a baby! Where're we going?" Kate asked, gladly playing his game.

He exited the causeway and drove toward Coral Gables, giving Kate a new set of possibilities.

"Ok, would *Casa Xoán* be too obvious? Am I getting warmer?" Kate went along with the charade, feeling gratitude for the elaborate schemes he was inventing to please her. They were behaving like two adolescents on their first date and promised each other to never let their hearts grow old. The maze ended at 21 Almeria Avenue. They were going to dine at Miami's culinary pinnacle.

"What a great surprise! *Norman's* is my favorite restaurant. Dad brought me here for dinner when I earned my black belt in *Aikido*." Kate embraced Enrique and started to cry. "Oh darling, I've been thinking about dad all day. I believe he guided you here tonight. I am so in love with you." Enrique held Kate in silence. Just letting her grief speak through tearful eyes with hues of green the ocean unveils after a storm.

Often privy to intimate vignettes, the parking attendant waited patiently for the keys. For a high school kid, vicariously enjoying amorous scenes, parking exotic cars and making generous tips was the epitome of part-time employment.

Chef Norman Van Aken is the author of his restaurant's sustained excellence. Arguably the best cuisine in South Florida, *Norman's* was a fortuitous choice for that evening. The décor melded Old Spanish stucco with Latin nouveau; harmonizing stylish elegance with modern trends. They were led to their table and Enrique asked for Laura to discuss the evening wines. Laura is the sommelier responsible for *Norman's* numerous wine awards from prestigious publications.

"Hi Laura. It's great to see you again. I'd like you to meet Kate Holland."

"Pleasure to meet you Ms. Holland. Welcome to *Norman's*. Dr. Lugo, you're going to love what I have for you from Galicia."

"You remembered?" Enrique asked, impressed with his favorite sommelier's attention to details.

"Kate, last time I was here, Eric Connery and I challenged Laura to add some worthy Galician wines to *Norman's* extensive cellar and, like a true professional, she delivered."

"Thank you Dr. Lugo. If you'll permit me, I'll start your evening with the *Vi-a Godeval 1999* that I was able to find for you."

"An excellent white from Valdeorras" Enrique added, pleased with Laura's new addition.

"Enrique, you glow when you talk about Galician wines. I relish those moments." Kate said noticing her mood lifted as it flowed with his.

"I am so glad you liked my surprise."

"I love your choice of restaurant…" Kate stopped suddenly with an expression of amazement. "Enrique, I just realized the significance of what I told you about my dad guiding us here tonight."

Enrique looked puzzled trying to figure out what she meant, and waited for her to explain.

"Oh, my dear mystic. What are we celebrating tonight?" she asked rhetorically.

"We're rejoicing my sweetie masterly kicking *Aikido* derrières… Of course!" Enrique blurted as the portal flash ignited his words. "Kate, you're so on target. Your dad brought you here to celebrate your black belt, and years later I bring you to the same place for another *Aikido* triumph!"

Kate was gleaming with pride. The two most important men in her life had honored her with synchronistic grace. The chilled bottle of *Godeval* arrived to underline the benevolence of *the drift*. They toasted to their good fortune and decided what to eat. They started with the conch chowder and the soft-shell crab with shrimp hash. After the appetizers, Enrique suggested a bottle of *Opus One 1993* to move from Galician white to Californian red. For their main course he ordered the rum & pepper painted snapper with Habanero-mango mojo, and Kate chose the Mongolian barbequed breast of chicken on annatto reddened rice. Each dish was a culinary masterpiece worthy of the superlatives critics select to describe *Norman's*.

"Enrique, there's something I want to discuss with you."

"Sure, darling. What is it?"

"Tonight before you picked me up, I tried a very unusual Tibetan ritual to free myself from an old hang-up."

Kate described the emotional progression she experienced in the shower and how it led to a new understanding of belongingness where partners participate in the inclusion without ownership. She felt she was opening her heart to a degree she had never done before and hoped he would appreciate the risk she was taking.

"Kate, one of the many things I love about you is the caring you put into our relationship. But I have often wondered if my Spanish sense of maleness offends you."

"If I didn't know you intimately, I could misconstrue some of your statements as being possessive, but I truly interpret them as your loving ways."

"And that's how they're intended," Enrique responded with kindness in his voice.

"I believe you. But the most interesting part of the ritual was how the mantras transformed my emotional reaction from repulsion to tenderness. Of course, a few years ago I would have stayed quite hostile."

"Thank the Lord I met you in your wise old age." They laughed and held hands under the table enjoying their solid dedication.

"Enrique, I want you to know that when Claudia and I went to Fisher Island for lunch, you and Máximo were the main topic of our chat."

"Oh really? And what did the ladies have to say about their handsome *caballeros*?" Enrique asked with the look of a little boy waiting for his favorite story.

"If you promise not to let that big head of yours continue to grow, I'll tell you that Claudia and I feel very fortunate to have found you two rogues. Claudia was so adorable the way she described how Máximo made the *grand dame* in her feel quite naughty."

"Kate, what a winner! Especially since Máximo is crazy about that woman. He speaks of her with such fondness. It's really inspiring to see them taking chances with their hearts."

"And tell me Dr. Lugo, are you taking chances with me?"

"*Mi deliciosa*, when it comes to you, I am Christopher Columbus."

"My dear, you're pushing that Galician luck of yours. But I am dying to know what you mean by your oxymoron *empathic machismo.*"

"I'll do my best to explain it, and then I want to hear your reaction. Agree?"

"Deal."

"You know that I am a bit long-winded at times, so bear with me." Enrique took a deep breath and continued. "As my learned mate knows, the word *macho* simply means *male* in Spanish and, although the term has taken a despicable connotation, the historical Spanish male was respectable, protective, honorable and lived by his word. And those attributes especially applied to their treatment of women. In fact, the word *hembra,* which is the female equivalent, carries inherent connotations of beauty and strength. When a Spanish gentleman uses the expression *'que hembra!'* He's really saying, *what a female!* Relating to her good looks, character or strength. Unfortunately, the word *macho* has lost its equivalent complementary meaning because of the gender wars that have, in my opinion, confused the hell out of men and women alike. So I propose a metamorphosis from the maligned *macho/*male to the exulting *hombre/*man, giving birth to *hombrismo* as we bury *machismo.*"

"So, as you live your *hombrismo,* will you ever say *'que hembra',* referring to me?" Kate asked letting Enrique know with her light humor that she was supporting his contention.

"Kate, I'll respond in Spanish since you understand it better than Galician. *Cuanto hembra eres al permitir hombrismo en nuestro amor.*"

"Enrique you're such a beautiful man. Tell me if my translation is true to my poet's intention: *how female you are to permit my maleness in our love.*" Kate's pronunciation was pure Castilian when she repeated his words in Spanish.

"Not only is it correct, but coming from your lips the words are consecrated. So you see, my love, by recognizing an empathic quality in *machismo,* the maligned term could have a chance to grow in the hearts of honorable women as *hombrismo.* It seems to me your view of belongingness goes quite well with my *empathic man.* If men and women freed themselves from the sociopolitical roles that inhibit their unique magic, and claimed their manly and womanly endowments, romance could be restored to its divine order. I really believe when men live their manliness, they ascend to venerate the admirable in women."

"Enrique, *of all the gin joints in all the towns in all the world, I thank God you walked into mine.*"

"Darling, is that what Bogie really said about Ingrid at Rick's?"

"Not quite. That's what this *hembra* is saying to you at *Norman's.*"

They were feeling the buoyancy of the wines and the sensuality of their trust. All was well with their covenant of safety.

Chapter 13

"The pain turns to tranquility within the storm."

It was Sunday morning and Enrique invited Michael over for brunch to discuss new developments with the book-in-progress. The food was prepared and served by a chef who made house calls: one of the many small business enterprises in South Beach that specialized in bringing the finer rituals of life to homes of clients willing to pay for care-free luxury. Enrique liked to share his abundance with friends like Michael, who appreciated the aesthetics of wining and dining. When Michael called, he seemed excited about the news he wanted to share, but he also hinted, with his sighs between sentences, that something was wrong.

The table was set on the balcony with a bottle of *Cristal* champagne chilling on the side. Michael arrived punctually and after *abrazos* they went to the living room where the chef served them a glass of the *Cristal.* Michael was dressed as he called it *smart casual,* which for most people would be high fashion.

"Enrique what a delightful surprise. You can't imagine how much I needed this kindness from a dear friend. I simply love *Cristal.*" Michael's usual effervescence was more subdued, hinting he wanted to discuss something personal in addition to business as usual. He trusted Enrique's judgment and felt emotionally safe around him.

"Thank you for coming, Michael. I hope you like the little meal I put together."

"Enrique, please be nice and give that wonderful chef credit. Cooking is not your forte, but I love the idea of brunch on your balcony."

"Brunch is ready, gentlemen," the chef announced as he refilled the champagne glasses and led them to the table. They started with escargot sautéed in olive oil, thyme and roasted pine nuts wrapped in thin slices of smoked salmon.

"Enrique, I want to hire this chef for my next dinner party. The appetizer is food for the gods. Well, dear man, let me tell you how fortune has descended upon you. I spoke to Liliana and she informed me, with her customary histrionics…" Michael imitated her gesticulations to add his own drama to the moment and continued, "that a major producer wants to purchase the film rights for your precious

The Man from Autumn." Michael started clapping and laughing. He could not drink much without becoming bubblier than the *Cristal* he was enjoying.

"Michael, that's wonderful news. I can't wait to tell Kate."

"Oh yes, you must tell *that woman.*" In a very benign way, Michael was jealous of anyone who dared to enter Enrique's emotional world. Growing up a pampered only child, Michael did not know how to share his friends well, but dealt with it by exaggerating his possessiveness with good humor.

"Michael, what else can I tell *that woman* about the film deal?" Enrique always enjoyed teasing him without hurting his fragile feelings.

"Alright, I'll behave. Enrique, they're talking megabucks. I would tell you that you're going to be very wealthy, but alas, you already are! Liliana's attorneys are doing the preliminary negotiations, and then you can jump in."

"But Michael, how can they offer a movie deal for pre-published work?"

"Well, they rarely do, but the *Faustus* film association with your Breogán mystic has given them a fertile product to develop. And listen to this," Michael brought his hands to a prayer position and started an inaudible fast clapping that he frequently did when he got excited, "Hollie Berings wants to play Sabela. How fun!"

"And how in the hell do they know about Sabela?"

Before responding, Michael gave him the look of a child caught being naughty. "I guess a little bird told them."

"And may I ask the name of the *little bird*? Is he in my presence now?" Enrique was pretending to be upset, not letting on that he already knew Liliana was the culprit. He had given her permission to discuss the manuscript with Hollywood.

"Not I! The little bird is a female. Shall we say…"

"Michael, could it be Liliana when she met with Hollie Berings?" Enrique interrupted to bring a crescendo to the guessing game.

"What? Liliana met with Hollie Berings and she didn't invite me? I am going to pull that witch's hair. Enrique, what an infamy has been perpetrated. I simply adore Hollie Berings."

Enrique's raucous laughter brought the chef out thinking more champagne was needed to accentuate the good cheer.

"Not to worry my friend. You'll be included when I meet with her."

"Oh Enrique, are you serious?"

"Of course. I don't attend important book-related meetings without my agent."

Although Enrique responded in the light spirit of the moment, he trusted Michael's judgment implicitly. Michael withdrew to an expression of introspection and gave Enrique a smile intended to be appreciative, but unable to disguise his pain.

"Listen Michael, we have time to celebrate this wonderful news later, but at the moment, I am more concerned about you. I knew there was something wrong when we spoke on the phone and now, seeing you hardly touched your favorite dish, confirms it." Enrique had asked the chef to prepare smoked haddock *gnocchi* to surprise Michael.

"No Enrique, the *gnocchi* is the best I've had and I am so pleased you went to all this trouble for me," Michael's eyes watered as he spoke, "it's times like these that I realize there's nothing more precious than a dear friend like you. Let me unload my burden and ask for your council. Sometime back we discussed this gorgeous woman I met who swept me away, and you told me to take a chance with my heart. I had been feeling these confounding emotions, until finally I let her know. We met for coffee a few times and had wonderful conversations. Then yesterday I went to the yoga class she teaches and, as I walked her to her car, I told her how I felt. I was panicking when my words were coming out, but I had a sense of propriety about what I was doing that gave me strength."

"And how did she react Michael?" Enrique was asking an obvious question but wanted to give his friend pause to collect his thoughts.

"She looked at me with kind eyes and told me she had a boyfriend. But you know? Rather than the devastation I expected from her response, there was a serene connection, although not necessarily what I wanted to hear." Michael stopped and looked perplexed at Enrique.

"My friend, although you didn't receive what you expected, you lived what I call the *rightness of the moment*."

"Enrique, for some unexplainable reason, your term gives me comfort. I have no clue. It's like the first relief you feel from a migraine when the medication begins to take effect," Michael took a bite of his *gnocchi* with little interest and continued, "but please tell me more about this *rightness of the moment* concept."

"Ok, but I'll have to be mystical to explain it, and you know how you react when you think I am getting weird," Enrique cautioned him with the prerequisite humor mystics use to disengage from linear thinking and jump to discovery mode.

"Right now, you can do your hocus-pocus as long as you can make sense of my predicament." Michael had a naïve view of mysticism, but his keen intuition guided him to the receptiveness Enrique was expecting.

"The *rightness of the moment* is action based on an essential truth that has universal connectiveness. It expresses the best our humanity has to offer because the decision to act is always honorable. Nations go to war, civil servants risk their lives to rescue victims, and ordinary people endure intolerable tortures for the rightness of the moment. In your case, your heart needed a voice and your action spoke its truth. But it's imperative to understand that acting on the rightness of the moment, is based on living a revered symbol rather than dependent on the response. If that were not the case, then no one would enter harm's way to live their truth."

"Enrique, that path you're offering gives me perspective to endure my pain. Before we spoke, I was into self-pity, and now I am beginning to feel I can care for this person at a level she can reciprocate."

"Michael, that's exactly what happens when you recognize the rightness of the moment. The pain turns to *tranquility within the storm*. One of my mentors is a priest and, I am reminded, he fell in love with a woman he met in graduate school after he had been ordained. The situation was complicated--not only was he unable to act on his feelings, but he also concluded it would be devastating to tell her, even if she wanted to reciprocate."

"And what did he do?" Michael asked with the bewilderment of innocence.

"Actually, what he did started me thinking on this *rightness of the moment* idea. He told me he raised his untenable feelings to a level of love they could both share without compromising his faith or her honor. They remain platonic friends to this day and care deeply for each other within a space that doesn't violate their symbols of love."

"But let's supposed you love someone who wants nothing to do with you?" Michael asked to test the limits of Enrique's theory, or perhaps bring light to some haunting memories.

"That happens when the recipient refuses to accept the implications of your gift. In that case, rather than invalidating the nobleness of your offer, *love at a distance* until the lack of reciprocity extinguishes the flame with grace. Distancing yourself, without denying your feelings, respects the recipient's boundaries and sets a gentle pace for your heart to heal from the stings of unrequited love. Honoring boundaries is one of the key components of mature love. For example, stalkers don't respect limits because they obsess rather than love."

"Enrique, I've decided to do something that I believe will bring me peace. But first, I want to thank you for the burden you've lifted. I am going to love this woman within the accorded boundaries until my predestined partner shows up to fill the void. Although it still hurts to know she's not going to partake as I expected, I can almost taste this *tranquility within the storm* you mentioned."

"Michael, forgive me for asking, but is she willing to be your friend after your disclosure?"

"Oh yes, she asked me to not regret what I felt, because she thought there was a great lesson to be learned if we remained friends."

"It seems to me you have the makings of a powerful friendship."

"Indeed. Enrique, could the good chef nuke my *gnocchi*? I am famished."

They laughed and cheered as the chef returned with the bottle of *Cristal*. Good servers can time the interjection of food and drinks by the rhythm of their customers' conversations. The meal was shared in the rightness of the moment, both men valuing the significance of friendship during emotional storms.

Enrique had immutable house rules about alcohol consumption, and he made the options very simple: if after indulging in adult beverages, a guest could not pronounce flawlessly the words *Methodist-Episcopal,* they would have to either take a nap or take a cab home. Michael giggled when he failed the test and went dutifully to one of the guest rooms to enjoy his nap.

Being an anthropologist, Enrique saw the rooms of a house as stations to perform the *biocultural rituals* that transitioned us from the forest to the cave. His kitchen was spacious, with large windows bringing nature into the preparation of nourishment. The bathroom showcased a steam room of blue marble for exorcising internal demons and road rage. His bedroom was the safety station, its calming shades of blue welcoming intimacy and sleep. And so it was that each room contributed to the richness of the collective space he called home. To this day, we insist on bringing plants to our dwellings because a part of us has never left the forest.

Adhering to his house rule, Enrique took a steam bath and a long shower to prepare for his nap. He slept deep and long, awaking late afternoon, with enough time to witness from his balcony the folding of another South Beach day. He walked to the kitchen and found a very gracious note from Michael, who was the prince of propriety. Enrique believed gratitude was the ultimate gift.

After a light meal, reminiscing about his chat with Michael reminded Enrique that the deadline to complete the manuscript was coming too fast for comfort. It was time to collaborate with Breogán once again.

Breogán and Sabela returned from their morning windsurfing and

after a hot shower and breakfast, Breogán began to read his accumu-
lated emails. There were the usual fans and the clever advertisements
that escaped the anti-spam software. Then he noticed an out-of-pattern
cue. He remembered how U.S. Special Forces are trained to look for
straight lines in the wilderness to identified man-made danger, because
nature does not produce straight lines. The out-of-pattern signal that
Breogán detected was an address containing the abbreviations fr. *and*
va., *signifying a priest was writing from Vatican City. He opened the*
email and found a Monsignor Emilio Balducci writing from the Secre-
tariat of State's Office of the Holy See.

Monsignor Balducci explained he had attended Breogán's lecture
on "a most relevant topic" at the University of the Holy Cross and,
given the expertise that Signore Breogán had so eloquently exhibited
on the subject, which was corroborated by prudent inquiries, the Curia
urgently sought his counsel on an internal matter of the utmost impor-
tance. The Monsignor appealed to Breogán's Catholic devotion to treat
the request with delicate confidentiality.

Breogán's schooling, with the Brothers of La Salle, taught him to
decipher Church language well enough to conclude that Monsignor
Balducci was counting on him to help his brethren with a case of stig-
mata involving one of their own. Considering that Saint Francis was
not an ordained priest, if the stigmatic needing Breogán's assistance
were indeed a priest, it would be the fourth credible instance after Pa-
dre Pio in the almost eight-hundred year history of such phenomena.

Monsignor Balducci proposed a meeting the following Monday at the
Palazzo San Calisto in Vatican City and he asked Breogán to confirm. The
surprise came when Breogán read that the man he was scheduled to meet
was Fr. Carlo Fellini! Immediately, Breogán thought of their conversation
about the medieval concept of suffering, and wondered why this particular
priest had been assigned to meet with him.

Breogán explained what he could to Sabela, who kissed him,
packed his bags, and drove him to Santiago for his flight to Rome. She
was staying with her uncle in Santiago until Breogán returned. Sa-
bela's native city inspired her best work, and her agent arranged a
meeting with an art dealer from L.A. to negotiate a commission for an
American Bank. After all, felicitous timing was becoming commonplace
in Sabela's autumns.

"Breogán, I have a little gift to protect you on your mysterious mis-
sion," Sabela said with affected drama to masquerade the anxiety she
felt about this trip.

"My dear wife, what a lovely Celtic cross." Breogán took the small silver cross with the thin rawhide necklace and put it over his head. In addition to the Celtic circle on the cross symbolizing the eternal life of Christ, it had three dots on each of the planes representing the resurrection after three days.

Breogán arrived at 10:30 pm at the Leonardo Da Vinci International Airport on a drizzling Roman night. After clearing customs, he was greeted by a priest he was able to recognize from the picture attached to the email from Monsignor Balducci.

"Signore Breogán I am Fr. Corrado. Welcome to Rome. I trust you had a pleasant flight?" The priest carried himself with the fluidity of a diplomat from an organization that could proclaim St. Peter as their first CEO. Fr. Corrado had a tall and frail physique, in a Don Quixote sort of way.

"Thank you for meeting me at this late hour, Father." Breogán knew better than to ask any specifics, well aware that a need-to-know basis was the protocol for sensitive Church business.

"If it's acceptable, we have made arrangements for you to stay at Casa di Santa Marta, *where we believe the accommodations will be quite adequate."*

Breogán knew this facility was the only hotel permitted within Vatican City. It was built by order of His Holiness John Paul II at a cost of $20 million, and available only to guests conducting business with the Holy See.

"Thank you Father, Casa di Santa Marta *will do fine."*

To relieve travel fatigue, Breogán could imagine humor in almost any situation. Hearing Fr. Corrado use the royal we, *as he explained the living quarters, made Breogán think of Mark Twain's prerequisites for the use of that pronoun: it was permitted only for the Queen of England, the Pope, and people with worms. Breogán was grateful Fr. Corrado could not read his private thoughts--sparing the good Father a most unpleasant diagnosis.*

They were driven in a black Mercedes with Vatican plates to a hotel of 108 suites and 23 single rooms equipped with every modern convenience. Casa di San Marta was originally built to house the Conclave of Cardinals that meets to elect a new Pope. Nuns run the hotel with apostolic care. Sister Clementina greeted Breogán and Fr. Corrado with restrained warmth, and proclaimed their guest had been assigned a suite where several blessed Cardinals had stayed.

Fr. Corrado walked Breogán to his suite with the conspiratorial tension of someone waiting for the proper moment to disclose sensitive information.

"Oh yes, one more thing... we beg your indulgence for a slight change of itinerary. Rather than meeting your host at Palazzo San Calisto, he will join you here for breakfast at 9 am. Of course, the meal will be served in your suite for the sake of prudence, as it were."

"I am looking forward to the meeting," Breogán answered, wondering if one could look forward to witnessing stigmatic suffering.

"Signore Breogán, we are relieved you understand our imposed inconvenience. It was my pleasure to meet you. God bless you." Fr. Corrado made the sign of the cross, as his credible humility governed the blessing ritual.

"Thank you Fr. Corrado. You're very kind."

Breogán woke up at 6 am with enough time to prepare his disposition for the possible turbulence that might lie ahead. He was glad Fr. Fellini was assigned to work with him. During difficult times, Breogán practiced a meditation he learned from the works of the Christian mystic St. Teresa of Avila. In a deep contemplative state, he performed the Prayer of Quiet. St. Teresa warned that people with poor constitutions could die from the intensity of the experience. She called that stage of deep meditation a "sleep of the faculties": in modern cognitive science it would be termed consciousness without contextual reference, which could indeed be dangerous for people suffering from dissociative disorders.

"Hello? Oh yes, sister, please have Fr. Fellini come up," Breogán answered the phone, hoping the mystery would soon be revealed.

"Carlo it's so good to see you again." Breogán took the liberty to hug the priest and felt the risk was rewarded with reciprocal warmth.

"My dear Breogán, I am so thankful that we meet again." Fr. Fellini looked energized, with vigor waiting to unfold.

An elaborate breakfast was brought in and the aroma of freshly brewed Italian coffee and pastries filled the room. Graceful presentation of food can stage the mood for confronting any of Dante's demons.

"Breogán, I am sure you are replete with questions and we apologize for the suspense, but as I brief you on the delicate incident we will face, I am certain you will understand why we were so reluctant to discuss it other than in person. You are most kind devoting your precious time."

"Carlo, I am assuming that we're dealing with a case of stigmata. Is it clergy?" Breogán did not want to mince words.

"My friend, you are very astute, so I will respond to your directness without further delays." For the first time Fr. Fellini looked anxious.

"We have a priest who is exhibiting symptoms of the invisible stigmata on both wrists and feet. Four out of the five classic areas."

"So there're no wounds for now, but there's pain?" Breogán asked, beginning his checklist method of inquiry.

"Precisely. But the pain is excruciating; and sadly, no amount of pain medication has been able to alleviate it."

"It doesn't surprise me. Has there been any tissue damage?"

"No, but the painful areas are turning red with a diameter of about ten millimeters. What can you make of this Breogán? I gave the priest a battery of psychological tests and he came out well within normal limits." Although Fr. Fellini had no experience with stigmatics, as a clinical psychologist he knew that hysteria and other psychiatric disorders needed to be ruled out.

"That's very valuable data and I am glad you anticipated the requirements." Breogán was beginning to see this was not going to be an easily dismissed case.

"Breogán, what do you suggest we do?"

"Where's this priest?"

"He is at a villa outside Rome. To avoid attracting attention at Vatican City, we moved him to the country a week ago."

Breogán told Fr. Fellini he was going to need medical history, blood labs, including immune cells profile, to rule out diabetes and other disorders that could explain problems with wound healing if the priest were to advance to the next stage, as well as to know how his immune system responded before and after the wounds manifested. Fr. Fellini had anticipated the requests from what he learned in Breogán's lecture about the biological elements of stigmata and had most of the information ready for him.

"Breogán, attending your lecture has helped me immensely. In fact, the physician assigned to the case wants to learn more about your work. But let me answer your questions. The results show no evidence of diabetes, hemophilia, psychogenic purpura, or neuropsychological deficits." Fr. Fellini looked pleased with his report.

"Carlo, I am impressed. You're a quick study."

"May the Lord hear you, Breogán. We are certainly going to need His guidance here."

"I agree. We're going to need all the help we can get. Let me suggest how I think we should proceed. Stigmata is a complex phenomenon where cultural and spiritual beliefs can influence biological function. We need to first rule out the self-inflicted possibility and then move on to see what else could be causing the symptoms."

"Breogán, why did it not surprise you that the pain medication was not working?"

"Because the cases I've seen have been very resistant to pain relief. Although the recipient is horrified, there's a self-punitive element that blocks the effect of analgesics on the body's pain receptors: the power of mind over pharmacology at its best, or perhaps at its worst."

"Amazing how Divinity endows. Breogán, my superiors have asked me to assist you with anything you need. I should tell you they trust you completely and are grateful for the pro bono cases you have investigated so prudently for the Vatican."

"Thank you Carlo. Of course we need to meet the priest as soon as possible to get started, but let me tell you how I approach the problem. We need his physician and his ecclesiastic superior involved to address the person from a psycho-spiritual medical model. In the case of a priest, we would of course, need a Bishop to intercede."

"Breogán, I was waiting for the right moment to, shall we say, drop the bomb? And when you assumed that a Bishop would be the appropriate superior, I thought the time had come," Fr. Fellini responded with apologetic anxiety.

"What's wrong with his Bishop? Is the stigmatic more pious than his boss?" Breogán asked, attempting theological humor, but Fr. Fellini was unaffected.

"My dear Breogán," Fr. Fellini stopped to catch his breath before continuing, *"in this case, a Bishop could not serve as his superior because our potential stigmatic is a Cardinal!"*

"I'll be damned! Sorry, Father." Breogán's attempt to excuse his profanity made Fr. Fellini cough to suppress laughter.

"Breogán, in your place, I would have responded the same way. May God forgive us." Both men laughed to help their collective reality absorb the tension.

"Carlo, how many people know about it?"

"Cardinal Allegro, Monsignor Balducci, the physician assigned to the case, you, and your humble servant. There are Cardinal Bishops, Cardinal-Deacons and Cardinal-Priests. Our man is a Cardinal-Priest."

"So that means he serves as Cardinal outside Vatican City, most likely in another country."

"Breogán, you know our Roman Curia well."

"And now my dear, Fr. Carlo Fellini, let's pin down the country. Where does he serve?" As soon as Breogán asked, he could sense the second bomb was going to drop.

Fr. Fellini started his answer with a measured delivery, using the

Cardinal's official title: "His Excellency Alonzo Cardinal Diaz Umap serves as the Archbishop of San Cristóbal in Havana, Cuba. And His Eminence is most simpatico to the Conclave that will choose the next Pope."

"Carlo, I am stunned for a multitude of reasons. Independent of his condition, can you imagine the geopolitical impact of electing a Pope from the only Communist country in the Western Hemisphere?"

Fr. Fellini nodded, validating Breogán's implications and added: "You can also imagine what would happen if Cardinal Diaz Umap's condition were leaked to the press. You know how the Vatican has avoided the potential circus atmosphere that cases of stigmata can generate. When I was asked to assist you on this case, I learned how you honored the confidentiality of the previous two instances you investigated for the Holy See. My question to you is: who can serve as the spiritual director in this case?"

"Well, the reason for the involvement of a superior is to maintain coherence between the physical and spiritual intrusions required to assess and hopefully resolve the condition. Due to his high position, we'll have to let Cardinal Diaz Umap decide whom he wants as his spiritual director."

"Breogán, I must ask you a pertinent question hoping you can answer it without violating confidentiality: are there cases where the wounds have reversed?"

"There are some where the wounds appear and disappear around sacred holidays, there are others that just disappear on their own and..." Breogán stopped to consider how to conclude, "there was one case where the wounds healed from psycho-spiritual intervention involving a multidisciplinary team of professionals."

"And to abate my own anxieties, were you a member of that team?"

"Yes, I was, Carlo, and I know that with your assistance we'll succeed when challenged by the circumstances."

"Breogán, I am most grateful for your confidence and faith."

"Thank you, Father, but my faith is in the power Divinity has bestowed our minds."

"While we were enjoying this delectable breakfast, I took the liberty of having the sisters pack your bags because, if you do not object, a driver is waiting downstairs to take us to the villa directly."

"You Jesuits are the epitome of efficiency. Let's go face the drift."

"The drift?" Fr. Fellini asked, as if derailed from reading a set of directions.

"Carlo, I'll explain later. It was just my esoteric Self seeking guidance."

"Patience is my humble gift," Fr. Fellini said with a pleasing smile as they stepped into the black Mercedes.

Both men sat in the back and before Breogán could speak, Fr. Fellini assured him the glass partition in front of them would permit conversations that would not reach the chauffeur's ears. Once again, Breogán's humorous imagery surfaced to entertain him. This time, he was a Galician James Bond, speaking Spanish to a Cuban Cardinal in Italy, solving a mystery that transcended language.

"Breogán, given the present scenario, please tell me more about the task of the spiritual director."

"Well, as we confront the cognitive, biological and cultural variables that influence the stigmata, the director serves as a mediator to bring spiritual context to the recipient. The objective is to resolve the conflict between healing and betraying the gift."

"That makes perfect sense. I see now how our conversation about the models of suffering will be very helpful in mapping our assessment and intervention."

"Absolutely." Breogán recognized Fr. Fellini's words had unfolded a feedforward event that would serve them well. Once again, the auspiciousness of the drift proved infallible.

"Carlo, I meant to ask you, where's the villa?"

"We are almost there. I guess I should tell you that I used the term 'villa' loosely, as you will see in a few minutes, our destination is Castle Gandolfo,*"* Fr. Fellini responded with an apologetic gesture for withholding the venue until then.

"The Pope's summer residence?" Breogán asked rhetorically knowing that Castle Gandolfo has been the summer home of Popes since the 18th century.

"Yes, His Eminence was brought here to provide the most private and secure place outside Vatican City."

Although modest as castles go, the Gandolfo residence boasts a spectacular view by the edge of a volcanic lake. The temple of Zeus stood on the opposite shore until Emperor Constantine destroyed it when he converted to Christianity in the 4th century, giving birth to the Catholic Church.

Breogán and Fr. Fellini entered Castle Gandolfo. Two Swiss Guards in blue uniforms and berets, and wearing SIG pistols, flanked the imposing brass door. The more dazzling tunic, with the red, blue *and yellow colors of the Medici family and the menacing halberds, are the ceremonial version worn only in Vatican City and public appearances. While the design of the uniforms has been incorrectly attributed to Michelangelo, it was most likely influenced by fellow artist Raphael.*

Fr. Fellini explained to Breogán that the Papal Palaces are traditionally guarded by the Corps of Gendarmes, but given the delicate geopolitical implications, the Cardinal's personal security had been assigned to the Swiss Guard.

The two men were met by Dr. Mario Scola, the physician assigned to the investigation. They went to a small reception room where they were served espressos and biscotti. Dr. Scola started the conversation without further delays.

"Signore Breogán, as a physician and priest, I find these ..." Dr. Scola stopped to decide how to label the condition of his patient, "symptoms shall we say, beyond the medical parameters we are trained to diagnose and treat. Case in point, I am baffled by the dosage of intravenous analgesics required to bring minimum pain relief. Also, the redness around the wrists and feet shows no inflammation or warmth to the touch, unlike the usual immune response to infection or foreign body detection. Have you seen such clinical presentation?" Dr. Scola drank his second cup of espresso as if the caffeine could paradoxically calm him.

"Yes, Dr. Scola. What you're seeing at this point are psychosomatic signs of invisible stigmata moving to its secondary manifestation. This particular sequence starts with pain without visual or lab corroboration, progressing to the redness you described. If it moves to the next phase, you might find secretion of a clear fluid, most likely progressing to torn tissue with bleeding. But tell me, what did you make of the lab results?"

"Nothing significant: sputum, urine, blood; all within normal limits."

"Did you include interleukins 1 and 8 in your lab work?" Breogán was asking from experience with his previous case.

"No, I did not. I saw no clinical reason at the time. But please tell me why?"

"Of course, I agree there was no justification at the time, but if the wounds appear, interleukins will be key to our investigation."

"You're thinking as they relate to inflammation and wound healing?" Dr. Scola asked with visible excitement.

"Yes, research in psychoneuroimmunology shows that stress slows the healing of wounds, because the high levels of cortisol released suppress interleukins 1 and 8, those involved in the inflammation

responsible for containing the infection and signaling the production of adhesion cells that close the wound. Interestingly, the production of neutrophils, which are the first line of defense against infections, is not as affected during stressful conditions."

"This is simply mesmerizing, Signore Breogán," Dr. Scola responded, getting up from his chair to pace around the room.

"Dr. Scola, Breogán has a theory on what may be happening with the wounds of stigmatics," Fr. Fellini interjected to facilitate a mindset of multidisciplinary cooperation.

"I beg you sir. Please tell us." Dr. Scola stopped pacing and returned to his chair like a curious student.

"Gentlemen, given the research I mentioned, I argue that the trauma of stigmata, whether divinely ignited or not, is certainly a stressor that can induce high levels of cortisol. But unlike the complications with slow healing of common wounds during stress, stigmatics may trigger a selective immunity with sufficient levels of protective leukocytes to fight infection while suppressing interleukins to prevent wound healing."

"But Signore Breogán, with your theory one has to assume that a belief could micromanage immune function," Dr. Scola responded, his inflection wavering between question and statement.

"Exactly. And that's what I think happens. We know, for example, that research participants can selectively increase T-cells vs. neutrophils using imagery rehearsals."

"Signore Breogán, can you direct me to the research in that area? I am very interested."

"Oh yes, Dr. Scola, there's substantial evidence in the psycho-neuroimmunology literature that I can provide you. Since stigmatics interpret their condition as a sign of divine intervention, their biology will adjust to the psycho-spiritual belief that the wounds should remain open and free of infection in order to accept the gift without compromising health. A pact of sorts between Creationism and Darwinism to maintain mind-body-spirit harmony," Breogán added, startled by his own conclusion.

"I guess there is nothing else we can do medically at this point, so I suggest we meet with His Eminence," Dr. Scola concluded.

A Swiss Guard led the three men to a large living room, where they were asked to wait by the welcoming warmth of blazing logs in the arched fireplace. They were served brandies as they discussed the works of Dutch masters that decorated the stucco walls. The double doors opened and a tall priest appeared, wearing the black cassock trimmed in red signifying a prince of the Church had entered the room. Despite his impressive elegance, Cardinal Diaz Umap carried himself with a simplicity that inspired trust. He had the presence of a holy man in turmoil.

"Your Eminence, may I present Fr. Fellini and Signore Breogán," Dr. Scola made the ceremonious introduction in perfect Spanish, the agreed language.

"Gentlemen, please sit down. I am most grateful for the time I am requesting of you. Dr. Scola explained the need to confront this situation without a moment to waste, so I am at your disposal."

Breogán outlined briefly their objectives and asked His Eminence if he had chosen a spiritual director.

"Yes, I have indeed. I would like Fr. Fellini to serve in that capacity." Cardinal Diaz Umap turned to Fr. Fellini to address him. "I asked Cardinal Allegro for his permission to involve you, given the laudable work you have done in theological psychology at the University of Milano. I do apologize for waiting until this moment to inform you and I pray you will accept my humble request."

Fr. Fellini was visibly shaken, and honored, by the opportunity to assist a man who had endured sustained hardship as head of the Catholic Church in a Communist country. "Your Eminence, I am deeply touched and, although I feel unworthy of your confidence, I will do my best to fulfill my duties with the help of our Lord."

"God bless you gentlemen," The Cardinal proffered as he sat exhausted from the relentless pain.

Breogán briefed Cardinal Diaz Umap on the examination he was going to conduct before moving on to other relevant areas of inquiry. Breogán noticed a red spot without the usual warm-to-the-touch found with inflammations. The red areas of about nine millimeters formed an irregular sphere with border variations on each of the four abrasions. The affected spots were between the wrist bones on an area called Destot's space. But rather than the arch of the feet, as usually depicted, the other two spots were on the heel of each foot. Fr. Fellini and Dr. Scola looked at Breogán in unison seeking explanation, but waited, following their agreement not to bias the Cardinal's perception with their interpretations. Breogán contended that stigmatics manifest their wounds based on where they perceived were inflicted on the body of Christ.

"Your Eminence, what do you make of these four skin irritations?" Breogán asked, using a generic description of what he had observed.

"Well, I think they are simply skin irritations, as you called them. One could argue a stigmatic connection with the wrists but the heels debunk the theory, no?"

"What is your understanding of how the Romans crucified?" Breogán answered with a question to identify the Cardinal's conceptual biases before giving more conclusive explanations.

"I am cognizant that the Shroud of Turin and other scientific evidence suggests the Romans drove the nails through the wrists rather than the palms, but I am relieved to know that the spots on my heels do not correspond with a stigmata profile."

"Your Eminence, have you seen any art or read anything that would support the location of your irritations on your heels as something more than a common rash?" Breogán continued to use dermatological terms to maintain scientific objectivity.

"No, I have not, but I have a feeling that what you are about to tell me may not be pleasant."

"I am afraid you're right. Modern archeological digs in Jerusalem uncovered skeletons of crucified victims that had their feet nailed to the cross sideways."

Cardinal Diaz Umap covered his face with cupped hands, and looked up with the expression of a sentenced prisoner to ask the three men: "what now gentlemen?"

Before anyone could respond the Cardinal began to hyperventilate with other symptoms indicative of a panic attack. His Eminence held his hand up to stop any intervention from his doctor. "I will be alright Dr. Scola, I've been suffering from these spells for years and, if I remember to breathe slowly, they subside." But this time the breathing technique did not work and he began to perspire profusely. Then a most phenomenal transformation happened. The pain in the four areas intensified and the perspiration secreting from the red spots began to turn red simultaneously. Cardinal Diaz Umap was horrified as his breathing became more labored. The men carried him to the nearby couch, where Dr. Scola gave him 2 mg. of Ativan I.V. After a few minutes, Cardinal Diaz Umap began to relax and his breathing returned slowly to normal. The body perspiration stopped but the reddish sweat continued to ooze from the four spots. Upon inspection, Dr. Scola noted there was no tissue tear, indicating the bleeding was coming through the pores.

"Your Eminence, there's an explanation for what's happening, but for now, please try to rest. We'll be in the other room if you need us,"

Breogán reassured him and walked out of the room with his two colleagues.

The men were served coffee in the smaller adjacent room, giving Breogán time to collect his thoughts. Fr. Fellini and Dr. Scola waited, trying to imagine what he would say.

"My friends, we're very fortunate to have witnessed a most spectacular set of events. I can tell you that although extremely rare, I believe the bloody perspiration was caused by a medical condition called hematidrosis. *During situations of overwhelming stress, such as facing death in a concentration camp etc., a very powerful sympathetic nervous system reaction can tear the small blood vessels that feed the sweat glands, and the victim bleeds from the pores that normally release sweat. In fact, an eminent forensic pathologist at Columbia University has speculated Christ may have suffered from this condition on the cross. The pathologist cited Luke 22: 42-44 describing how in His agony, 'Christ's sweat became like great drops of blood falling upon the ground.' But more exceptional is the specific areas where the Cardinal bled. It was a case of* selective *hematidrosis where the mind-body endowment pushed a highly unlikely biological occurrence to the edge of Divinity. Of course, I leave the theological implications to you two gentlemen of the cloth."*

"Well, this gentleman of the cloth is speechless," Fr. Fellini added.

Dr. Scola said nothing, perhaps trying to reconcile his medical and ecclesiastic training.

"Dr. Scola, I am glad you collected samples of saliva and the sanguineous fluid from the four areas of secretion. I am sure the lab results will provide important clues." Breogán was thankful for the assistance he was getting from these two dedicated men.

"We will have the results by tomorrow afternoon. I will order all the tests you requested and a few of my own," Dr. Scola replied.

"Breogán, what do you propose to do, beyond assessing the physical manifestations?" Fr. Fellini asked

"Good question. Although the data we're collecting will document the biology of stigmata, our most important task is to help His Eminence conceptualize what he's experiencing within his cultural and religious background. Before we can help him, we need to know the attribution he gives to his suffering and how it will affect his personal journey."

"I can tell you, His Eminence is no stranger to suffering. He spent

close to three years in a Cuban concentration camp," Dr. Scola related
*with an expression of indignation he subdued before continuing, " and
during his internment, he began to have panic attacks and night terror
typical of post-traumatic stress syndrome seen in war veterans and ca-
tastrophe victims. His symptoms had been in remission until now."*

*"Dr. Scola, this history you're giving us is very useful, because
stigmatics assume a victim soul mindset that compels them to suffer for
others as Jesus did for mankind. So there is suffering to identify with
Christ, as well as suffering for others, to imitate Christ. And the key to
solving the stigmatic conflict lies in isolating the dynamics of both
modes of suffering and replacing them with the love of Christ. Then the
physiology of suffering can heal with the biology of love,"* Breogán was
*slowly mapping the sequence of interventions required to assess how
mind-body could reconcile spirit within a cultural history.*

*The men were cohering their expertise to approach their next level
of involvement as a team. Dr. Scola went back to check on his patient
and found him peacefully asleep. The sanguineous fluid had stopped
secreting, leaving patterns of dried rivulets around the four affected
areas. Dr. Scola left orders to not disturb His Eminence, and went to
the dining room to meet Fr. Fellini and Breogán for a late lunch.*

*After a typical Roman meal and wines were served, the three men
resumed their discussion, energized by the sustenance.*

"Signore Breogán," Dr. Scola began, *"do you believe stigmata
manifests through divine intervention?"*

*"Well, if one acknowledges Divinity, one would have to entertain
that it could intercede in human affairs at any time. But since I believe
free will is our only divine endowment, when potentiated by faith, we
can commune with Providence. And in that state of Grace, we become
stewards of Divinity where nothing is impossible."*

*"Breogán, then what you are proposing is that rather than divine
intervention, it is our intervention with Divinity."*

*"My dear Carlo, you have surmised very eloquently what I was try-
ing to say."*

*"Signore Breogán, your exchange with Fr. Fellini reminded me of
something His Eminence told me about his nightmares that might have
great relevance here,"* Dr. Scola interject *with the pensive hesitance of
someone about to disclose intimate information...*

Chapter 14

"A moment in time and space when self disowns motive."

Enrique woke up mid afternoon. He had a clock shaped like a pyramid by his bed and when he pressed the tip, a synthesized voice with a Japanese accent would tell the precise time. There was a block of hours in the middle of the night where the accent was so thick he was unable to track his patterns of insomnia. He had been writing for twelve hours until he decided to stop at 6 am and get some rest. He tested his internal clock every morning against the programmed voice and, this time, he was notably off when it announced it was three twenty-six pm.

Enrique's first coherent thought was to ponder what Dr. Scola was going to say about the Cardinal's nightmares. A precursor impulse to call his mentor Fr. Simon surfaced and, like a devoted student of *the drift*, he picked up the phone and complied.

"Hi Jonas, do you have time to talk?"

"Enrique? It's so good to hear from you. What's up?" Fr. Simon always had time for his favorite former student.

Enrique explained where he was going with the book and how he got stuck after delineating the suffering attributions of stigmata. He wanted to expand on their previous conversation about the suffering of Eastern vs. Western mystics. The stigmatic suffering appeared to have different contextual elements.

"Now Jonas, I want you to know that you'll be given proper credit as spiritual adviser for the book."

"Don't you dare screw up the serenity of my pseudo-retirement. I don't want to hear from the *Congregation for the Causes of Saints,*" Fr. Simon quipped with his energizing style. He and Enrique had joked about how the film *Stigmata* stretched the facts with a Hollywood twist. In the film, the main character was a priest who investigated supernatural phenomena for the Vatican's *Congregation for the Causes of Saints*. Although the Congregation exists, rather than scrutinizing cases of stigmata, its duties involve authenticating miracles, acts of martyrdom, and heroic virtues attributed to those who are being evaluated for beatification and canonization. Hollywood intelligentsia ignored that stigmata is not part of the criteria for sainthood. More importantly, unlike the afflicted actress in the film, no stigmatic has ever been possessed by troubled spirits.

"But Jonas, although the *atonement archetype* we identified in our previous chat could certainly be part of the stigmata fabric, it seems to me there's more."

"You mean the *atonement archetype* that *you* so aptly named. Regardless, I think you're right. Stigmata involves more than suffering for either past deeds or future gains. The pain serves to emulate Christ in His suffering for others. The Germans have the word *weltschmerz,* literally meaning *world pain,* to label the experience of identifying with world suffering."

"Jonas, do you recall your lecture on Nietzsche and *Weltschmerz?*"

"This old priest is no fool. I didn't retire my neurons to Florida precisely so I could keep alive the brilliant material the Lord provided for my lectures."

"Oh, wise master, pray tell," Enrique countered, humoring his mentor.

"You know Nietzsche believed Christianity numbed present suffering with metaphysical promises of a better afterlife. He felt this numbing effect prevented the possibility of conquering suffering by transforming it into something beautiful. For example, overcoming suffering from envy by turning it into competition. But the limitations of his existentialism kept him chronically depressed, and prevented him from seeing the redemptive world of Kierkegaard. While both men despised the insincere virtue of those who gloss over life's vicissitudes, unlike Nietzsche, Kierkegaard believed metaphysical detachment from worldly goods facilitated enjoying the gifts of life without guilt."

"Now we're getting close to an epiphany, right?" Enrique asked in his jovial way of gaining wisdom.

"Well, we can use your terminology and call it a *portal flash.*" Fr. Simon had been keeping up with Enrique's intellectual development, confirming that people who love you take interest in what you love. "For Nietzsche, Christianity distracts us from life's sufferings with transcendental promises, but with Kierkegaard, the transcendental empowers us to resolve the temporal nature of suffering with the infinite essence of divine love. In other words, knowing that an aversion does not last forever makes it possible to overcome it with a quality that does."

"Jonas, the distinction you've presented gets to the core of *weltschmerz* and its place in the stigmatic expression."

"Alright, so run with it and show me what you got."

"Ok, we agree the atonement archetype functions in all cultures, through episodes of suffering, to cleanse personal past deeds or ensure future gains. But stigmatic suffering endeavors to atone for the sins of others rather than self: a case of vicarious atonement where the symbolic *weltschmerz* acquires physical form.

"What can be done for them, Enrique?"

Enrique beckoned a gift from heaven--wisdom to answer the stigmata enigma, for the man who taught the wave-dancing surfer to sail the mystical winds of compassion. *Why does my chat with Andres Vitón come to mind? Is it the inner force we discussed? Should I flow with his image and see where it takes me?* Enrique pondered in rapid sequence.

"Are you still there, *wonder-boy*? Fr. Simon broke the internal inquiry using his old nickname for Enrique.

"Sorry Jonas, I was thinking about a conversation I had with my agent that may have relevance here."

"About stigmata?"

"No, but like most things I do these days, it may have coincidental meaning. I was wondering… *if* free will is activated by an inner force and *if* all emotions are subsumed under love and fear, then what could move the will to manifest stigmata?"

"Are you asking or getting ready to tell me? But before you do, your assumptions are not including divine intervention as an option, right?"

"Jonas, I am sort of thinking out loud. And yes, I am excluding divine intervention as a cause of stigmata, deferring that interpretation to theologians. But as a scientist, I am looking for what my psychologist friend calls *biocultural* explanations." Enrique was beginning to feel the lightheadedness that preceded discovery through a portal flash. He was entering the suspension of linear thinking where precursors of coherence come as fractals, with each piece containing the totality of the information needed to assemble holographic wisdom.

"Yes, you told me about your friend's theory of Biocognition." Fr. Simon's memory served him well at any age.

"Well, according to Biocognitive theory, we exist in a vibrant field that contains all the information accumulated from the beginning of time. And within this bioinformational field, we have access to our individual cultural history as well as the collective intelligence relevant to our species. The biologist Rupert Sheldrake calls these species-specific fields *morphic resonance.*

"Oh yes, I am familiar with Sheldrake's work, but I recall biocognitive theory expands the concept by addressing the role of culture within these fields of information.

"Jonas, you have a precise memory. And no, I am not going to say *for your age.*" Enrique responded confident that his humor would not offend his beloved mentor.

"So now your wit includes *apophasis*?"

"Jonas, you've succeeded in humbling me with that esoteric word. What in the world does *apophasis* mean?" Enrique asked, reflecting a smile in the tone of his voice.

"That'll teach you not to play with the elderly."

"Somehow the term *elderly* sounds unconvincing when applied to you. But please tell me what that professorial word means."

"*Apophasis* means alluding to something by denying that it will be mentioned."

"Oh, you mean like attorneys do to slide in damaging evidence not admissible in court?" Enrique asked to pause for the powerful physiological reaction the word had triggered, rather than to confirm its meaning. He felt the familiar sensation of energy swirling around him, announcing a portal flash. He didn't hear Fr. Simon when he explained that judges have no mercy for attorneys who dare to use *apophasis* in their arguments. Enrique knew he needed to give this precursor of coherence immediate audience or he would miss the portal flash. He quickly thanked Fr. Simon for his wise counsel and excused himself for ending the chat so abruptly. Enrique hung up the phone and closed his eyes to witness the rush of fractals assembling holographic wisdom: a flashing jolt that signals entrance to a portal.

His stream of consciousness entered *the drift* and he began to absorb the assembling gift: *apophasis claims the unspoken; a negation of what is; a moment in time and space when self disowns motive.* But before the epiphany exploded, a haunting memory surfaced: *Dad, I don't want you to know how much I'll miss you if you ever leave me.* Yes, it finally came to pass. Apophasis is *the epitome of misguided will.* And stigmata is the body expressing a denied intention of the mind: *a psycho-spiritual apophasis!*

Chapter 15

"Only a high priest of poetry can marry science and soul."

*D*r. Scola brought his right index finger to the side of his chin, hoping that his pensive stance would help him describe, with veneration, the Cardinal's dream.

"Signore Breogán, as I disclosed earlier, His Eminence suffers from panic attacks and night terror from the inhumane treatment he endured in the concentration camp. Although he was not physically assaulted, his captors attempted to shake his faith with unremitting psycho-political indoctrination. What struck me as odd were the recurring words he kept hearing in these nightmares. Or, I should say, the words that brought him out of the hellish nightmares into a state of engulfing serenity."

"And what were those words Dr. Scola?" Fr. Fellini interjected as if expecting a monumental ending to a painful saga: an Omega Event.

Dr. Scola exhaled and slowly uttered: "tu es Petrus."

"Oh dear God, I was afraid of something like that," Fr. Fellini said, exclaiming to himself.

Breogán and Dr. Scola looked at Fr. Fellini, waiting for some theological insight.

"I am confident you remember your Latin well enough to know the words mean 'you are Peter'. Christ told the apostle Simon that he was to be known as Petrus. Of course, Petrus comes from the Greek word 'Petra', meaning rock. Christ was commanding Simon to become the rock foundation of what became the Catholic Church. After Christ's crucifixion and resurrection, Simon, henceforth Peter, became the first Pope. Thus, the Conclave elects Popes to be successors of Peter," Fr. Fellini explained wearing exhaustion on his face.

"But why are you so troubled by the words appearing in the dream?" Breogán asked hungry for clues.

"Gentlemen, what I am about to disclose here you must take to your graves." Fr. Fellini aged before their eyes as he stipulated secrecy.

Both men obliged and waited for Fr. Fellini to continue.

"The significance of Cardinal Diaz Umap's dream will be obvious when you learn that he is one of the strongest candidates to succeed

His Holiness. Of course, the Cardinal is not aware of his status and that's what makes it so ominous."

"Forgive me Fr. Fellini, but how do you know all of this?" Dr. Scola asked, alarmed with the news about his patient.

"Besides teaching psychology, I work for the Vatican's Secretariat of State. I would not be privy to this information if His Eminence had not been afflicted with his predicament. I was instructed to inform you only if critically necessary. Given the circumstances, I decided it was imperative to tell you."

"Carlo, I am sure Dr. Scola will agree that we're honored to have your confidence and that we pledge to do our best to help His Eminence," Breogán said solemnly.

"But of course, I entirely concur with Signore Breogán's sentiments," Dr. Scola added.

The three men sat around a mahogany coffee table, and Fr. Fellini began his debriefing in a low voice.

"Not only is His Eminence the first Cardinal with the signs of stigmata, but he may become the first Hispanic Pope in the history of the Catholic Church. The papacy will never be his, however, if his affliction is not resolved. In fact, I venture to say, his laudable career will be ruined if his condition were to reach the public. As you gentlemen know, the Church does not sanction stigmata and, in this particular case, it would create insurmountable chaos due to the high office of the recipient." Fr. Fellini scanned the room to reassure himself no one else was privy to their covenant.

There was a startling knock at the door and, before it could be opened, a Swiss Guard entered the room with a grim expression.

"Dr. Scola, you must come immediately to His Eminence's quarters," the guard asserted, with alarmed authority.

Breogán and Fr. Fellini waited for Dr. Scola to grab his medical bag, and rushed with him to the Cardinal's bedroom at the end of a long hallway. The Swiss Guard let them in and stayed outside as if protecting the entrance to the Cardinal's bedroom from some unimaginable intruder. His Eminence was sitting in a chair next to his bed. His face was pale with suspended emotions, and his arms were extended palms up, gesturing for someone to confirm that blood was dripping from his wrists.

Dr. Scola checked airways, breathing and circulation: pulse was rapid and blood pressure low, indicating shock. He started the Cardinal on I.V. fluids and began to examine the wounds. The slow-bleeding wrists presented irregularly torn tissue, ruling out self-mutilation with a sharp object. Notably, the afflicted areas in the ankles were not bleeding and the redness was almost gone. With Dr. Scola's permission, Breogán inspected the wounds and found they were somewhat diamond-shaped, approximately 9 millimeters wide and 10 millimeters deep, with the sharp odor of iron unique to normal blood: no fragrance of roses there. Anticipating Breogán's request, Dr. Scola took blood samples before cleaning and bandaging the wounds. Although Cardinal Diaz Umap did not appear to be in pain, he retained the unfocused stare of shock.

While Dr. Scola and Breogán were attending to the Cardinal, Fr. Fellini stepped out of the room hoping to gain some information from the Swiss Guard.

"May I assist you, Father?" the guard offered, as he saluted the priest.

"Can you tell me what happened when His Eminence called for Dr. Scola?" Fr. Fellini inquired with the equanimity of a Scotland Yard inspector.

"At your orders Father," the guard saluted again and continued, "I heard a loud scream that justified my entrance to the room without waiting for permission."

"Of course my son, please continue," Fr. Fellini validated the guard's judgment.

"Father, when I walked into the bedroom, I saw His Eminence standing arching his head back, with his arms extended out angling at ninety degrees." The Swiss Guard was trained to report observations with meticulous objectivity, but his description left little doubt he was depicting a crucifixion stance.

"What else do you recall?" Fr. Fellini asked hoping for clues that could help them comprehend the phenomenon unfolding before their eyes.

"I heard His Eminence say something, in Spanish, that I will never forget."

"Are you fluent in Spanish?"

"Yes, Father."

Although the official language of the Swiss Guard is German, most are multilingual.

"Please tell me, if you can, what he said verbatim," Fr. Fellini asked, thankful that he too was fluent in Spanish.

"Father, although His Eminence appeared to be in great pain, he kept repeating: 'sufro por mi pueblo Señor.'"

Knowing the Swiss Guard's code of honor, Fr. Fellini thanked him for the information without concern for breach of confidentiality. In the Swiss Guard tradition, new recruits are sworn in on May sixth of every year. On that day, almost five hundred years ago, one hundred forty-seven Swiss Guards lost their lives protecting Pope Clement VII during the Sack of Rome. In the ceremony, recruits kneel placing their left hand on their flag and, raising three fingers of their right hand to symbolize the Trinity, they swear a sacred oath to protect the Pope and the Church with their own lives.

After Dr. Scola and Breogán tended to the Cardinal, they joined Fr. Fellini for a late dinner. During the meal they kept their conversation light in deference to the fatigue evident in their faces. They intuited it would be prudent to withhold the information they had gathered until a good night's rest could replenish them.

Early next morning, the men checked on Cardinal Diaz Umap, who was sitting in his favorite chair. Dr. Scola noted the wrist wounds continued to bleed in a slow flow, with no signs of infection or healing. The irritations on the ankles had disappeared, giving all small relief. Dr. Scola explained to the Cardinal that, after evaluating the findings, they would return with a full report. The men retired to an adjacent study, eager to approach the lab results like a Rosetta Stone *ready to reveal a great mystery.*

The first lab report showed nothing remarkable in the usual indices. At Breogán's request, Dr. Scola had ordered an additional test to measure blood levels of endorphins: the body's natural painkiller, more powerful than any narcotic. Surprisingly, the levels of endorphins were significantly low, considering the intense pain the Cardinal had experienced during his initial phase of the signs.

"Signore Breogán," Dr. Scola began slowly, "I am eager to hear your thoughts about the lab results. Expectedly, the blood work ordered would be normal, given that at that time the stigmata signs were not visible, but what puzzled me were the low levels of endorphins in light of the Cardinal's excruciating pain. That finding makes little medical sense."

"Dr. Scola, I believe what you are seeing is the biocultural elements of stigmata," Breogán answered, introducing how culture may shape biology. "By that I mean, the interpretation of pain, rather than the actual pain, is what determines the secretion of endorphins. Psychoneuroimmunology research is beginning to clarify the mind-body-culture connection in pain management. The expectation of how long the pain will last, the attribution given to the pain, and other contextual elements are the main determinants of how much natural anesthesia the body will release to pain receptors."

"Breogán, are you saying that, if the mind attributes the pain of stigmata to a divine or justified cause, the body would be more reluctant to relieve the suffering?"

146

"Carlo, you have a rare gift for explaining complexity." Breogán's compliment made Fr. Fellini's face shined with joy.

"Splendid, Signore Breogán, your thesis addresses why His Eminence required so much pain medication when I started treating him. If his interpretation that his pain was worthy inhibited the secretion of endorphins, then a larger dosage was needed because the mind was unwilling to relieve the body of its suffering. I am beginning to gain respect for this psychoneuro...what do you call it again?" Dr. Scola asked, with an inquiring smile.

"Psychoneuroimmunology, or PNI for short," Fr. Fellini interjected, pleased he had attended Breogán's lecture.

"Yes," Breogán added, "PNI is a multidisciplinary research area pioneered by my dear friend Dr. George F. Solomon. He coined the word psychoimmunology in the nineteen-sixties when he found that thoughts and emotions could influence immune system regulation. Although psychoimmunology was later modified to the present term of psychoneuroimmunology by Dr. Robert Ader, the scientific community owes a great debt to Dr. Solomon for his stellar contributions to mind-body medicine."

"Breogán, hearing you speak about PNI brought to mind your insistence to approach this case as a team. Now I can see why we are bringing our three different disciplines together to help His Eminence," Fr. Fellini affirmed, as he wondered how Breogán was going to proceed.

"Fr. Fellini, your words about Signore Breogán's thesis are timely, because I am also beginning to see how science and theology can cooperate to address dissonance between flesh and spirit."

"Dr. Scola, you're a poet embodied in a physician," Breogán responded, confirming how the team was reaching coherence. His old adage came to mind: only a high priest of poetry can marry science and soul.

A collective intuition brought silence to the room, marking the moment when their histories would bond to confront the suffering of a pious man. Fr. Fellini and Dr. Scola turned to Breogán cuing him to begin.

"Gentlemen," Breogán spoke with prudent confidence, "I believe we're ready to help His Eminence. Let's discuss what we've gathered so far."

Fr. Fellini related how the Swiss Guard observed Cardinal Diaz Umap in a crucifixion stance repeating softly, "Lord, I suffer for my people." Dr. Scola asked if that statement could be related to the tu es Petrus – you are Peter locution the Cardinal heard in his dream. After a brief discussion, Breogán suggested they approach Cardinal Diaz

Umap within a framework that included the theological, cultural, psychological and medical contributions to the affliction. Fr. Fellini interjected that even PNI was not comprehensive enough to encompass the colossal task ahead of them. The men agreed to follow the proposed plan of action and headed for the Cardinal's bedroom.

His Eminence was sitting by his bedside, and smiled weakly as he saw the men enter. The wrist bandages were painted with red circles from the slow but consistent bleeding. After attending to the wounds, Dr. Scola began to describe, from a medical perspective, the most concrete signs the mind had imposed on the body. "Your Eminence, we are prepared to present our findings and how we believe we need to proceed with your condition. Signore Breogán has dealt with these matters before and he will be guiding us throughout our time together. But before we discuss our views, please tell us how you are feeling?" Dr. Scola spoke with the assurance of a man who was sharing the burden of his decisions with colleagues he could trust.

Cardinal Diaz Umap took a deep breath to gather his strength. "I am still feeling considerable pain despite the medications taken, but I am hopeful that with our Lord's guidance, you gentlemen will be able to bring clarity to this ordeal." The Cardinal expressed his suffering with humbling honor, more like a wounded hero than those who use their misfortunes as currency to control others.

"Cardinal, we will ask you respectfully, very difficult questions. Did you pray for what you are experiencing?" Fr. Fellini asked with delicacy in his voice.

"Fr. Fellini, if my suffering is divinely ordained, I will accept it resolutely, but I do not believe I have consciously wished it, if that's what you are asking."

"Your Eminence, do you recall what you were doing when the Swiss Guard came to your aid?" Fr. Fellini continued with his questions.

"I remember I was in excruciating pain and I had to stand quickly to catch my breath."

"Do you recall saying anything when you were standing?" Breogán interjected.

"No, I only remember the piercing pain on both wrists. I wanted to sit for fear of passing out, but the only way I could breathe was in that standing position."

"Your Eminence, and how would you describe that position?" Dr. Scola asked, gaining awareness the team had become a cohesive instrument of inquiry. Like asking with one voice and seeing through one set of eyes to reach a truth they already suspected.

"I am not sure I understand what you are asking. I just remember standing, feeling consumed by the pain."

Breogán saw the confusion in the Cardinal's face as an opportunity to begin the interpretive phase of their work. *"Your Eminence, we realize you were in great pain, but it's important to determine if you remember saying anything while you were standing."*

"I am sorry Mr. Breogán, I have no recollection of saying anything."

"Your Eminence," Breogán was about to test the Cardinal's presumption of what transpired, *"when the Swiss Guard entered your bedroom after hearing your scream, he saw you standing with your arms spread in a crucifixion stance repeating the words: 'Lord, I suffer for my people'."*

"Oh Mr. Breogán, I have no reason to doubt the guard, but I am truly unable to confirm what he observed."

"Your Eminence, it's quite possible to have lapses of memory under intense pain. But do the words in question mean anything to you? More precisely: if you could consider that you said those words, what would they mean to you? It's very important that you search your past to find meaning." Breogán could not afford to be vague because time was running against them.

"Your Eminence," Fr. Fellini interjected adding preciseness to their inquiry, *"we believe your condition can be influenced by your personal history and beliefs. That is why Breogán asked you, so decisively, to find personal meaning. Needless to say, your comments will be held in strict confidentiality."*

Cardinal Diaz Umap's expression turned to sadness as he prepared to revisit a past he thought he had buried.

"Well, I am certainly pained by the injustices perpetrated in our increasingly godless world, but I believe you gentlemen want me to be more specific. Very well, I can honestly tell you that I have suffered deeply..." the Cardinal paused and debated an inner voice giving him permission to weep, but decided to maintain the composure expected of his position, and continued stoically, *" yes, I suffer very deeply for my people in Cuba."* He looked at the three men, with eyes asking for answers, his heart knew they could not provide.

"Your Eminence, as a physician I can tell you that I am not trained to make sense of what your body is manifesting, but I have learned from Signore Breogán and Fr. Fellini that our biology can be affected by our beliefs beyond what psychosomatic medicine would predict."

"Dr. Scola, I am ready to hear what you gentlemen have in mind." Cardinal Diaz Umap spoke with a glimpse of hope the team had not seen before.

"Thank you for your receptiveness." Dr. Scola began the presentation as planned: a multidisciplinary protocol, starting with the physical/psychological implications and moving toward the spiritual within a cultural history. He explained why sutures would not help a wound that did not heal and why it did not show infection. How endorphins were not secreting at the normal rate to relieve the pain, thus requiring more analgesics. And he expounded on how the interpretation of biological manifestations could affect immune function. Paradoxically, as scientists, the team had to entertain all causes, including the possibility of divine intervention: to consider scientifically an event beyond the scope of science. But Breogán had pointed out that, although we cannot measure spirit, we can record biological activity during spiritual experiences.

Cardinal Diaz Umap listened with a dissecting ear that had to reconcile physical proof before permitting it to enter his ecclesiastic reality. His apprehension turned to inquisitiveness, letting the team know they were dealing with a man who could harmonize religion with empirical evidence: the qualities of a true theologian. Breogán wondered how much suffering Copernicus and Galileo could have been spared if the Church had relied on men like Diaz Umap in those dark days. But even the Holy See has a right to be judged without revisionist historians.

"Your Eminence, we believe the locution 'tu es Petrus' that you heard in your dream and your statement 'Lord, I suffer for my people' are interconnected. But more importantly, they bring contextual meaning to your ordeal," Fr. Fellini explained, building the paradigm for Breogán's psycho-spiritual intervention.

Taking Fr. Fellini's lead, Breogán presented his observations: The locution in the dream told Cardinal Diaz Umap he was Peter – the rock. Later, while in shock, the cardinal's own words revealed the source of his suffering. He was the foundation and similar to the arcane sin eaters, *who absorbed the transgressions of dying men; he wore the suffering of his people on his wounds of Christ.*

After a valiant attempt to assimilate the biocultural interpretation Breogán offered, Cardinal Diaz Umap was ready to engage the team with a new perspective. He addressed Dr. Scola first.

"I must admit that, just like you lack medical reference to ground what is happening to me, I am not able to draw from my theological studies as well. The Church does not take a position on the cause of stigmata and medical science cannot explain it. If it is not divinely bestowed, and if I did not inflict the wounds, then what are we to conclude?" Cardinal Diaz Umap scanned the men's expressions,

knowing each could only offer part of the solution to a multidimensional puzzle. Then, moving through the conundrum without waiting for answers he was not ready to hear, he responded to Breogán.

"I can tell you that while I was in the concentration camp, euphemistically known as a 'production support center', the locutions in my dreams gave me strength to endure my internment. And I did not see them as anything more than solace at the time. But I dread asking a question that keeps haunting me."

The three men leaned forward in unison to hear the unexpected.

"We have not discussed the worst scenario, if I may use that modern vernacular to describe a calamitous possibility: what if my affliction was caused by the Evil One?" The Cardinal's words brought a somber cadence to the hearts of all present. Breogán and Dr. Scola turned to Fr. Fellini, confirming in silence that they were entering the province of a spiritual director.

"Your Eminence," Fr. Fellini spoke with a pained expression, "as much as we tried to avoid that scenario, as you called it, the theological component of our approach must include all possibilities within your religious beliefs. Breogán taught us that our biology responds to the totality of our personal reality. I am certain you realize how our differing fields of expertise must converge to grasp the complexities of your affliction."

"Yes, I am beginning to see what you are trying to do as my spiritual director."

"Fortunately, we can draw from the wisdom of St. Teresa of Avila to answer the alarming question you posed. Although she did not allude to stigmata in her writings, she offered a test to rule out locutions from a source of evil," Fr. Fellini explained with confidence.

"I can assure you gentlemen that I revere our blessed St. Teresa, although I am not as well versed in her mystical theology," the Cardinal responded, appreciating the combined insight the men were offering.

"I believe her wisdom will be a blessing in this matter. Let's begin with the content of the locution. Would you describe the words you heard as a statement or a command?" Fr. Fellini was presenting St. Teresa's requirements in order of importance: the locution must convey a sense of power and authority.

"The words were commanding in the most unusual combination of tenderness and strength. They gave me great comfort." The Cardinal responded without hesitation.

Fr. Fellini suppressed a smile of approval to avoid biasing the responses. The Cardinal's answer was better than expected. It passed the first and second test at once when, in addition to possessing strength, the words gave him tranquility. Now Fr. Fellini was ready for the third and last test: how enduring are the words in memory? He had to ask without influencing the response.

"Your Eminence, are you certain the words you heard are indeed 'tu es Petrus'?"

"I have no doubt."

"And what makes you feel so sure about what you remember? You first heard those words years ago, years possibly diminishing the accuracy of your memories." Fr. Fellini felt he had to create doubt in order to gain a reliable answer. His line of questioning made him wonder how frightening it must have been for some suspected Satanists, who were tortured into confessing what the Inquisitors wanted to hear. Fr. Fellini was brought back from his medieval musing by Cardinal Diaz Umap's precise answer.

"Few days go by without me thinking about those words. They continue to bring me comfort and hope that there is some divine purpose for my people's suffering."

"Your Eminence, I am pleased to inform you that, according to St. Teresa's directives, the locution from your dream is not tainted by the Evil One. Your answers ruled out what we were dreading. The words met the criteria for exuding strength, bringing tranquility and persisting in memory," Fr. Fellini said, with a hint of triumph in his voice.

"Thank the Lord for His benevolence and for the brilliance of you gentlemen." Cardinal Diaz Umap smiled as the heaviness of dark energy lifted from his weary soul.

"As your physician, I can tell you that it is common to have lapses of memory during a state of shock. Not remembering your statement about suffering for your people is due to what we call retrograde amnesia: similar to being under anesthesia," Dr. Scola clarified while he pulled two folded pieces of paper from his coat pocket. "We have the results of the second blood samples and, rather than give you a conventional medical interpretation, I will let Signore Breogán explain it in the mind-body context we are presenting."

Breogán scanned the lab results one more time before proceeding: the alarmingly high levels of cortisol found reflected the intensity of the stressful condition. Endorphin levels were lower than expected, considering the excruciating pain. Neutrophils were high to fight infection, although the usual inflammation that surrounds a wound to contain the damaging intruders was not present. And the interleukins responsible for signaling wound healing were significantly lower than expected in normal tissue repair.

It was up to Breogán to take the biochemical evidence and make mind-body sense within Cardinal Diaz Umap's cultural history. These incongruous findings, where biology suspends its internal logic in deference to biocultural beliefs, kept surfacing in Breogán's investigations of psycho-spiritual phenomena. And in cases like the Cardinal's, there was a recurring stigmata profile. *Breogán cleared his throat and began to speak in a soft tone to promote a calming mood.*

"Your Eminence, the information I am about to share with you is at the edge of science. We know that our biological regulators are affected by the context and strength of our beliefs. But sometimes, physical manifestations seem unrelated to our thoughts because their connection does not reach our awareness. In the case of your wounds, we have ruled out self-mutilation and a malevolent source. Since we're not able to entertain divine intervention, the only other option left is what I call the 'stigmata profile'. Breogán paused to allow Cardinal Diaz Umap time to assimilate the reality shock he was being dealt.

"Mr. Breogán, at this point I am open to any explanation you gentlemen have to offer," The Cardinal responded with an expression that wavered between resignation and hope.

"Good. The lab report shows that your body is protecting the wounds from infection, while refusing to initiate healing. There are medical conditions that can delay or prevent healing, but the configuration of your lab results does not fit any known pathology. Let me explain: something is not allowing your wounds to heal and your pain to subside. And we suggest that this 'something' is a belief that you should suffer for your people, as Christ did for us. But you must understand that this can occur without your conscious permission."

"Does that mean that I am giving my body permission to wound me without my awareness?"

Breogán knew that question would come up inevitably. He had heard it before in other cases, and he understood that at that moment, candor had to replace diplomacy.

"From all we can gather so far, the answer is yes. And our job is to help you resolve whatever cognitive dissonance created the command to wound you without reprieve."

The Cardinal was pensive for a moment and then smiled; hinting he was ready to collaborate with the team, to expose that part of him that was unwittingly tormenting him. The smile remained as he responded to the challenge. "Can I conclude from what you are saying that, if my mind commanded my body to cause a physical disturbance, I can also command the disturbance to cease?"

Fr. Fellini stood up from his chair thrilled to respond. "Cardinal, your brilliance is going to make my job a spiritual delight!" The comically quixotic stance he took as he spoke brought much needed laughter to all.

"Fr. Fellini, you're a most stirring spiritual director," Cardinal Diaz Umap praised him with the strength of hope and the tenderness of gratitude.

"Your Eminence, I have done little to earn your kind words, but I am gratified by your encouragement." Fr. Fellini knew it was his turn to intervene, and took on the challenge with renewed energy. "Cardinal, may I speak freely?"

"Please do, my son."

"To begin my humble spiritual contribution to Breogán's stigmata protocol, I submit that when the inner force of will is propelled by love, it offers compassion to the body and joy to the soul. But if that inner force is fueled by guilt, the body can only find suffering, compelling the soul to approach God with dread." Breogán and Dr. Scola nodded in consensus.

"Then what is loving God through suffering?" The Cardinal asked with genuine concern. His theological training had never confronted the apostolic model of suffering, still prevailing in contemporary ecclesiastic teachings.

"Your Eminence, with all due respect, we propose that suffering, as an expression of love for our Lord, is a form of denied joy." Fr. Fellini spoke confidently, knowing that Breogán and Dr. Scola shared his view. Although the authors of this bold statement would have burned at the stake for heresy during the times of St. Francis of Assisi, over three hundred and fifty cases of stigmata and seven hundred and eighty years later, this heresy had to be chanced to reverse the wounds. It was clear to the group that when cultural history interacts with the evolution of consciousness, the unspeakable can find a forum to transform presumed evil into benevolent healing.

"How can it be denied joy, if the love is felt so profoundly?" The Cardinal retorted, knowing he had to examine the foundation of his faith.

"Because suffering misguides the intention of love," Breogán interjected quickly to affirm the theoretical solidarity of the team.

"Cardinal," Fr. Fellini continued with the contentious theme, gratefully aware his superior had a flexible mind, "if God is pure love and the greatest joy is the love of God, then loving Him through self-imposed suffering misses the mark. To honor the pain Christ endured for us, we must clarify that He suffered to absolve our transgressions, rather than perpetuate our misery. We were invited to evolve from disciples of pain to recipients of joy."

"So you contend the pain I am experiencing from these wounds is denied joy?"

"Your Eminence, are you familiar with the term survivor's guilt?*"* Fr. Fellini asked, without addressing the Cardinal's question.

"No, I can't say that I am."

"I think what Breogán has to say about this subject will be very relevant here," Fr. Fellini suggested with uncanny sense of timing.

The three men understood that, to solve the Cardinal's mind-body riddle, the protocol required introducing perspectives from their diverse disciplines at the most opportune moments. And one of those vital moments had just arrived. The team was crafting a reality where a noble belief that was unwittingly punishing the body could evolve to a higher level of consciousness and reverse the imposed penance.

Breogán stood and spoke with delicate emphasis. "Survivor's guilt is a prime example of how a righteous thought can misguide emotions. When we lose someone we love to an unexpected death, we have a tendency to feel a type of guilt that comes from asking: 'why not me instead?' It happens when a soldier loses a compatriot in battle or when a parent experiences the death of a child. The death of a soldier is sudden, whereas the death of a child happens out of the natural order of life. Both circumstances disrupt our sense of existential timing, and we react with survivor's guilt to question our place in the universal design. It is one of those supreme moments when we are one with our noble symbols: willing to make the lives of those we love more precious than living without them."

"Mr. Breogán, what you say is compelling because it speaks to my heart, but please explain how survivor's guilt applies to me?"

"Your Eminence, we believe that in the case of stigmata, there is a unique expression of survivor's guilt. The guilt is felt for the suffering, rather than for the death of those we love. But instead of asking 'why not my death instead of theirs, the question becomes 'will my suffering end theirs?' Both conditions are grounded on displaced nobleness, as if atonement could negotiate death and suffering through quid pro quo." Breogán was helping orchestrate a double bind where the only viable psycho-spiritual resolution was for the mind to rescind the misguided order it had given the heart.

"Your Eminence, I want to bring up a medical observation that might help us understand the mind-body implications we are confronting here," Dr. Scola offered, hoping his contribution would open a new line of inquiry. "Do you recall how the red spots on your ankles disappeared?"

"Yes I do. In fact, I was thinking about it this morning wondering if it had any significance."

"I was also pondering their possible implication, and I can tell you that symbolic dermatitis is not uncommon. When a child has been physically abused, the abrasions can reappear years later under hypnosis or highly stressful conditions. And now, I am thinking a loud: could a vicariously traumatic memory have the same power to affect tissue?"

Breogán and Fr. Fellini looked at each other wondering where Dr. Scola was going with his line of thinking. But they had come to trust each other implicitly, and waited, anticipating a breakthrough.

Dr. Scola continued sharing thoughts as they surfaced in his consciousness. "I have a suspicion that if cell memory is capable of storing a traumatic event for future expression, it may also archive the observation of someone else's trauma, with similar consequences."

"Well, if your hypothesis is correct, let me ask His Eminence a question," Breogán stood up and placed his hand on Dr. Scola's shoulder to show his gratitude for the new perspective, before continuing, "have you ever seen anyone with abrasions on the ankles?"

"No, I don't think so," Cardinal Diaz Umap responded hesitantly.

"Do you recall anyone you loved who had ankle abrasions or sores?" Dr. Scola added, with emphasis on the word 'loved.'"

The Cardinal frowned, forcing his memory to produce relevance, until it suddenly delivered abruptly. His eyes swelled with tears, and he covered his face with cupped hands to contain the emotional avalanche.

"Dear friends, I am beginning to see how our minds can disguise our sorrow," the Cardinal cleared his throat hoping it would return strength to his voice, "I distinctly remember now, one of our elderly parish priests suffered from diabetes, and how we were unable to control his illness due to lack of medicines. He bruised easily and developed sores on his ankles from wearing sandals made of old tires. His doctor warned him about the consequences of his wounds not healing, but he kept doing God's work, walking for miles all over Havana, ministering to the needy without ever complaining.

"One morning, when he failed to show up for breakfast, I went to his room looking for him and found him on his bed in a coma. Now I remember so vividly kneeling by his feet and, after praying for him, looking up when the ambulance arrived, and noticing the sores on his ankles. At that moment, I was very angry with God. And now that I know about survivor's guilt, I recall that, at that moment, I wished

God had given me the suffering of that noble man." Cardinal Diaz Umap closed his eyes, fatigued from reliving the sorrow of his past.

"Your Eminence, please let us know if we are moving too fast. We can only imagine how difficult this ordeal must be for you," Breogán offered with empathy.

"Thank you for your concern, but I am ready to continue. I do want to pose a question, or perhaps expose my great dilemma. Our Church was built on the suffering of martyrs. St. Peter taught us to rejoice when we participate in the suffering of Christ. And St. Paul said 'now I rejoice in my suffering'. But I am also aware that St. Paul cautioned we should balance our suffering with our joy. Then how does my mind-body state, as you gentlemen call it, reconcile the painful stigmata I am experiencing with the joy I feel for serving our Lord?"

Cardinal Diaz Umap had reached what Breogán viewed as the crossroad of the mind-body-spirit conflict. He had discussed this critical junction with Dr. Scola and Fr. Fellini, and they were ready to help the Cardinal decide his fate. The crossroad was the critical moment when the afflicted either relinquished their penance, or carried it as disciples of pain for the rest of their lives.

Fr. Fellini knew that words have transforming power when heard by those who trust the speaker. He honored the magnitude of his task and addressed the Cardinal with Church formality. "Alonzo Cardinal Diaz Umap, we have reached a critical moment. The question you pose is critical, because its answer must provide spiritual harmony before your mind can release the burden it has imposed on your body.

"It is true that suffering was essential to build our Church. Christianity had to be defended at any cost. And many of our martyrs certainly paid the ultimate price with their lives. In the early days, to suffer and die for the Church was more than a symbol. It was a way of life.

"That era of apostolic suffering served us well for two thousand years. But like any body of knowledge, dogma must face the new challenges of our evolving consciousness. And we respectfully submit to you that the advancement of our Church depends on our willingness to relinquish agony as a measure of faith. Rather than identifying with Christ through self-imposed suffering, we can begin to emulate His joy and honor His pain for the atonement it was meant to serve." Fr. Fellini looked at the medieval crucifix on the wall, before continuing with his confrontational thesis.

"Your Eminence, in the Apostolic Era, suffering was a consequence of action taken to save the Church. It had a vital function. But punishing our bodies to commiserate with the suffering of others has no corrective purpose and perpetuates misery. If we could reverse your

stigmata, it would be an act of expiation. We would be colluding with ascending love." Fr. *Fellini waited for a reaction from the theologian he was inviting to redefine penitence.*

Cardinal Diaz Umap nodded with a troubled expression, as if debating jumping off a burning building to save his life. "Gentlemen, if we follow your line of thinking, we have sanctioned apostolic suffering beyond its intended function. And if we accept that the Church must progress through joy, perhaps the literal meaning of the word 'gospel' could symbolize the next stage of development."

Breogán glanced at Fr. Fellini and Dr. Scola, confirming the beginning of the last stage of their work. Cardinal Diaz Umap was now ready to enter an uncharted personal space where entrenched beliefs are confronted with intellectual honesty. Not unlike the time when it was no longer tenable for the Church to defend geocentricism, after Galileo proved the earth revolves around the sun.

"Cardinal, your point is well taken. The word 'gospel' translated from the Greek 'euangelos' does mean to bring good news. Your suggestion to embrace its essence, would shift our focus from penitence to celebration." Breogán felt the weight of the responsibility he had accepted, as he listened to his own words.

"Well, gentlemen, I am prepared to celebrate the good news and, if it's the will of our Lord, I am also ready to relinquish the punishment my body has endured. What do you propose?"

Breogán knew it was time to confront his greatest fear. Could he help the Cardinal after convincing him to change his interpretation of suffering? As he gathered his thoughts, the words of his Tibetan mentor came to mind: 'it is easier to cure disease than to give up the consciousness that permits it to exist.'

"Let's see where our scientific training and our faith will take us." Breogán always tested his intellectual limits when it came to his work. Now, he was ready to challenge his own faith. "Cardinal, you've seen how our biology can follow our beliefs. How you manifested the sores on your ankles in solidarity with the pain of your beloved priest. And how you're carrying the ultimate symbol of suffering with the stigmata on your wrists. Do you recall when your ankle sores disappeared?"

"Yes, I do, and I was hoping you could explain why the ankles and not the wrists as well?"

"Indeed. I've also wondered how our mind-body communication could be so selective in damaging and repairing tissue," Dr. Scola added, as he turned to Breogán for an answer.

"It's fascinating to consider how the mind can wound and heal the body so precisely," Breogán marveled, "and this pathway that the

mind uses to transform thought into biology is what we need to access in order to reverse the damage. Obviously the process is not conscious, but it is symbolic and culture-specific. Let me explain what I mean. Consistent with the medieval crucifixion paintings, old stigmatics had their wounds on their palms, whereas the contemporary stigmatics, with knowledge of modern archeological evidence, have their wounds on their wrists. The locution in your dream about Peter was in the Latin you studied in seminary school, so you heard Petrus, *instead of his original Aramaic name,* Kepha. *And over ninety-percent of stigmatic cases have been Roman Catholics, rather than randomly occurring independent of religious denomination.*

"Cardinal, you are a modern theologian, fluent in Latin, and a prince of the Roman Catholic Church. Your beliefs were shaped by your cultural history, and their symbolic expression is an evolving process amenable to change. That change can only take place, however, in the symbolic space where mind and body resonate with spirit."

"And what can I do to find that place where my mind is misguiding my intentions?" Cardinal Diaz Umap asked Breogán, but intuitively looked at Fr. Fellini for an answer. The theologian was appealing to his spiritual director.

Fr. Fellini stood from his comfortable chair, as he frequently did when he had something significant to say. The teacher in him preferred to think on his feet and pace. He remembered telling his students how movement could break stagnant thinking. Now, he paced, searching for a tool to end the symbolic purgatory the Cardinal's mind had conjured.

"Your Eminence, the Prayer of Quiet is our answer." Fr. Fellini noticed the conviction in his suggestion was not coming from experience. He was voicing an intuition that leaped to action, commanded by faith.

"Carlo, St. Teresa's Prayer of Quiet is an excellent idea," Breogán affirmed Fr. Fellini's timely contribution. He could not recall discussing that powerful contemplative method with either Fr. Fellini or Dr. Scola.

"Thank you Breogán, but although the idea came spontaneously, I know very little about the practice. In fact, I have a very odd feeling about what I've just done."

"My friends, I believe there's a cogent explanation for Carlo's suggestion. The four of us have engaged a field of vital information to achieve a worthy objective. The strength of our intention, created a mind-body coherence that gave us access to our collective wisdom. Although Carlo proposed the Prayer of Quiet without experiential reference, I have practiced that method for years. Yet, the idea did not

reach relevance until he brought it to our collective consciousness. We coauthored the rightness of the moment with our shared intentions." Breogán knew they had found a pathway to the wounding mind.

Chapter 16

"The drift was a matrix of fine lines..."

nrique had been writing for two solid weeks without much rest. He could not remember the last time he had worked as hard and as isolated from the people he loved. Yet, his self-imposed solitude brought him appreciation for his creativity and gratitude for those who respected his priorities. His body needed rest, but his mind was ready to discover the secrets of stigmata in the surreal world he had crafted with Breogán. A steaming bath refreshed his fatigue and, after barely drying his body, he jumped into bed for a deep surrendering sleep.

The *Penny Lane* door chimes ended his twelve-hour rest. He hit the tip of his pyramid clock, and the synthesized voice with the Japanese accent told him it was 6 pm.

He rose in slow motion and put on his black bathrobe to answer the door. It was Máximo.

"Enriquito, were you asleep? We did agree to 6 pm, right?"

"Hi Máximo, I completely forgot about our meeting. I am so sorry."

Máximo had invited Enrique to meet Jude Fouché. Máximo and Claudia visited the Voodoo priest on several occasions and had befriended him. Fouché expressed an interest in meeting Enrique, after learning he was an anthropologist. That evening, Máximo and Enrique were to meet with Fouché at his home for a gentlemen's chat.

"Not to worry my boy, there's plenty of time. We can dine at one of the restaurants on *calle ocho* and meet Fouché at 8:30 pm. You'll be pleased to know that he shares our taste in *Larios* and fine Cuban cigars."

"*Larios* brandy?" Enrique asked, pleasantly surprised.

"Yes indeed. Now, go get dressed and lets hit the road. If we're late, Fouché may cast a spell on our virility, and then what are we to do?" Máximo was in a playful mood and Enrique loved it.

"I'll hurry because we can't let that happen. We must uphold our Latin lover image." Enrique was thankful to have Máximo in his life, and rushed like a schoolboy trying to please his father.

"Enriquito, why don't you drive my Cayenne so you can experience a family man's Porsche?" Máximo suggested, as they walked out of the house.

"So now you're a family man?"

"Well, Claudia and I will be a family soon, and who knows, we may want children in the future."

Enrique went along with the games Máximo played to remain young. Máximo believed the aging process was determined by cultural agreements about how a person's biology should respond to the passing of time. But he cautioned that his strategies to fight aging would only work if beliefs were consistent with life styles, and if one could acquire a healthy disrespect for the cultural invitations to live in fear. No one could contradict Máximo's theory, considering the energy, enthusiasm and youthful demeanor he exhibited at seventy-three.

"In that case, I accept the invitation to drive your *family car*," savoring the moment, Enrique answered with feigned resignation. "But if I drive your beloved Cayenne, will you let me choose where we eat?"

"Enriquito, you ask too much. I admit you have excellent taste in restaurants, but you lack my gift to discover *calle ocho's* culinary secrets."

"You found another treasure on *calle ocho*? That's impossible. Kate and I have tried them all."

"I beg to differ, Dr. Enriquito."

Both men laughed and accepted the joyful possibilities that exist when friends celebrate the moment. Máximo had taught Enrique *the drift* was a matrix of fine lines that divided the mundane from the exquisite, and heaven from hell.

"Then tell me where I need to drive us tonight."

"Go to *calle ocho* and Sixteenth Avenue, and you will be pleasantly surprised." Máximo accented the instructions with his distinctive wink.

Enrique drove up to the corner Máximo had suggested and stopped in front of *Casa Panza*: A Cuban fusion restaurant considered one of *calle ocho's* crown jewels.

"Well, what do you think Enriquito?"

"I am sorry to disappoint you, but Kate introduced me to this place a couple of weeks ago."

"Where is your faith my boy? Let's see what unfolds." Máximo's second wink and head tilt meant he was up to something special.

They walked to the front of the restaurant, and were met by a portly man in his sixties who seemed to be expecting Máximo.

"*Saludos Máximo. Que hay de nuevo?*" The man greeted Máximo with a Spanish *abrazo*.

"*Hola Luis*. I want you to meet my dear friend Enrique Lugo. By the way, is Doña Josefa ready for us?"

"Oh yes, she knows you're coming. Follow me." Luis guided the two men through a small patio in back of *Casa Panza*, leading to a charming two-story Mediterranean home. Máximo kept looking at Enrique and smiling like a naughty boy ready to reveal a secret.

Doña Josefa's husband greeted them at the door and the *abrazo* ritual started again as Máximo introduced Enrique to Don Fernando.

"Welcome *señores*. Josefa and I are honored with your presence. Máximo, you don't age. What's your secret?"

"Fernando, you know damn well my secret is to never tell my age."

They all laughed, lifting the mood for the evening. Máximo and Enrique were shown to a charming dining room with an elegant table set for three. Fernando opened a bottle of *Taitinger* from a chilling bucket and poured with impressive dexterity.

"Señores, welcome to our home. As Máximo can attest, our concept is one of Miami's best-kept secrets, and we prefer it that way. My wife and I serve a select group of customers affectionately known as *Los Cincuenta Bacanes*. These fifty *bon vivants* and their guests are the only patrons we care to have. No more, no less. Please enjoy the evening." Fernando left the room ceremoniously, giving Máximo time to explain.

"Máximo, you never cease to amaze me. How long have you been a part of these fortunate fifty?" Enrique admired the way his friend celebrated life.

"I became number thirty-eight, when I was invited to join four years ago."

"Máximo, what a marvelous idea! But how do they make money with so few customers?"

"Fernando and Josefa are quite wealthy and love what they do. They're also astute entrepreneurs. Each member pays a hefty yearly fee to dine as many times as reservations can accommodate. They only serve one member and up to three guests per evening. Fernando told me they net around $300,000 per year. Abundance means to be rewarded for playing. Not bad for doing what you love."

"Not bad at all. Speaking of guests, I noticed our table is set for three. Is that by design?"

"Enriquito, let's say it was *the drift*'s design." Máximo sat back and smiled.

"All right, I'm game. What are you up to?"

"The sequence of tonight's events is a classical example of the synchronicity we have come to appreciate. Initially, I made plans for us to meet Fouché at his home after dinner. At that time, Fernando had already booked a party for tonight, so I asked him to put us on a waiting list. Then last night, Fernando told me the other guests cancelled, so I took their reservation for tonight. But while you were getting dressed to come here, Fouché called me to reschedule our meeting because of a power failure in his neighborhood. I saw that event as a sign of *the drift*, and invited him to join us for dinner instead."

"Did he accept?"

"He did with pleasure, and will be joining us in a few minutes. But the most telling part is that Fernando assumed we were a party of three and set the table accordingly."

"Máximo, when it comes to you, the synchronism of this evening seems like the most natural thing."

"I agree. I constantly impress myself." A burst of laughter from both men coincided with Fouché's entrance to the dining room.

"My friends, how auspicious to walk into your joy. Ah, you must be Dr. Lugo. A pleasure to meet you sir." Fouché shook hands and apologized for arriving a few minutes late.

"Mr. Fouché, thank you for joining us for dinner. Máximo speaks very highly of you." Enrique took an instant liking to the man. He saw a tender elegance rarely found in powerful men. It was clear Fouché understood the nuances of prudence and the essence of his journey.

"You're both most gracious. Máximo, I am an aficionado of Cuban restaurants, but I was not aware this place existed."

As Máximo explained the concept of *Los Cincuenta Bacanes,* Don Fernando returned to pour the *Taitinger* for Fouché, and refill the other two glasses.

"*Señores,* allow me to explain our menu. We offer game, beef or sea fare, and two light courses of Cuban fusion prepared to compliment your choice of entrée," Fernando explained with his eyes closed in ecstasy, from merely imagining the delicacies that awaited his customers. "If you will permit me, I would be honored to suggest the wines for the evening. Knowing Máximo's taste, my selections would include some of the best Galician wines."

"My friends, you're in excellent hands with Fernando: rack of lamb for me," Máximo ordered.

"I'll have the pink abalone." Enrique selected one of the house specialties.

"Fouché, I can tell you there is no better rack of lamb than Doña Josefa's," Máximo suggested, with a wink.

"In that case, rack of lamb it is." Fouché decided.

"Excellent. I will convey your compliments to my wife, Josefa."

"Fouché, Enriquito and I are very fond of Galician wines. I hope we didn't impose on your taste."

"Máximo, although I have not had the pleasure of visiting your lovely Galicia, I am looking forward to her wines. Being a fan of *Larios* does predispose one to delight in the finer exports of Spain, yes? "

"I agree Mr. Fouché." Enrique lifted his glass inviting a toast.

Subdued lighting and fine Persian rugs punctuated the erudite mood the room had taken. Wisdom and levity were their dining companions. The first course included *tapas de morzillas, queso cabrales* and *calamares al ajillo,* with a sprinkle of Iberian herbs to awaken the palate and stimulate the mind. Fernando accentuated the *tapas* with a bottle of *Terras Gauda* 1998 that confirmed how wines could transform sustenance for mortals to ambrosias for gods. Enrique was jolted: that particular wine and vintage was what Sabela ordered for their first course when she and Breogán met Galician folksinger Paulo Zas! The night was a tribute to *the drift.*

Enrique was ready for dialogue. He marveled at how writing *The Man from Autumn* was like birthing an oracle for his life. He wished Breogán could join them.

"Mr. Fouché, after Máximo told me about your work, I looked forward to meeting you and hearing about your rich culture and its rituals."

"Dr. Lugo, you are too kind. It is I, who look forward to learning from you. Admittedly, I am a frustrated anthropologist at heart. And tonight, I can ask a true professional questions that have intrigued me for years."

"Fouché, I can attest, Enriquito is one of the best in his field," Máximo interjected, at the expense of embarrassing his protégé.

"Mr. Fouché, let me ask you a question before I let these undeserved kudos go to my head. I understand you worked with *bokor* black magic, before practicing the healing force of the good *loa.* What made you shift so drastically?"

"That's a grand question, and I appreciate your knowledge of our lexicon." Before answering, Fouché frowned and puckered his lips, as if expecting a kiss of clarity from some imagined Voodoo goddess. "One late night, a woman came to my home in Haiti, carrying her dying little girl. She thought I worked in the healing dimension, and asked me to reverse a spell cast by my strongest rival. The child was burning with fever, and when I saw her gasping for air, I remembered a disturbing dream I had the previous night, compelling me to serve the immaculate light. That's when I decided to help the child. From then on, my life changed for the best." Fouché relaxed his facial expression and smiled.

"And what did you do to help the little girl?" Máximo asked, anticipating Enrique's interest in the cultural aspects of Voodoo healings.

Fouché considered the question with the discretion of a magician about to divulge his trade secrets. "Although Voodoo curing relies mainly on medicinal herbs and faith healing, we are slowly incorporating Western medicine to our practice. There are some clinics in Haiti where Voodoo priests and medical doctors work together to treat illnesses related to malevolent curses. Unlike your Christian angels and demons, we have spirits that embody both positive and negative forces, relatively independent of God."

"I understand some of the hexes include poisonous potions and powders that can make the victim very ill, or even die. What can you tell us about that?" Enrique asked, hoping Fouché would not be offended by the directness of his question.

"Yes, you are correct. In addition to taking hair or personal belongings from the victim to initiate the malevolent action, the hexes can include toxic concoctions. But let me tell you what I did to help the little girl. There was no time to assemble the ceremonial drummers and other rituals, so I had to perform the healing by myself. Fortunately, I knew how to look for signs of poisoning and damage done by evil spirits. I lit several Voodoo lamps to burn an antidote powder. When the room was filled with smoke, I lifted the child over my head, so she could breathe the concentrated air. She started to cough, and slowly began to breathe normally again. The toxic elements were neutralized. But I still had to deal with the spiritual aspect of the hex." Fouché stopped in time for Fernando to serve their second course. The pause brought them back to the next culinary surprise. The three men picked up their glasses of wine and drank in unison, confirming the cohesiveness they had created. Enrique felt the connection, and smiled at Máximo, who in turn nodded to Fouché.

"Men, our spiritual guardians are in harmony tonight. *Bon appetit,*" Fouché stated, without explaining himself.

"Here, here, Fouché! I am delighted we're meeting tonight. Both Enriquito and I are intrigued by your work."

"I confer with Máximo. Your work is of great interest to me." Enrique looked at their plates to see what Fernando had chosen for the second course. Fouché and Máximo were served grilled hearts of Romaine with grated *Manchego* cheese *mojito*: a Cuban fusion of Caesar's dressing. And Enrique was offered slithers of cucumbers and capers over smoked herring, sprinkled with balsamic vinegar. Fernando also excelled with his choice of wine: *Conde de Albarei* 1997 from the *Rias Baixas* region of Galicia. Made from the *Albariño* grape aged in oak, this elegant white wine had the intense citrus fruit and the racy acidity that harmonized with the pronounced flavors of both dishes.

"Máximo, we're witnessing the selections of a master," Fouché commented, as Fernando stood by showcasing the bottle of wine like the father of a newborn.

"Yes indeed. He makes me proud," Máximo added, while patting Fernando's arm.

"*Señores*, you spoil me. But Josefa's cooking is what makes our establishment unique," Fernando responded and walked away smiling, with equal measures of embarrassment and pride.

Fouché leaned forward to speak in a conspiratorial whisper. "I have not had the pleasure of meeting *Doña* Josefa, but if I were married to her, I can assure you, I would be morbidly obese." Fouché's expression of mischievous delight ignited roaring laughter and a spontaneous toast.

"Mr. Fouché, as you were explaining your remedy for the poisoned child, I wondered if the effects of the curse were limited to the toxic substance. How did you determine if spiritual forces were involved as well?" Enrique's question returned the attention to the candid discussion that was bonding them.

"I think that is a key consideration in my work. I detected several signs. The child was six years old and, in her delirium, she kept calling her grandmother's name, although she had never met her. The grandmother had passed on before the child was born. That information, along with the dirt the mother found on her doorsteps, led me to conclude evil spiritual forces were involved.

"Why would the spirit of the grandmother want to harm her granddaughter?" Máximo asked.

"Please forgive me for getting ahead of myself without explaining. When a lump of dirt is found at the entrance of a home, it means it came from a graveyard to signal the location where the evil spirit is doing harm. But the child uttering her grandmother's name without having known her meant that the departed relative wanted to help from the other side. You see, we can summon good *loas,* or the spirits of relatives who have passed on, to help us with the healing. The grandmother's spirit guided me through the rituals to discharge the malevolent forces that possessed the child. Fortunately, her grandmother had been a powerful *mambo* and could stand up to the culprit spirit. To this day, she continues to brings me wisdom for having saved her grandchild."

"Mr. Fouché, you mentioned your rival cast the hex. How did you know? Did the mother tell you?" Enrique asked, one of many questions churning, in his anthropologist's mind.

"Men, we are drinking a fine wine. *Viva España.*" Fouché was softening his forthcoming answer with praise for his hosts. "Let's say that his signature was evident all over the curse. But most interestingly, he met a violent death two days later."

"What happened to the son of a bitch?" Máximo asked, looking for retribution.

"The fellow slipped and impaled himself through the chest, while climbing a cemetery fence." Fouché had a most unusual look as he explained. His facial expression depicted poetic justice, sharing space with the triumph of good over evil.

"Any evidence of foul play?" Enrique winced as he asked.

"Yes, there was foul play. He played with the wrong spirits."

"Well said, Fouché." Máximo's head-tilt and wink brought the comic relief needed to welcome Fernando's red wine selection for the main course.

"*Señores*, at this moment, I will be at your mercy if I fail to please you. I must admit, finding the proper wine that could dance with pink abalone and rack of lamb was a serious challenge, but thanks to the grapes of Spain, I may be able to satisfy your palate."

"Fernando, you have never failed me. We're ready for your wisdom to come forth." Máximo spoke with deliberate drama.

"Señores, this wine is Spain's answer to *Chateau Latour*." Fernando ceremoniously presented a bottle of *Vega Sicilia Unico* 1987.

"My friend, you're absolutely right. But I should have known you were up to no good when you said the grapes were from Spain, rather than from the province of Galicia. But we must admit that although Galicia has outstanding whites, regrettably, we are not up to par with your supreme choice of red from Valladolid," Máximo responded in jest, vindicating Fernando's audacity to choose a wine from Galicia's neighboring province.

"Máximo, the *Vega Sicilia* is a sweet surrender," Enrique offered.

"Yes my boy, you're right. But I had to pretend disappointment to humor Fernando. He knows I am impressed with his choice."

"Men, in that case I will be forced to drink a wine that has been compared to a *Latour*," Fouché added to the charade.

A server brought the main course, as Fernando opened the wine that would waltz with pink abalone and rack of lamb.

"Life is good when fine food and wine can be enjoyed with old and new friends," Máximo added, while pointing his glass in a gentle sequence toward Enrique, Fernando, and Fouché.

Savoring the main course took precedence over discourse, inducing a silence chefs often dream about. Guava soufflé was the dessert, and Cuban espresso the closure to their gustatory trance. The assisting waiter cleared the table, and Fernando served warmed snifters of *Larios,* signaling the men it was time to light their *Cohibas.*

"I will say, when it comes to cigars, nothing beats a *Cohiba*," Fouché commented.

"Mr. Fouché, listening to your story about the little girl, reminded me of a subject I wanted to discuss. Are you familiar with the term *mass sociogenic illness*?" Enrique's question shifted the attention from the taste buds back to the brain.

"Is it something like mass hysteria?"

"Yes, it's a term that replaced mass hysteria, because of what we're learning about how shared beliefs can affect biology.

"Enriquito, I read an article about Legionnaire's disease being an example of mass sociogenic illnesses," Máximo interjected.

"Yes, there's some merit to that theory. Members of organizations or sports teams that share a purpose or strong interests are more susceptible to false alarms from their peers. For example, a member of a group, responding to a harmless odor as if it were toxic fumes, can trigger a chain reaction of vomiting or shortness of breath in the other members. The power of shared suggestion creates an illness by observation." Enrique paused and looked at Fouché to ask a delicate question. "As a Voodoo priest, do you think the mass sociogenic element is relevant in hexes and healings?"

Fouché frowned to weigh the implications of his intended response. "Dr. Lugo, I have struggled for many years with the dichotomy of cultural beliefs vs. spiritual intervention in our Voodoo tradition. I can tell you, there are evil and benevolent forces that exist beyond our physical dimension. But there is no denial that those who give the forces credence are the most affected."

"Mr. Fouché, I like your assessment. You truly *are* an anthropologist at heart."

"Thank you, Dr. Lugo. Unfortunately, not all my colleagues would agree with how I view our calling. As you men are aware, some practitioners use poison in their hexes to impose a fear of evil spirits on nonbelievers. Yet, I have seen hexes causing severe illness where toxic concoctions were not used, and the victims did not know they had been cursed. So I must caution, there is more than meets the eye when it comes to entities of good and evil."

The night had grown old graciously. It was time to leave.

"Fouché, I am so glad you were able to join us for dinner. It was grand to share this exquisite place with you and my dear Enriquito."

"Máximo, I cannot thank you and Dr. Lugo enough for your charming company and erudite conversation. We must do this again."

"I am sure we will, Mr. Fouché. It was indeed a pleasure to meet you." Enrique added.

Fouché left quickly, and Enrique followed Máximo to the kitchen, where they congratulated Doña Josefa for her sumptuous cuisine. The chef was pleasantly embarrassed, and her husband glowed with pride.

On their way home, Máximo and Enrique said very little for the first few minutes, trying to assimilate the wisdom of the night. Then, as if on cue from some ethereal stage director, the dialogue resumed.

"Enriquito, I'd be very interested in hearing your take on Fouché's world."

"I would trust his powerful mind. But I know there is much more we could learn from him. I thought he was candid with us and I sensed his great respect for you. Like any stimulating conversation, it left me with more questions to ponder. Máximo, you and I share a Catholic history, strongly influenced by the Christian mystics. Although our interpretations may be different than Fouché's, the origin of evil remains a mystery. Whether we attribute it to Satan, malevolent spirits, or our own deeds, evil remains a force of destruction, that can only be confronted with faith in the strength of benevolence."

"I agree. Fouché has chosen the path of goodness, and I admire him for that. I wonder how the anthropologist and the mystic within you will reconcile the cultural and metaphysical influences in your book?"

They arrived at Enrique's home. Máximo parked his Cayenne in front of the garage, and waited for a reply.

"Dear friend, I'm going straight to bed, and when I start writing early next morning, I may ask Breogán. But you will not see me again until I finish the manuscript."

"Well my boy, good luck to you and Breogán. May God help me for contributing to the delusions of my protégé." Máximo could make Enrique laugh any hour of the night.

Chapter 17

"Acts of faith were making their presence known."

Office of the Camerlengo, Vatican City

C amerlengo is the Italian word for chamberlain, *and the Cardinal who heads that office gains importance when a Pope dies and before a new Pope is elected. The Cardinal Camerlengo is responsible for certifying the death of the Pope with the ritual of calling the Pontiff by his name three times without response. During the vacancy of the Holy See, all heads of the Roman Curia are suspended from exercising their authorities, and the Cardinal Camerlengo takes on the responsibility of governing the Church. His interim duties include arranging for the funeral and burial of the Pope, as well as directing the election of a new Pope.*

Evelio Martin Somal, from Spain, was the Cardinal Camerlengo. Although Cardinal Martin Somal prayed daily for the longevity of the Pope he loved, His Holiness was a frail 84 year-old man in failing health. The transfer of power can bring out the worst in the best of us. Reluctantly, the Cardinal Camerlengo was busy with the informal preparations for the inevitable. And in those anticipatory days, he could sense the forlorn climate of the Vatican. Decent men encounter guilt when they curse God or thank God for taking those they loved instead of them, but the Cardinal confronted his losses differently. He loved his friends and colleagues by his daily actions, leaving nothing to lament when it was time for them to go.

"Fr. Fellini? The Cardinal Camerlengo would like to speak with you."

"Yes, of course," Fr. Fellini responded anxiously. *Given the condition of the Pope, a call from the Camerlengo's office could be ominous.*

"Hello, Carlo. We need to speak in confidence. Are you alone?"

"Yes I am, Your Eminence."

"Good. Cardinal Allegro briefed me on what has transpired and how you are assisting us. Given the gravity and timing of the circumstances, you have our full support. How are you progressing?" *The Camerlengo spoke in precise Italian with a pronounced Spanish ac-*

cent, giving the sound of his words an academic cadence. Although the Camerlengo was calling from a secured phone line in the Vatican, his circumspect style of communication reflected the old school of clergy, who placed little faith in modern technology.

"Your Eminence, I believe my colleague Signore Breogán may have a way to resolve the matter satisfactorily."

"Signore Breogán is from Spain. Is he not?"

"Yes, Your Eminence, he is Galician."

"I am encouraged by your report. Unfortunately, time is of the essence. You will keep me abreast?"

"I will, Your Eminence." Fr. Fellini smiled, knowing the Cardinal Camerlengo was also Galician and proud of his heritage, despite years of prayers to free himself of such worldly emotions.

That evening, the team was meeting with Cardinal Diaz Umap to begin the intervention phase of their work. Breogán would guide the contemplative Prayer of Quiet, with Fr. Fellini assisting as spiritual director, and Dr. Scola attending to any medical emergency. Given the power of symbols in the healing process, the session would begin at sunset: a time known in ancient Catholic rituals as the canonical hour of Vester.

Breogán walked into the monastic study and found Fr. Fellini chatting with Dr. Scola by the fireplace. Strategically arranged pillar candles lit the center of the room like a stage for a sacred ritual. The aroma of burning frankincense brought serenity to a place where inclusive compassion would implore a wounding mind.

The previous evening, Breogán had clarified that, rather than active meditation, the Prayer of Quiet was a passive state of contemplation to invite God's presence. It did not involve concentrating on breathing or on anything else, because even focusing on nothingness was a willful act of concentration. Since the contemplation was a mystical invitation for the soul to meet God, it was not accessible to the faculties. Grounded in the senses, the experiential self was limited to confirming the physical. But when it came to releasing the faculties to beseech a hidden God, the soul had to relinquish experience and embrace Presence. By freeing the soul from the faculties, the contemplation would set the conditions to receive God.

And from the perspective of spiritual director, Fr. Fellini explained that the soul has its own ontology, ready to meet God through faith. But it was not faith in a belief, because that would still be a thought coming from the faculties of memory, intellect, or will. Instead, it was a degree of faith that transcended belief by freeing the will.

"Fr. Fellini, I was intrigued with your comments last night about the ontology of the soul. I am not sure I understand how the language of the faculties can explain...uh," Dr. Scola was searching for the right word that would do justice to the imagery he was trying to convey, *"well, explain the indescribable."*

"Your point is well taken, Dr. Scola, and it reminds me of how Archbishop Luis Martinez addressed that dilemma. He was a theologian mystic strongly influenced by St. John of the Cross, and in his book Secrets of the Interior Life, *the Archbishop argued that faith penetrates all recesses. In his view, God is concealed in all things except faith,"* Fr. Fellini responded.

"Good evening Signore Breogán, you came in at the right moment because I would like to address my next question to you. If we know with our faculties, how can we recognize the presence of God without them?"

"Dr. Scola, the difficulty in answering your question arises when we attempt to describe a dimension that exists beyond language. Our language is of the mind, and when we move beyond the faculties of the mind, we lose our descriptive instrument. But the mind can allude to conditions that transcend our faculties. The objective of the mystic is to enter Presence through faith, but that can only be accomplished by suspending the need to know. Faith detaches from the known and embraces the mystery, without expecting feedback from the faculties."

"Please forgive me Signore Breogán, but as a physician, I must push the limits of your premise. If we reside in a biological body that gains knowledge through our mind, how can we leave the faculties to gain and retrieve wisdom from God's presence?" Dr. Scola asked, with apology in his voice.

"Dr. Scola, I welcome your question, because we should not get lost in sophistries when it comes to our beliefs. If we accept that mind, body and spirit are inseparable, we can consider that, while the experiential world is sensed by the body and is known by the mind, the soul recognizes God through faith. But knowing the physical world is different than infusing His presence. We can discourse and have feelings about our worldly experiences, but when our soul is in His presence, we can only recognize the undulation of the experience. So rather than leaving our body to know God, our mind suspends the need to know through the faculties, and frees our soul to receive His presence through faith."

"Signore Breogán, I could not help overhearing your compelling treatise, so I must ask. What is the undulation of the experience?" Car-

dinal Diaz Umap had entered the room and remained silent until Breogán finished.

The team looked in unison toward Cardinal Diaz Umap. He was standing by the door dressed in a priest's black soutane without the trace of red that signified his high office.

"Good evening Cardinal. I'll defer your question to your spiritual director," Breogán responded without thinking. It reminded him of when Fr. Fellini suggested using the Prayer of Quiet without knowing the method. Acts of faith were making their presence known.

Fr. Fellini looked at Breogán with a smile, and turned to Cardinal Diaz Umap with joy. "Your Eminence, rapture is the undulation of the experience."

"Yes, rapture," Dr. Scola repeated the word, nodding as if he had asked the Cardinal's question. By suspending the physician from the man, the doctor was beginning to understand St. Teresa's work. Perhaps the Cardinal could also understand if he released the man from the priest.

"Carlo, I am certain you can see now the wisdom of your suggestion to use the Prayer of Quiet. It's the only way I know to reach a mystical presence, where the mind wounds and God heals." Breogán's words had the reassurance of experience.

The night before, Breogán had taught Cardinal Diaz Umap to prepare for the Prayer of Quiet. According to St. Teresa, God invites the soul to His presence by infused contemplation during the Prayer of Quiet, but given the magnitude of the meeting, the soul feels unworthy of the invitation. Paradoxically, the unworthiness that the soul admits through the faculties does not allow it to be released from the faculties. St. Teresa proposes the Prayer of Recollection to resolve the impasse. This prayer enlarges the soul's worthiness, and prepares it to gain freedom from the mindset that precludes the invitation.

A wide leaded window filtered the diminishing light coming from an inner courtyard. The canonical hour of Vester was nearing. Two pair of armchairs faced each other in the candle lit circle. Breogán and Cardinal Diaz Umap sat next to each other, and across from Fr. Fellini and Dr. Scola.

Following the ancient ritual of Vester, Fr. Fellini blessed the canonical hour with its corresponding supplicant prayer: "Deus in adiutorium meum intende. Domine ad adiuvandum me festina."

Breogán was not familiar with the prayer, but he translated the Latin words in his head: O God, come to my assistance. O Lord, make haste to help me.

"Your Eminence, are you ready?" Breogán asked softly, and as he

looked at the Cardinal's hands in prayer, he could see how the candle-light danced on the bandaged wrists with crimson circles.

"Yes, I am ready."

"Then let's begin. Although the Prayer of Quiet could take years to master, I believe your priestly experience with supplicant prayers and your strong faith can overcome that obstacle. We're going to use your knowledge of active meditation to call back the faculties from remembering, interpreting, or choosing external content. This recollection will provide the solitude needed for the soul to enlarge its worthiness and accept the invitation of Presence." Breogán closed his eyes and asked the Cardinal to do the same before continuing.

"Please bring awareness to your breathing and connect each breath with a silent prayer. When your memory, your intellect, or your will begin to distract you from quieting them, let the silent breathing prayer do the recollection without conscious effort. The centering will take place faster if you let faith replace reason, because trying to detach from your faculties will have the opposite effect. Just like breathing is conscious when you think about it and autonomous when you forget it, the silent prayer will follow the same course. When your breathing and your silent prayer become one, they will be recollected from your awareness, giving the soul freedom to enlarge without distractions from the faculties."

Fr. Fellini understood Breogán's incidental teaching method. By grounding silent prayer with each breath, when faith frees breathing from awareness, it will also trust God to hear prayer without invocation.

Breogán gave the Cardinal a few minutes to adjust, before continuing the instructions. "You will notice that, as the sub-vocal prayer is repeated with each breath, your attention will fluctuate between breathing and praying. This awareness-shifting slowly becomes the center stage. When your mind wanders, let the breathing prayer do the recollection. Initially, the competing awareness created by the breathing prayer will take attention away from other mind activities, but when all distractions cease, the breathing prayer must also be suspended from the faculties. Since faith is an act of relinquishing, it can set the conditions to detach intention from breathing and praying. The breathing prayer quiets the mind, and faith quiets the breathing prayer. Awareness is suspended in a consciousness without context that can assimilate the invitation from boundless God."

Before elaborating further, Breogán looked at Fr. Fellini and Dr. Scola and felt their anticipation weighing on him. The thought of wind-surfing in his beloved Galicia came to mind, as he wondered how well the Cardinal would navigate the impending mystical hurdles.

"As you detach from internal and external distractions, you will be engulfed by a commanding serenity. Do not let fear dissuade you from going deeper into the silence. The fear comes because the faculties are unable to categorize the experience. At that critical junction, you must engage your faith and release your mind. If you succeed, your soul will enter a portal where God speaks without words, and infuses His wisdom without thoughts. Since the faculties remain outside that space of profound stillness, the senses can only register the undulations of what is taking place as the Prayer of Quiet unfolds. The rapture that Teresa of Avila describes is merely the ripples of the mystical joy the soul assimilates. The body would be pulverized if exposed to that degree of ecstasy.

"One final caution. When your soul is ready to reunite with the faculties, do not attempt it abruptly. It could be very dangerous to your health. To do it safely, simply bring your awareness from suspension back to the breathing prayer until you can feel oriented in the present. Then slowly open your eyes and take a deep breath. We will be here waiting." As Breogán concluded, he followed his own counsel and took a deep breath with a silent prayer for the Cardinal.

"Yes, Your Eminence, we will remain with you in spirit and await your safe return." Fr. Fellini interjected, knowing Cardinal Diaz Umap was about to test the horizons of faith.

Cardinal Diaz Umap took a deep breath, letting his thoughts wander before starting the silent prayer. He mentally scanned his body and relaxed the tension around his shoulders. The candlelight that defied his closed eyes diminished at the speed of rice paper absorbing black ink. And slowly the layers of darkness brought haunting memories from archetypal wounds of shame, betrayal and abandonment. Acts perpetrated against him, and suffering he had inflicted on others. Recollections of his first unrequited love, and lies to protect his pride, were paled by his first lapse of courage. His internal judge was relentless, retrieving ghosts of old wrongs.

His experience with meditation prayer taught him that as the body relaxes, accusatory debris surfaces to pummel self-worth. A punitive mind-body template crafts a consciousness where the soul can only reside in oppression. But now he understood how the Prayer of Recollection could exonerate, and prepare the soul for infused contemplation in the Prayer of Quiet. Having a spiritual compass gave him the mystical direction he lacked.

It was time to settle the unruly mind. He remembered what Fr. Fellini taught him about choosing the silent prayer: it had to recall the faculties rather than petition God. The Cardinal searched until a *burgeoning cognition surfaced from a cacophony of thoughts. Something between an image and a symbol. More like an annunciation that could be surrounded by words but never captured. Slowly evolving, until his consciousness recognized it was Christ ascending without crucifixion wounds. He had found his silent prayer.*

Each breath depicted the ascension from a new perspective, with the complexity of a hologram. Multiple angles defied the depth of meaning and the boundaries of images. Unable to compete with the diligence of the silent prayer, distractions capitulated and punitive memories lost their sting. The soul was on its way to stillness. But the Cardinal knew that, in addition to quieting the faculties, the symbolism of the Prayer of Recollection served a more vital purpose.

The Ascension without Wounds image was an invitation to desist from emulating Christ through stigmatic suffering and to promote healing through His joy. Yet, there was more to the symbol than the interpretative mind could apprehend. And after exhausting his faculties to no avail, the Cardinal had a flash of clarity: The faculties could only go so far into the mystery of the Ascension. He had reached the moment of recollection when the mind accepts its own limitations and frees the soul. Then, in the pervasive stillness of the Prayer of Quiet, the soul is infused with a mystical wisdom that transcends cognition.

Contemplative quieting *came without warning, suspending the field of awareness with a jolt. At once, the Cardinal felt the terror of releasing his consciousness and the love that bound his intentions. He recruited the power of his faith and permitted his will to be guided by an impending force. His body began to sway like sea oats dancing with the wind. Tears of joy poured with a loving warmth he had never felt before. Fear was no longer an obstacle to conquer.*

Dr. Scola saw his patient hyperventilate, Fr. Fellini prayed for spiritual guidance, and Breogán empathized from his own experience with the Prayer of Quiet. The three men could only see the Cardinal's body reflecting a mystical moment. And the Cardinal could only sense the undulations of that mystical moment. Wisdom infused in the profound stillness remained a mystery to all present.

First light of morning arrived to compete with illuminations from the circle of candles. One man's rapture had fatigued the other three. A collective exhaustion permeated the room. Dr. Scola was the first to awaken. He scanned the room and saw Breogán and Fr. Fellini still asleep on their chairs. Almost afraid to check on his patient, he walked toward the Cardinal's chair mesmerized by what he encountered.

Cardinal Diaz Umap was staring at the massive crucifix on the wall. His eyes expressed the joy of tranquility seen in patients who awaken from a near-death experience. His black soutane was lined with thin layers of salt, tracing his hours of heavy perspiration. Dr. Scola's medical reality could not assimilate what he was about to witness. He examined the dressings and noticed the crimson circles had not enlarged. He held his breath and cut the bandages. The deep punctures were now covered with the light pink tissue seen only after months of slow healing. The wounds had healed completely.

Dr. Scola tried to make sense of the evidence in light of the normal process of tissue repair. His mind raced through the three stages of wound healing: the inflammatory phase during the first few days, when blood vessels around the wounded area constrict to control the bleeding so that platelets and thromboplastins can make a clot, followed by the proliferation phase, lasting about three weeks, when granulation occurs with fibroblast cells, making collagen to fill the wound. But he was most astounded when he considered the maturation and remodeling phase. This final stage can take up to two years to reshape the wound with new collagen and to strengthen tissue in the area.

The overwhelming medical evidence against anything other than a miracle volleyed between the mindsets of Dr. Scola, the physician, and Fr. Scola, the priest. His right hand lost strength to hold the scissors, and the loud clatter of metal hitting tiled floor brought Breogán and Fr. Fellini out of their sleep.

Dr. Scola signaled the two men to meet him in the adjoining study, to avoid disrupting the Cardinal's emotional unfolding. He described the medical improbability -- two years of normal healing had been compressed to a few hours. Breogán admitted he had never witnessed anything as radical in his previous work with stigmata. Fr. Fellini fell to his knees and began to pray in whispers.

Without going into details, Fr. Fellini requested the Camerlengo's presence, most urgently, at Castle Gandolfo. The team and the Cardinal waited for the Camerlengo in the study, each wondering how the Vatican would respond. He arrived two hours later, giving Cardinal Diaz Umap time to stabilize his emotions and absorb the extraordinary experience he had endured.

"Gentlemen, I can only imagine what I am about to witness. His Holiness is most anxious to hear my report." The Camerlengo attempted to conduct business as usual, but his hand trembled when he made the sign of the cross to bless all present.

Dr. Scola related from a medical perspective what had transpired and, as the Camerlengo listened, Cardinal Diaz Umap held out his arms, exhibiting the evidence with gratitude. Fr. Fellini and Breogán took turns describing the contemplative method selected and its spiritual and psycho-

logical implications. But as each man lauded the significance of the event, none was ready for the Camerlengo's response.

"My dear brethren, this momentous news confirms the infinite power of faith, but we must exercise decisive prudence in our response. As you well know, the Church does not consider stigmata a product of divine intervention. And although this spontaneous reversal of the wounds is unprecedented, we must resist the impulse to make it public knowledge before its proper time."

"Your Eminence," Breogán began to pace before continuing to address the Camerlengo, "with all due respect, what we have witnessed here must be shared with the scientific community. Would you not agree that, in addition to the medical contribution, the news would galvanize Christian faith at a time of scandalous grievances against our Church?"

"Breogán, we are most appreciative for the expertise and discretion you have so graciously given us. And you are correct with your assessment about the ethical dilemmas our Church is facing, but we implore you to consider our position with the utmost care," the Camerlengo spoke without a trace of coercion in his voice.

Before Breogán could respond, Fr. Fellini stood up and addressed the Camerlengo. "Your Eminence, when Cardinal Diaz Umap asked me to be his spiritual director, I could not fathom the ethical ramifications that I would confront. We have witnessed an act of supreme benevolence, and now we must decide how to respond. But most importantly, we should consider how the beneficiary of this grace wishes to proceed. After all, independent of our wishes, Cardinal Diaz Umap is the recipient."

Cardinal Diaz Umap followed the conversation, patiently weighing the arguments from all sides, before offering his opinion. Fatigue was evident on his face, but this was a man who knew how to gather strength from his soul when there was none to be had from his body.

"Camerlengo, I am convinced what these men have done for me was guided by Divinity and they will remain in my prayers of gratitude for the rest of my days. I certainly cannot take credit for this extraordinary gift. I only want what is best for the mission of our Church and, as such, I defer to the wisdom of His Holiness on this matter. Since my ordination, I have found infinite comfort in accepting that God's wisdom is seldom bestowed directly. If it were, there would be no need to exercise faith."

Dr. Scola posed a question in the name of science, knowing Cardinal Diaz Umap would respond without subduing what was in his heart:

"And what is the indirectness that you see in the Lord's message? It seems to me this miraculous occurrence is a clear opportunity for science to learn more about how the mind can wound and heal the body through the power of belief."

"My dear Dr. Scola, I trust the significance of His message will unfold with impeccable timing. In the words of Albert Einstein, 'God does not play dice with the universe'. But if you gentlemen will excuse me, I am in dire need of sleep."

"Yes, of course you must get some rest," Dr. Scola agreed with his patient.

Cardinal Diaz Umap walked toward the door with the burdened pace of exhaustion and left the room. He knew his presence would inhibit the discussion that needed to take place. But if the others' body language competed to break the burgeoning silence, the Camerlengo's expression of apprehension tempered with prudence was the winner.

"Perhaps if I offer some historical perspective, you might see why the Church must consider the geopolitical consequences of its actions. When Cardinal Karol Wojtyla was elected pope and took the name John Paul ll in 1978, he had been working diligently to support Lech Walesa's labor movement, which led to Poland's emancipation from the Soviet Union. By electing the first Polish pope and also the first non-Italian pope since Pope Adrian VI in 1522, our Church supported a bloodless revolution that established a democracy and afforded the Polish people the right to worship without government retribution." *The Camerlengo spoke with conviction, pausing long enough to look at each man in the eye before entrusting him with highly confidential Vatican strategy.*

"And now gentlemen, we believe the opportunity for another peaceful liberation is approaching faster than we would like to admit. Cuba is the only Communist country in the Western Hemisphere, and Cardinal Diaz Umap has paid a dear price for defending its people's right to worship. If he were elected pope, it must be for his potential to exalt freedom, rather than what would be concluded if stigmata appeared to be the reason for electing the first Hispanic pontiff in the two thousand-year history of our Church. So you see gentlemen, we must consider moral as well as spiritual consequences when we elect the leader of our Faith."

The Camerlengo's perspective brought receptive nods to a mood of oppositional tension: a moment in discourse when the prevailing logic shifts from winning arguments to finding unconditional truth.

"I don't know about the rest of you, but I always wanted to partici-

pate in a bloodless revolution." Fr. Fellini's words drew cheers from Breogán and Dr. Scola not unlike what follows a passionate speech that touches the soul. Unable to maintain his trademark stoicism, the Camerlengo reacted to the unexpected enthusiasm with a broad smile.

Breogán waited for the excitement to subside before presenting his view: "I see the geopolitical wisdom of electing a pope from a totalitarian country. And Cardinal Diaz Umap could certainly rekindle the quest for freedom in Cuba, with moral support from millions of Spanish-speaking Catholics throughout the world. The Vatican's strategy is brilliant, but the knowledge we gained working with Cardinal Diaz Umap should not be discarded if he is elected pope."

"I agree. The healing effects of the contemplative methods could be tested with serious illnesses without disclosing our sources." Dr. Scola added with a jubilant smile.

" Gentlemen, now that I see your willingness to support our position, I think you will be pleased with what we are about to offer: The Vatican is prepared to fund a small research clinic where you men could continue to investigate how spiritual beliefs affect health and how the knowledge you gain from your investigations could be applied to illnesses impervious to conventional medical treatment. The patients would be assured anonymity, and when you accumulate convincing evidence, the results would be made available to the scientific community." The Camerlengo's proposal was met with instant approval.

In the morning, the Camerlengo invited the team and Cardinal Diaz Umap for a farewell breakfast. They broke bread in an atmosphere of fellowship and gratitude, with each man committing to what they called the stigmata covenant.

Fr. Fellini returned to his teaching at the University of Milano, Dr. Scola resumed his duties as Vatican physician, and Breogán went home to love Sabela, with the wisdom he could gather every autumn of his life. As for the fate of His Eminence Alonzo Cardinal Diaz Umap... only the Holy See could tell.

Chapter 18

"Enrique felt a cold sweat invading his body..."

*T*he *Man from Autumn* made the *New York Times* bestseller list faster than most books in its genre. Critics pronounced the work a resounding success for Enrique. The two months following publication were filled with interviews, book-signing lectures and guest appearances on popular talk shows. Paradoxically, Enrique, exhausted from months of writing under deadline stress, was replenished by the physical demands of the book tour. He knew the economy of emotional energy had more to do with validation than expenditure. A worthy goal transcends physical limitations by drawing energy from love, whereas working without meaning makes the simplest task insurmountable. And he wondered: *if the stigmatic mind wounds the body to express love through suffering, what could be achieved if disciples of pain learned to love from joy?*

Enrique was cognizant of how the joy of triumph is best assimilated in solitude with a loving partner. What could better satisfy those conditions than celebrating with Kate in the land of Breogán? The idea brought him a jolting laughter that confirmed the *rightness of the moment.* Considering how society responds when joy is expressed without an audience, Enrique was thankful there was no one around to question his sanity.

Enrique and Kate flew to Santiago de Compostela and drove to Breogán's town of Estaca de Bares, with the clear intention of letting life imitate art for two weeks in the heart of Celtic Spain. Void of news and celebrity status, they cooked their own meals, took long walks by the ocean, and brought idyllic days to an end sipping *Larios* by a roaring fireplace. The seaside cottage they rented, was their only companion. It was easy for them to imagine Breogán and Sabela dancing in the picturesque town where the man from autumn was given life.

On their last night, Enrique and Kate decided to go into town for dinner and, once again, bring people into their world. Enrique's publisher had given him a pocket PC to stay in touch, knowing he would not comply; but Liliana was not easily dissuaded, so he accepted the gift graciously to avoid her histrionics.

When they arrived at the restaurant in the neighboring village, two weeks of abstinence from telecommunication piqued his curiosity, and he scrolled the list of emails.

"Would you believe I have twelve emails, and one marked urgent, that I am reluctant to open?" Enrique told Kate with a worried look.

"Can you tell from the address who it's from?" Kate asked, joining him in the stress that technology triggers when it disrupts serenity.

"It's from Andrés Vitón."

"Your publicist?"

"Yes, and it must be something personal because he always protects my privacy."

Enrique exhaled the breath he was guarding, and read the email:

> *Urgent! I've been trying to get in touch with you for the past two days! Call me as soon as you can.*
>
> *Un abrazo,*
> *Andrés*

"Kate, please forgive me for interrupting our seclusion, but I think there may be something wrong with Andrés. Last time we talked, he was anxious about his upcoming birthday, approaching the age his father died."

"Of course, darling. Do you need privacy?"

"No, please stay," Enrique implored, wanting to share the moment with her.

"Andrés?"

"*Torero*, where the hell have you been hiding? What do you think about the big news?"

Enrique was relieved, hearing the nickname Andrés used when they humored each other.

"Thank God, he's ok," Enrique whispered to Kate, and returned to the conversation with a lighthearted tone.

"My dear *gaucho,* what's so important that it can't wait till I return to *stress city?*"

"You must be living in a cave if you haven't heard the news."

"Ok, now that I am out of the cave, I am sure you'll end the suspense and tell me."

"Enrique, the Pope died."

Enrique felt a cold sweat invading his body, so apparent that Kate braced herself to prepare for the worst.

"The Pope died? When? What's the Vatican doing?"

"My friend, you better be sitting when I tell you," Andrés warned before answering. "The Pope died four days ago. The Conclave of Cardinals met and elected the new Pope in seventy-two hours, bypassing the minimum nine-day interregnum. But the most astonishing news is their unprecedented choice. For the first time in the history of the Catholic Church, we now have a Hispanic pope."

"Andrés, I can't believe this is happening."

"What you're not going to really believe is what the new Pope decided to do. Also another first for the Catholic Church, because up to now no one had the audacity to take the name he chose."

Enrique held his breath, and waited for Andrés to tell him.

"Oh my God! Andrés, this is surreal."

"Enrique, the media picked up on the coincidences, and all the news networks are looking for you. They're beginning to call your book *the oracle*. Of course, your publisher is delighted and is desperately looking for you."

"Don't tell anyone where I am until I can sort this out. Thanks, Andrés. I'll call you as soon as I can."

Enrique hung up, and saw Kate gesturing anticipation and words without sound, as if Enrique were still on the phone.

"Kate, you heard me say the Pope died and that his successor is Hispanic, but the momentous part is the name he chose."

"Darling, what name did he take?"

"The new pontiff will be known as *Pope Peter II...*"

Prolepsis

pro-lep'-sis Gk. A preconception. The anachronistic representation of something existing before its proper or historical time.

    The injustices and traumas we endure on this personal journey we call life can condemn our existence to a private hell of despair. Pain descends upon us unexpectedly when our novice hearts are unable to reach emotional perspective, and our young minds are incapable of finding meaning.

    But the instant we gain awareness that our wounds of profound shame, abandonment, or betrayal were impetus for all our deeds of honor, commitment, and loyalty, we enter an Alpha Event. *And when we begin to live with gratitude for the wisdom extracted from those acts of injustice, our despair ends with an* Omega Event.

Breogán

Mario E. Martinez is a clinical psychologist, who specializes in the ways cultural and spiritual beliefs affect health and longevity.

He lectures worldwide on his theory of Biocognition, and on the investigations he has conducted of alleged cases of stigmata for the Catholic Church. Dr. Martinez lives in Nashville, Tennessee and spends his autumns in Ireland and Celtic Spain.

For more information on his lectures and publications, visit his website at www.biocognitive.com or write him at manfromautumn@biocognitive.com

Printed in the United States
77319LV00003B/148-150